THE MERE WIFE

MARIA DAHVANA HEADLEY

MCD

FARRAR, STRAUS AND GIROUX

NEW YORK

MCD

Farrar, Straus and Giroux

175 Varick Street, New York 10014

Library of Congress Cataloging-in-Publication Data

Names: Headley, Maria Dahvana, 1977– author.

Title: The mere wife / Maria Dahvana Headley.

Description: First edition. | New York : Farrar, Straus and Giroux, 2018.

Identifiers: LCCN 2017058628 | ISBN 9780374208431 (hardcover)

Subjects: LCSH: Mothers and sons—Fiction.

Classification: LCC PS3608.E233 M47 2018 | DDC 813/.6—dc23

LC record available at https://lccn.loc.gov/2017058628

Designed by Jonathan D. Lippincott

Our books may be purchased in bulk for promotional, educational, or business
use. Please contact your local bookseller or the Macmillan Corporate and
Premium Sales Department at 1-800-221-7945, extension 5442, or by e-mail at
MacmillanSpecialMarkets@macmillan.com.

www.mcdbooks.com • www.fsgbooks.com

Follow us on Twitter, Facebook, and Instagram at @mcdbooks

1   3   5   7   9   10   8   6   4   2

For Anonymous
and all the stories she told

I make this song   about me full sadly
my own wayfaring.   I a woman tell
what griefs I had   since I grew up
new or old   never more than now.
Ever I know   the dark of my exile.

. . .

The man sent me out   to live in the woods
under an oak tree   in this den in the earth.
Ancient this earth hall.   I am all longing.

—Anonymous
"The Wife's Lament," ca. 960–90

translated from the Old English by Ann Stanford

SELECTED TRANSLATIONS

AGLÆCA (Old English, noun, masculine): fighter, warrior,
hero

AGLÆC-WIF (Old English, noun, feminine): wretch, monster, hell-bride, hag

HWÆT (Old English, interrogative pronoun, disputed
translations): Say, Listen, So, What, Attend, Hark, Tell,
Behold, Ah, Lo, Yes, Sing, Now

THE MERE WIFE

PROLOGUE

Say it. The beginning and end at once. I'm facedown in a truck bed, getting ready to be dead. I think about praying, but I've never been any good at asking for help. I try to sing. There aren't any songs for this. All I have is a line I read in a library book. *All shall be well and all shall be well and all manner of thing shall be well.*

There's a sack over my head, but I'm seeing the faces of dead soldiers. I'm watching the war in slow motion, and then too fast, a string of men, a line of blood and baffled eyes—

We got lost. All of us got sent to the wrong country, and everyone but me is dead. Now I think all countries are the wrong country, and I'm out here, two minutes from gone.

My guys are ghosts, and my girls too. My best friend Renee got killed a week ago, slipped on a step, made a noise, and bullets, fast as wasps. I had her in my arms when she died. Three days ago, I was riding in a truck with Lynn Graven from Gulfport, who told me the Mississippi River had wandered according to its own hungers, changed its path in order to drink up land it wanted to claim, and then told me that there was a river like that in this desert too, and we should swim in it and see if it drank us. He dove out of the truck we were in at eighty miles per hour, thinking he'd land in water. Raul Honrez grew up in Idaho, his parents fruit pickers. He got halfway through med school before the planes flew into the towers and he joined up. I watched his body blow apart, right before someone grabbed me and threw me into this truck.

Two months ago I was on leave, far away from all this.

"*Listen!*" Someone shouted from the sidewalk, and she held on to my ankle. She had a sign that read YES. I GOT LOST. ANYTHING HELPS. She'd come from the same war I'd come from. Tin dish, rattling for change.

"Listen, lemme tell you what's gonna come for you," she said. "Gimme five bucks."

"You can have everything," I told her, and dropped the contents of my wallet into her dish.

"Then I'll tell you everything I know," she said.

"No, thanks," I said, and walked.

"You're gonna live forever!" she shouted after me. "You're the one who gets away! You're gonna lose some shit, though, so you better watch out."

"I don't have anything to lose," I said to her, cocky for no reason.

You go into war knowing you're signing up to be a goner. Living is luck, not anything special. You're not magic. You're just lucky.

I figured I knew the shape of things. I'd been fighting awhile. I signed up right after people stopped volunteering, in the middle of a war that went on forever. They made me think it was about heroes. That's how they sell it to you when you're seventeen. Go out and save the starving, the war-torn, the children, and the women. Instead, you march in and roll down roads, close your eyes and shoot. Hungry people on rations, scared people, fucked-up people, shooting by clothes and color of skin, or by the way bodies send out heat. Bright blots on a map, hearts beating.

I figured I'd been lucky so far. I figured that if I died, I died.

I got on a plane and came back to the desert.

Now I'm rattling down the road, and there's nowhere I want

to go, no good option. If I'm being taken, I'm going into a prison, or I'm going up on a screen. My brain's shaking up old things, distractions, picking over the moments leading me here, grabbing things I should have paid attention to when people said them.

"*Listen!*" an old woman said to me ten years ago, on a Greyhound Bus. "Let me tell you a story!"

I didn't know that I could move away, so I listened. Windows full of places. Night and the highway, lights green and red, people in every car going somewhere, and beside me this woman, telling me her version of the story of the world, all the things that ever happened from the beginning of time to the end of it. Thirty hours.

"This is the thing about history," she said. "People lie about the parts they missed. They tell you they know what happened, the world exploded and they watched it, when really all they did was hear a sound so loud it shook the ground. You never understand the whole story until you're at the end of it. If you're the last one standing, you're the one who sings for everyone else's funeral. But at least you get to be the one who tells it. You tell it for the rest of us."

I looked at her, sitting next to me, her shaky hands and church hat. She looked old enough to have been born in the single digits.

I thought I knew everything.

I thought I knew what the Earth had in it. I thought I knew what was coming for me. Now I know all this was waiting, this desert, this sack, this stumble as they drag me out of the truck.

I hear the whetting of a blade.

I don't know who they are, whoever has me, but I'm their *them*, and they're mine. We are each other's nightmares. I'm on my knees in the sand. They give me words, and I say them for the video.

"My name is Dana Mills," I say. "America, this is your doing."

I feel the wind of the blade swinging back, and I'm in a thousand cities at once, *all shall be well,* and in a thousand countries, and I'm on a ship coming across an ocean, *and all shall be well,* and I'm an old woman dying on a mountain, the last of my family, the last of my line, *and all manner of thing shall be well,* and there's blackness, and in the blackness, there's a bright star, and it gets bigger, and bigger—

"Listen," someone whispers into my ear. "Listen to me."

Am I dead?

"Listen," the voice whispers. "In some countries, you kill a monster when it's born. Other places, you kill it only when it kills someone else. Other places, you let it go, out into the forest or the sea, and it lives there forever, calling for others of its kind. Listen to me, *it cries. Maybe it's just alone."*

I wake up, gasping, underneath sand. Grit between my fingertips. There's space around my face, but nowhere else. I feel my heart beating, though, and that tells me something.

The sand is heavy and hot. Sunlight through my eyelids. I move sand with my fingers, then with my whole body, until my hand comes into the air. I push myself out, and stand up, swaying. There's an unfamiliar weight, and I look down at my stomach.

I'm a tent in the middle of the desert, and someone's inside it, someone who doesn't speak and doesn't march, who just sleeps. I almost laugh. I almost cry. I don't know who the father is.

I'm the mother.

This is how I come back from the dead. Six months pregnant. This is what I have. This is what I own.

I look out across the sand, and there's movement at the edge of it, ripples of heat, silhouettes of people moving. I start walking.

Hours in, something blows up ten feet from me. A shard of shrapnel in my eye, blood running down my cheek, nothing else. I tie my shirt around my face and keep going.

I walk until I get to Americans. I look so bad no one knows which side I'm on. They freak out when they get close. They read my tags.

Shitfuck, it's Dana Mills. Get someone.

I wake up later, under lights, shaved all over, my head, my pubic hair, my legs, my armpits, like someone on her way to be cooked. There are bars on the windows. There's a patch over my eye, and I feel drugged.

"Tough luck," says the girl in the bed beside mine. She doesn't have legs. "Guess it's too late now," she says. "For all of us stupid fuckers."

"Guess it is."

"I made it out of where I came from and I'm never going back," she says. "I got no one out there in the whole wide world."

"Me neither," I say. "My mother's dead. I'm alone."

We both look at my stomach.

"You're not," she says. "You got that one. Whoever that one's gonna be."

She has freckled skin and a pointed nose, crooked lips covered in black lipstick like she's planning to go to a club and throw herself into a mosh pit. Maybe she's seventeen, the same age I was when I joined up. Her fingernails are longer than regulation and polished with glitter. I don't ask her what she did. She doesn't ask me.

"So, are you crazy?" she asks, without fanfare. "*I* am. I see things. Mostly I see my legs. Why am I alive, anyway? Is that what you're thinking? That's what I'm thinking."

I'm in the middle of replying when I see something light up in the center of her chest. A flicker. A flame?

"What's in there?" I ask, but she's gone.

Five men are in her place, making themselves at home, feet on the bed frame, one or two looming over me, looking at my charts. Letting me know I'm the only one in the room who can't run. Being barefoot, once you've been to war, is terrifying.

"What happened to you, soldier? Who took you?"

"I don't know," I say. I'm still looking for the girl, but there's no girl.

A guy kneels in front of me, looking at me with all sincerity, like I can't tell him from a good person.

"We saw you on television," the man says. "You were lucky. You were still pretty enough for video. The rest of your team got blown up."

I think about luck.

"We watched you die. It was convincing."

"I'm alive," I say. My skin's prickling all over.

"Execution by edit." He gestures at my stomach. "Whose child is this?"

"Mine." I don't expect to say that, but it's what I say.

"Rape? Or consensual?"

One answer means I'm a victim, and the other means I'm a collaborator, and I don't know, so I don't answer. I hear one of them say something about DNA tests. My brain is skipping like a record. They hypnotize me, insist I tell them everything. There's nothing to tell, except that I'm back from wherever I've been, that I'm alive, and that I'm pregnant.

I stay in the hospital that isn't a hospital for six weeks, and then I feel my baby under my ribs, kicking hard.

There are other soldiers working in the prison. I find a guy who was stationed where I was. He gets me out in the middle of the night, a key in my food, a map under my plate, and I run. When I can't find a train, I hide myself in trailers carrying horses. Go under a tarp in the back of a pickup. Wake up in a parking lot one night with someone staring at me, punch him in the side of the head, and take off into the dark.

I see the girl from the hospital again in a truck-stop bathroom. She walks out of a stall without the use of legs and says, "Hey," and I say *hey* back to her like I'm not worried about my sanity. Her fingers are nothing but skeleton. She's smoking a cigarette.

In the center of her chest there's an open wound, and through it I can see her ribs, her lungs, a candle lit, balanced on her solar plexus and surrounded by gilding.

"God get to you yet? God ask for any favors?" she asks.

"I don't know," I say. "Something happened to me. I don't know what. I don't know what's happening to me now, either."

"Something happened to me too," she says. "I started spitting fire, and then I turned to ice and melted and everyone around me said I was a martyr. I got painted by every painter. You've seen me on walls and on drugstore candles. Go get one if you want." She indicates the votive in her chest. "Might help you."

The girl takes a long drag, and her cheeks suck in so far I can see what her skull looks like.

"Still hurts," she says. "You don't want to go this way, even if you get famous. Your face shows up on burnt toast and you never stop feeling like you can't get a good breath. Still, it's better than the alternative."

"What's the alternative?" I ask.

"Oh," she says. "You know. Eternal flame."

She walks out of the bathroom, legless, leaving footprints made of fire, but then they're gone and I'm standing there, one hand wrapped in paper.

My baby kicks inside me, cars pull in and out of the lot, trucks make that grieving moan of too heavy and brakes half broken. I see a bunch of them pull off the highway and uphill because nothing works on a big thing, nothing but gravity.

I keep going. Why am I going home at all? It occurs to me that they'll know where I came from, and be waiting for me. But they aren't. Nobody's there.

I guess that's because where I came from is gone.

I'm having contractions, close enough together that I'm scared, and all that's left in the place where I used to live is a bright white light, a fence around new buildings, and a mountain.

Every life starts with the same beginning and ends with the same end. The rest is the story, even if you don't understand it, even if you aren't sure which parts are true and which parts are your brain trying to make sense out of smoke. I grew up in a house looking up at this mountain. I left this place forever, but forever is over. Now I'm coming home again.

I climb, stumbling up the slope, through the trees and toward the cave.

Listen, I think. Listen.

the mountain

The hall loomed

golden towers antler-tipped; it was asking for

burning, but that hadn't happened yet.

You know how it is: Every castle wants invading, and

every family has enemies born within it. Old grudges boil up.

LISTEN

Listen. Long after the end of everything is supposed to have oc-
curred, long after apocalypses have been calculated by cults and
calendared by computers, long after the world has ceased believ-
ing in miracles, there's a baby born inside a mountain.

Earth's a thieved place. Everything living needs somewhere
to be.

There's a howl and then a whistle and then a roar. Wind
shrieks around the tops of trees, and sun melts the glacier at the
top of the peak. Even stars sing. Boulders avalanche and snow
drifts, ice moans.

No one needs to see us for us to exist. No one needs to love us
for us to exist. The sky is filled with light.

The world is full of wonders.

We're the wilderness, the hidden river, and the stone caves.
We're the snakes and songbirds, the storm water, the brightness
beneath the darkest pools. We're an old thing made of everything
else, and we've been waiting here a long time.

We rose up from an inland sea, and now, half beneath the
mountain, half outside it, is the last of that sea, a mere. In our soil
there are tree fossils, the remains of a forest, dating from the
greening of the world. They used to be a canopy; now they spread
their stone fingers underground. Deep inside the mountain,

there's a cave full of old bones. There was once a tremendous skeleton here, rib cage curving the wall, tail twisting across the floor.

Later, the cave was widened and pushed, tiled, tracked, and beamed to house a train station. The bones were pried out and taken to a museum, reassembled into a hanging body.

The station was a showpiece before it wasn't. The train it housed went back and forth to the city, cocktail cars, leather seats. The cave's walls are crumbling now, and on top of the stone the tiles are cracking, but the station remains: ticket booth, wooden benches, newspaper racks, a café counter, china teacups, stained-glass windows facing outward into earthworms, and crystal chandeliers draped in cobwebs. There are drinking fountains tapping the spring that feeds the mountain, and there's a wishing pool covered in dust.

No train's been through our territory in almost a hundred years. Both sides of the tunnel are covered with metal doors and soil, but the gilded chamber remains, water pouring over the tracks. Fish swim in the rail river and creatures move up and down over the mosaics and destination signs.

We wait, and one day our waiting is over.

A panel in the ceiling moves out of position, and a woman drops through the gap at the end of an arch, falling a couple of feet to the floor, panting.

She's bone-thin but for her belly. She staggers, leans against our wall, and looks up at our ceiling, breathing carefully.

There's a blurry streak of light, coming from the old skylight, a portal to the world outside. The world inside consists only of this woman, dressed in stained camo, a tank top, rope-belted fatigues, combat boots, a patch over one eye, hair tied back in a piece of cloth. Her face is scarred with a complicated line. On her back, there are two guns and a pack of provisions.

She eases herself down to the tiles. She calls, to any god, to all of them.

She calls to us.

Tree roots dangle through the ceiling tiles. A wandering bird swoops down from the outside world, makes its way through the arch, and settles into a secret nest glittered with hoop earrings made of brass, candy wrappers, bits of ribbon.

The woman screams, and her scream echoes from corner to corner of the station, and there is no train, and no help. There is no one but us, silent, and this woman, alone underground. She grits her teeth, and pushes.

We watch. We wait.

The labor takes a day and a night. The sun transits the sky, and the moon slips through the skylight.

The baby latches fingers into the woman's rib cage, toes into her pelvis, and forces itself out breech, unfolding, punching, pressing against something that will not give, and then does.

She screams once more, and then her son is born, wet, small, bloody. He takes his first breath. He gasps, gagging on air, his fingers spread.

His mother's eyes flicker with fire, and her hands glow, as though a bomb has exploded in the far distance, not outside but in.

She breathes. She clenches her fists and brings a knife out of her pack. She cuts the cord and ties it off with a strip of cotton from her shirt. She looks at her child, holding him up into the thin beam of light.

The baby's eyes open, golden, and his mouth opens too. He's born with teeth. His mother looks at him, her face uncertain. She holds him carefully, her hands shaking.

Wonders have been born before. Sometimes they've been worshipped. There've been new things over and over, and some creatures have fallen groaning to the ground and others have learned to fly.

Never mind the loneliness of being on Earth. That will come later.

She touches the baby's face. She washes him with our water, and swaddles him in her shirt, tight against her body.

"Gren," she whispers.

In our history, the history of the mountain, of the land that surged up out of the darkness at the bottom of the sea, this is only an instant, and then it will be dark again.

"Listen," she whispers to the baby.

All the other things that have been born here rise silently in the water of the mere to listen with him, toothed, clawed, each with its own ridge of spiny gleam.

The mountain's citizens look at the infant for a moment, listen to his mother for a moment, and then dive back into the depths.

He is born.

2

"*Listen!*" Dylan's playing "Chopsticks" with all his might.

Willa doesn't want to listen. She'll never want to listen to people learning to play the piano, and yet other mothers claim to enjoy things in this category.

Dil practices, slowly climbing the keys, and then a mistake, and he starts over. She wouldn't allow him the clarinet. "Chopsticks" is his vengeance. He's only seven. When *she* was only seven, she was perfect.

"*Listen!*" he demands again.

"Let's go to the grocery store, Dilly!"

The piano lid slams shut, silencing the cries of ivory keys, probably made of elephants. Willa feels stabbed every time she hears it playing. Ebony too. Those trees make spears. The piano is an act of savage warfare disguised as culture. No one else seems to notice, but Willa's always been sensitive.

She checks the menu she's posted on the refrigerator.

Sunday: Pork Chops with Applesauce and Salad
Monday: Chicken à la King with Scalloped Potatoes
Tuesday: Clam Chowder with Cornbread (Homemade)
Wednesday: Green Pasta & Ravioli with Red Sauce
Thursday: Shrimp Cocktail, Fish Filet, Salad

Friday: Flank Steak in Marinade
Saturday: Pizza Night—Choose Your Own Toppings!
Every Day: Vodka Martini

This week is irrelevant, though, because it's a holiday week. She should have the Christmas menu up. It's two days till goose, though that may have been a mistake. She's never done a goose before. Who has? She could have a cook come, or subscribe to a service, but she does the cooking herself. It's part of her claim to fame. Other wives look at her and wonder, and she wants it that way. She photographs and posts. She dresses for dinner. It is a competition, even though it pretends not to be.

At 4:30 every afternoon she's in the kitchen, looking at her reflection in the appliances. At 5:30 she's pouring a cocktail for Roger, and at 5:33 he's walking in the door, his hand outstretched for it, kissing her, not entirely chastely. There's always something of an event in this kiss, in the way her dress bunches against his belt. She likes it when he does it in front of guests.

She looks into the mirror she keeps on the kitchen wall and assesses herself, thinking about a pair of fishnet tights she once owned, worn with a tunic that scarcely covered her bottom. The tights were printed with peacock feathers. Now she'd never. She straightens her sweaterdress and gathers the bags. She can stretch a grocery trip out for an hour, two, maybe more. The miles of aisles at the Herot Hall grocery store are wide enough that you could drive a car down them if you wanted to.

Willa wants to. Every day she doesn't.

She has an outing there in the afternoons and comes home with dinner, plotted and planned. She brings Dylan with her and he skids through the aisles, treating them like ice. No one minds. He's perfect. Everyone thinks so, the checkers, the stock boys, the other customers. The car is white, and that's tempting fate, but Dil's never sticky. He knows better.

Children are monsters, but there are ways to work around

them. Six miles from Herot Hall there's a playground where Willa can, if she likes, pretend Dil isn't hers and she isn't his. She can sit on a bench smoking a cigarette—she's not actually a smoker, of course—while Dil monkeys his way along the jungle gym with the rest of the little lords of the flies.

At the Herot playground, she has to sit with other mothers, and watch as they bring snacks from their purses. She's expected to feed children who aren't her own. It's a *community*, emphasis on the commune. When Dil was only a few months old, she took him to a mommy group where a neighboring baby latched unexpectedly onto her breast. The baby tilted sideways, mouth agape, a triangle of shocking pink.

Viper! she thought, then redacted.

There was, however, a momentary escapade inside Willa's head, a bad adventure during which she broke the offending baby's neck and served the infant as a snack, surrounded by sippy yogurt and smashed peas.

Herot Hall is a toddler empire. Everyone with any power is between the ages of zero and seven. All boys are born with Nobel Prize potential. It's the mothers who ruin it, by forcing the boys into gentleness. That's what one of the fathers told her at cocktail hour.

Willa's own husband is the heir to Herot Hall. Roger's last name, in fact, *is* Herot. He's of noble family. Willa says that only in her head, but it's the truth. Roger's family built Herot Hall according to their own specifications, the buildings high and gabled, the entirety of the community self-sustaining, with its own grocery and pharmacy, each house with a fireplace, and each fireplace burning gas, a clean blue flame flicked on with a switch, lapping at logs made of stone. Central heat and air-conditioning. Finished basements. Landscaping to look as though wildflowers had seeded themselves in neat rows. It replaced the town that was here before, falling down since the railroad stopped running this line. Old Victorian monstrosities became condemned messes, full of a bunch of people who didn't belong in such a beautiful place. It took years to get them out. Willa didn't know Roger then, but if she had, she thinks she would have enjoyed the demolition. She always enjoys improvements.

She thinks of the Willa that existed before Herot, a Willa in an acting class wearing a striped sweater, a boy across from her looking into her eyes. A wineglass full of cheap white wine, an exposed brick wall, her body smashed against it, his tongue in her mouth—

Sometimes, admittedly, she misses living in the city. She isn't that person anymore, though, who called herself an actor, instead of actress. Here, that'd make the neighbors laugh. Lots of the neighbors are former city dwellers. They all moved out to where it was better, owning rather than renting, who'd want to suffer the subways with a child? And the guns, and the knives, and the lack of human compassion?

Roger and Willa have the loveliest house of all, the showpiece. Once a month, for the fun of it, they go out to dinner in the city, pretend they're on their honeymoon and get a free crème brûlée. They don't need it to be free, of course. They can afford whatever they want. Willa wouldn't have married another man like her first husband. That one was annulled. He doesn't even count. She woke up the morning after that wedding with her mother standing over her wedding bed. Willa's mother knows how to get a job done. Diane will never forgive Willa for that heroic rescue. Nor for the fact that she then had to take Willa to the doctor, urgently spilling secrets and lies, and the doctor, old man, family practice, did what was necessary.

"No need to speak of any of this to your father," Willa's mother said. "It'll only disgust him. For heaven's sake, Willa."

In this section of the fairy tale, Willa drifted flat in the backseat of the car with an ice pack on her belly and another on her back, and what felt like an entire roll of paper towels in her panties, which were plastic, because of the leather upholstery. Once,

Willa was in a production of *Julius Caesar*, and the blood in that show? It came, it saw, it overcame. She bowed deep at the end, feeling like a living tampon. After the annulment, she felt like a—

Like a Jell-O mold, unset, tilting dangerously in the refrigerator.

Richie, Willa never saw again. He was a musician, was it any wonder? Willa had one tattoo by the time her mother found her, and it was Richie's name. After the abortion, her mother took her to the dermatologist, who turned the tattoo into a scar in the shape of someone Willa used to know. She went to bed in her childhood room for six months. Richie didn't try to find her. Instead, he got famous. Sometimes now she hears him on the radio, singing about hunger.

After the requisite recovery, Willa's mother handed her Roger's phone number, procured from Roger's mother.

"You're lucky," she said to Willa. "You're still pretty enough. You can get a doctor. There's a new community going up near the mountain. You won't go back to the city, Willa. You'll get married and have a child with Roger. I can see it. He'll want to be carried, and your knees'll give out on you. You'll never be able to wear heels again."

Their first date: cocktail bar, medium exclusive. Both of them laughed about their mothers meddling, while silently agreeing they looked good together. She checked his wallet while he was in the bathroom, to see if he was lying about anything. His plastic was platinum, and his driver's license listed his height accurately.

"To us, and people like us," Roger said, and raised his glass of champagne.

Willa looked at him, uncertain, but then she clinked. Everyone else could toast to themselves too, if they felt inclined. It wasn't as though she was stealing their luck.

They were married within the year. Now Willa's thirty-two. Her hair's blond of its own volition. Her face has high cheekbones, perfectly arched eyebrows, a mouth like rose-colored wax sealing something official. When there's anything that looks like a wrinkle or spot, her mother notices before she does.

"You can't let yourself go, Willa," Willa's mother says. "You have a man to keep."

She does. Willa's keep is this glass castle at Herot, and Roger's in private practice in the city, plastic surgery. He's done some work on Willa, just a little in the eyelids and the chin.

He sets his own hours, and they go on vacations. Once a cruise, once Tahiti, where the huts gave Willa a dismal feeling. She felt the bottom drop out every time she looked at the transparent floor. That'd been when she was unknowingly pregnant. She had one sip of a cocktail and vomited startlingly into the snorkelers.

Roger named Dylan after his own dead dad while Willa was passed out post-delivery. Now he's called Dil, because who can call a little kid Dylan? Shades of Bob and guitars, poets dead of drink in the snow, all of it. Besides, Dil and Willa, that implies a certain adorable familial quality. It also implies pickles.

She would've named her son Theodore, had she been given the opportunity. It isn't Willa's fault that Roger's dad, Dilly the First, died in a car accident during the building of Herot and needed to be commemorated. She never even met him.

Four days after Willa gave birth, two of her mother's friends arrived with a clenching device for revising her vagina. She didn't say no, though she was startled at the implication she'd need help. The mothers acted as though she'd lost vigilance, as though she were about to wander half naked through the streets, her pubis patchily shaven from childbirth, her breasts leaking, loinclothed in receiving blankets, but she was already, exhausted and faintly tearful, beginning to Kegel.

Dil wasn't a sleeper. She wasn't a sleeper either. No one was a sleeper, except for Roger, who slept for two years straight, through cries, howls, bouts of vomiting, diapers, diarrhea, and utter desperation, with a faint and intensely frustrating smile on his face. If she woke him, he pretended he'd never heard anything.

"Now, Willa," he'd say, and the baby would stop screaming, as if by magic. Then he'd go back to sleep, and the baby would screech like a bird of prey.

At least the baby years are done. Now Dylan's in school, and Willa has her days free, to do what? She hasn't found whatever it is. There must be a solution, but at present she does Pilates, and then sits in the kitchen, looking out over her domain, feeling faintly something.

The grocery store, at least, is cool and peaceful. It's gated into the community with the rest of the perks of Herot: cageless chickens, free-range beef, vegetables untouched by progress.

Dilly dangles from the ice-cream freezer, his face pressed against the glass. Willa looks around to make sure no one's watching, and then opens the door. Slowly, she prizes the lid from the top of a container of something artisanal, and offers it to him. He looks up, startled.

"You're allowed," she says. Little man.

She shows him with her own finger, and then he puts his into the ice cream too. Each of them eats their bite, and then she replaces the lid and puts the container back into the freezer surreptitiously, as though merely deciding on a second flavor. She thinks with dark pleasure about the person who will buy this pint of ice cream, take it home, and discover that someone else has been here first.

Dil has his whole hand in his mouth now, working it around, feeling his loose tooth. Willa has the sickly suspicion there'll be blood. She hands him a Kleenex.

"Now," she says, and waits.

He wipes his fingers with the tissue.

"That's not for telling Daddy," she says.

"Nothing is," Dil says, giving her a jolt. It isn't as though she has a secret life.

Back at home, Willa makes a marinade. She shakes steak in a plastic sack. She roasts tomatoes and roses radishes.

Dadadada DAdadada DA DA DA DA, Dylan plays, pounding the keys. Willa takes the bottle of vodka out of the freezer, pours herself a glass cut with a drop of orange juice, drinks it quickly, and pours another.

From outside, she hears a howl. The back windows of the living room are open onto the mountain, of course, to get the night air and the natural beauty. *Your backyard IS the mountain*, that's what it says in the brochures, and it's true.

"Chopsticks." Dil hammers away, undistracted.

The howl begins again, and Willa cocks her ear, uneasy. She thinks of trying to record it for Roger to hear. If the neighborhood needs a notification, if there's some animal out there, it's her responsibility, but then it's gone, and it's 5:32, and the sun is down, and there's no cocktail poured, and Roger's car is in the driveway.

Willa clicks into the living room, presses play, and raises the volume on something smooth but not too sultry, not likely to provoke despair. Ella Fitzgerald dueting with another of the dead, an electronic combination of voices, two singers who never met, singing separately together.

The ghastly piano drowns in it.

One more howl, and this time she thinks it's definitely human, a boy? But no, of course it's not.

It's coming from the mountain. There's nothing up there but trees.

3

"Listen!" my son says. "Someone's singing!"

Gren's been playing with the skin of a red squirrel, some pebbles, and a tin can, digging a hole in the ground and burying his rattling rag doll.

"What's that voice?" he says again.

It's not a voice. It's a piano. The player below us continues the alphabet, the scales rising, jarring, false notes. They sound like things I'll never be able to get for Gren.

"Listen," he whispers, his hands spread to catch the noise, like it's something he can keep and eat, like it's a bird or a frog. Like a song can feed him.

This is how the war begins: a piano lesson echoing up the mountain. This is how I start to lose him.

◆

Only one other person has ever seen my son. You figure out what you can do for love, and the answer, it turns out, is anything. You can hide for love. You can stay hidden.

Cash register, Army surplus, my son wrapped up in my coat. He was just a baby then. I thought I might be up here on this mountain for no reason. Maybe everything I thought was wrong in the world wasn't wrong at all. Maybe he'd be safe here. Maybe

I was just every mother ever, panicked, looking at her child and seeing all the ways he might get hurt. He was mine, and I wanted someone to tell me my son was beautiful, to tell me he'd grow into a man. I didn't want to be alone forever, with no one to help me, and no one but me to help him.

"Aww, you've got a little one," the woman at the checkout said, and pulled the blanket away from his face. She looked at me, and I looked back at her, and neither of us said anything, but all the worst things blasted into my head.

The look on her face was a look I'd seen in the war, soldiers bending to admire babies, knowing that in a week, a day, an hour, those babies might be dead. I saw bombs falling and obliterating my son, and I saw guns aimed at him.

I saw his body categorized as an enemy body, and I couldn't breathe. I wrapped him up again. I held him tighter.

I went up the mountain, trying to seem like I wasn't running, doubling back, hiding my tracks. She was the last person I spoke to. That was six years ago. I hope she's forgotten everything about it.

There's nothing wrong with him. He's perfect.

His eyes are gold. He's all bones and angles. He has long lashes, like black feathers. He's almost as tall as I am and he's only seven. To me, he looks like my son. To everyone else? I don't know. A wonder? A danger? A boy? A boy with brown skin?

Any of those things will make him a target. I know the world. I've been in it.

"Mama?"

"Gren," I say. "All is well and will be well." I simplified the line, and made it a lullaby.

He says the next line back to me reluctantly. He's distracted by the piano. "And the squirrels will be fed, and the trees will grow taller."

"The snows will come and pile up, but we'll be warm." I say the next line, and Gren says the next.

"Like the animals," he says. "All in their dens."

This mountain used to be a place where predators could survive, but the last mountain lion I saw out here was spread across the asphalt one morning, belly vibrating with flies. We're not predators.

"Like the fish sleeping beneath the frozen water."

"Like the children, safe in their beds," he says, and this isn't a line I taught him. This is something he's made for himself. Has he been watching the people down the mountain? Thinking about what he doesn't have?

I put it aside. He's still little. He doesn't know how to lie to me yet. I haven't always been here, but it's all Gren knows.

I can't panic. I can't think things could be as bad as the rabbit part of my heart suddenly insists they're about to be.

"We don't need to listen to the people down there," I tell my son. "They have their place, and we have ours."

"Listen, though! Listen!" my son insists. There's a little whine in his breath, the air catching itself in his vocal cords and singing through them. I worry about asthma. I worry about everything.

Everything in me says, *Get away from here*, but I know what I am. I'm a stack of broken dishes in the shape of a woman, and this is a flight response.

Nobody comes to this cave, and certainly not to the station below it. That's closed off, and no one even knows it's still there. I know that for sure, but I have to convince myself all the time.

When I was a kid, people didn't want to walk up this mountain at all. They thought it was haunted. It's full of steam springs, water rushing out of nowhere, cold breezes, strange sounds. The mere is half glacial freeze, half hot spots, mist coming up from the center. Everything about this place still exists because people are too nervous to break it open and see what's underneath. It's not a national park. Nothing protects it from progress, nothing but people being scared of ghosts. It's private land. It used to be owned by the train company, and now, I don't know. The people below us, maybe, the ones who surround it.

I stand up and brush the leaves from my jeans, feeling the wind coming in through them, too thin for the winter. I'm as thin as my jeans, my hip bones prodding my skin from the inside. Gren is no better. We strip the bark from the trees. We store nuts, and in the winter we roast them. I hunt with snares.

I tell him I'm checking our traps, but instead I go to the overlook and stare down at Herot Hall. The perimeter's lit up every night with streetlights so God can see them from heaven. I can see them too.

I stare down at the neatly plotted roads, the green grass, watered even on days when it rains. I can hear the people of Herot Hall, the way their appliances beep, the way their car motors move as they come home to wooden tables and identical chairs.

The gated community goes all the way around the mountain, except for the place where the lake is. There are pickets for each of the houses—not the kind of fences that keep anything out—but at the top of the exterior wall they've got barbed wire and cameras, lights detecting our motions when we come too close.

It isn't entirely walled off, though. The side facing us is unguarded. Whoever designed this put their backs to the hillside, like mountains weren't a threat.

Below us, a woman opens the front door of a house made mostly of glass. A child comes running out, young as my son, but fed on better things.

The cats from Herot Hall climb up here to eat our birds. I have a Siamese skinned and ready for the fire, but cat's nothing good to eat, and it isn't enough. The Herot child is dressed in furred pajamas with feet, and the feet have soft claws. The pajamas have ears. A bear. I can see how that'd be sweet, if you weren't me, and they weren't them.

From my vantage, I watch the child bouncing on the asphalt, warm enough, fed enough, safe enough.

Safe from people like me, people living on nothing. If he saw me, he'd be scared. That's how it goes.

The damage that shows: One eye. There's a part of my hair coming in white instead of black. The damage that doesn't show? PTSD, amnesia. Brain, shaken by explosions. Sight, full of shadows. Some people had it worse than me. Some people are dead. I'm alive and I think I'm thirty-four.

I felt like there was a miracle when Gren was born, when I survived it. *Look at my son*, I thought, wanting to show him to my mother, my grandmother, anyone, but there was no one left to show.

✦

My ancestors built the first houses in this valley, hauling materials up the river to the mountain. The mountain was famous for its springs, and the mere was famous for being the place people came to be healed. In the 1800s, people drank the waters and soaked in them, and thought they were being cured of every kind of disease. There was a train from the city, and they'd come out, stay in the hotels for months. My family staffed the resort grounds, cleaned, cooked. Went about their business.

Soon after the turn of the century, people lost their taste for the water and started wondering if it was poison rather than medicine. The tourist trade dropped to almost nothing, and so my family started working for the train line.

In the 1920s, the train stopped coming, and they closed up the station. My family stayed, living in the old hotels, working the scrap jobs in a place left over from the glory days. They knew about the station because they worked the line. They were the ones who closed it off from the world. There were stories about the mountain, people dying in these caves, but my family wasn't afraid.

I was seventeen when my mother brought me up here and rolled a rock off something I later figured out was a vent down into the station. She pretended she was leading me, but I had most of her weight on my shoulder.

This cave was part of the upper entrance, the one for maintenance, and out of it was a hidden staircase, metal, skinny steps, steep, spiraling down a long tunnel with a hidden door. She wouldn't let me take a flashlight. The first cave, this one, had a view of the outside world, but she took me farther in.

We crept along a clammy wall, ankle-deep in water for a while, and below us, on one side, there was a drop-off.

Finally, she lifted a panel from the floor and showed me what was underneath it. The real cave, the old station, was like climbing into the mouth of a whale.

We looked down into the water off the platform, a gurgling river covering the old tracks.

She cupped her hand and lifted the water to her lips and for a moment I saw her as maybe she'd always been, my mother. A skinny woman with blazing eyes. When Gren was born, I saw those eyes again. Wherever he came from, he came from my family too. I sipped from her hand, tasting rock, dirt, and tree.

She tossed a penny down from the ledge at the end of the platform, and I heard something cry out. The sound echoed against the walls.

"If they ever come for you," she said, "this is where you hide. There're things down here they don't know about. Old things."

We were ten years into her illness by then. I figured everything she'd been through, chemo, surgeries, radiation, had messed with her mind. She was always saying things like this, trying to convince me I was special.

That night I climbed out the window in my bare feet and went to meet a boy. I was desperate to see anything that wasn't my mother's shoulder blades under her nightgown. We drove to a party. Someone had music and dancing and lights, parents gone, couches, closets, but all I remember was that when I came home in the morning, ready to get in trouble, my mother's bed was empty, and by the time I got to the hospital, she was already in the basement, covered in a sheet.

Her grave is down there, underneath Herot Hall. I prepared her body for burial myself. I dressed her, and put her favorite things around her, like she'd have any use for them after she was dead. Her family's things, all of them kept generation to generation. I figured they belonged with her, not me. There was a goblet made out of silver, which I spent my childhood polishing. It had the family initials on it, and every night before bed I was the one who filled it with water from the spring. She loved it in a way that pissed me off, like she loved it more than she loved me, and most of the time I wanted to drop it in the mere, but when I found her empty bed, the goblet was sitting on her bedside table. That was what I ended up holding, like I was holding her hand. I put it in with her to go down. In my head, I was taking off forever.

There's no sign of her gravestone now. I don't know how they got permission to build mini-mansions on top of a graveyard, but I guess they did. The cemetery was almost two hundred years old. People never think, until it happens to their place, that all construction is destruction. The whole planet is paved in the dead, who are ignored so the living can dig their foundations.

I walked away from all of it, from the place I came from, and from anything that tried to be more than the usual world. I knew about the station, I knew why it was there, and that was all I wanted to know. I wasn't special.

Then my life happened.

If they come for you, this is where you hide.

The labor took a long time and it was as painful as any labor is. The birth was worse. Anyone who says it doesn't hurt, they're lying. He was born, and we both lived through it, and that's more than nothing.

Let him grow up, I was thinking the whole time. That's an old prayer. It comes in every language.

✦

I go back to the cave and hold the back of Gren's skull for a moment. I stroke his forehead. I give him a walnut and he chews it slowly. I can feel the cold of the cave floor through my jeans and his sleeping bag. There's wet on the wall, wicking upward.

There's a sound out there, clucking. Someone on the other side of the mountain has chickens. We got one last year, but I had to be quick, because they have dogs too. There's a family in Herot Hall that has a parrot, and sometimes I hear it telling itself stories. Once, Gren and I saw it fly over, its wings bright red and green, talking to itself.

"*Once upon a time!*" it screeched.

My son was terrified, but dazzled. So, it turned out, was I. I'd never seen a bird like that out here before, and I was worried it'd tell the world about us, but it just flew over, looked at us with a black and glittering eye, and in a very soft voice said, "*Once upon a time,*" again, before it took off into the morning.

"Hello," I said to the bird, and then closed my mouth. Apparently parrots grieve for the dead as much as humans do, and they're often a sad, speaking creature, capable of flying up into the trees to cry for you and all your neighbors for twenty years or more. I wish—

I can smell Herot Hall's dinner cooking. I wish Gren didn't hear or smell as well as he does.

He cocks his head and looks out into the dark. Laughter carrying up from Herot. The sound of music, louder than it was, and singing. Recorded. Ella Fitzgerald. I know this song.

"It hurts my ears," he says.

Gren doesn't know the words yet for how music makes you feel.

"It makes me want to sing," he says. He looks at me, his eyes darting around, looking first at one side of my face, then the other.

"You can sing quietly," I say. "In a whisper."

He whispers, "I'm singing."

He's shaking with excitement. I try to distract him with a story.

"You can never go down the mountain," this story begins. A lot of my stories begin this way.

"Why not?" he asks, every time I tell it.

"Down the mountain there's a town where everyone's a hungry monster. The monsters tear people limb from limb—"

"Like tree limbs?" he asks.

"Like I might tear bark."

He nods. "To chew," he says.

"They'd tear the skin from your arm," I say, "and eat it."

"What if I *want* to go down the mountain?" he says.

"Want and need aren't the same thing," I say.

"What if you're sick?"

"I'm not."

"You've been sick before," he says reproachfully, his fingertips on the scar on my face.

"That was hurt," I say. "Sick is something different."

"I don't think they're monsters. I watch them when you're hunting," Gren whispers. He hesitates a moment, then: "There's a little boy. He plays outside."

"A little boy?" I ask him. I know the one he means. There's a cold feeling in my stomach. "You can't go down there, Gren. You know that. Tell me you hear me."

He looks at me defiantly and howls in harmony.

"Shhhh!" I tell him, holding his shoulders hard.

He keeps howling, glaring at me, high-pitched, louder and louder.

"Do you want the monsters to kill your mama?" I don't want to say it, but I say it.

He hesitates, and then the howling turns to whimpering.

I stay still, checking, hoping. There are no sounds that say anyone's heard him. No sirens. No new lights flicking on where they face the slopes.

I point out into the sky. A shooting star streaking across the dark. Gren's sniffling, but he looks. I reach out my arms to my son, and he huddles into them, making himself smaller, his hard skull, his eyelashes on my face.

Over there, when you saw a star fall, you weren't sure if it was a star at all, or something sent from your country to blow up their country. There were, I was told, monitors showing all the people in every place, with names put to the dots. There were, I was told, when I was one of the dots, systems for making sure you killed only the monsters, not the good people.

Who are the monsters? Who deserves killing?

I wait for Gren to sleep. He's not a sleeper, and neither am I. But who can sleep in a time like this?

4

We're listening to a little boy at a piano, the keys halting under his fingertips.

Beneath the mountain, in the cave, the song carries, and someone's listening there too.

The people of Herot Hall eat dinner, drink wine and more wine and more wine until the entire place is sleepy. Snow falls, heavy and soft, insulating the roads and rooftops, and a boy emerges from a crack in the mountainside, moving quickly. He runs down, snow kicking up around him, clouds of cold. He glances back at the place he's come from, dodges out of sight of the cave entrance, and down the slope.

The lights blink over him, and then he's at the back of a house full of windows, tapping on the glass.

Another boy appears inside the house, smaller than the first, eyes sleepy, then wide.

They look at each other, one inside, the other outside. They put their hands on the doors and stare. The glass fogs up, and at last the boy on the inside slides his door open.

He puts a finger to his lips. The other boy nods, and comes into the house, easing the door closed behind him. They are known to each other, not strangers.

Silence here. The brightness of the snow, the shine of it under the moon. Nothing moves but tree branches weighted with ice.

The boys are out again, the smaller one dressed for the cold. Both of them run up the hillside, out of sight of the house. The moon silhouettes two shadows as they play in the drifts, the boy from inside teaching the boy from outside how to make a snowball, the boy from outside teaching the boy from inside how to throw the snowball, hard and fast enough to hit the treetops.

Their laughter carries up and away, and the birds consider the sound. We dampen the noise so the laughter is only murmurs, whispers, two boys at play.

They fall on their backs and roll. They angel, arms and legs flailing, and the snow melts around impressions of wings.

After a while, the boys make their way down again, back through the sliding doors, and into the house. The piano plays again, haltingly, four hands instead of two.

5

Listening halfway to the late-night news, Willa's sitting in front
of the TV in her robe and slippers, thinking about the scratches
she's just found on the kitchen door. Long and thin, and in the
glass the marks of something that scratched it. She tried to do it
with her own fingernails and couldn't. The marks were on the
inside. The housekeeper must have brought her dog. There'll be a
discussion.

She looks up at the holly on the mantel. Holy, holly, thole.
Thole = suffering. That drifts up from somewhere, some college
intro to lit, Canterbury, something.

Scrooge is on the screen suddenly. She's always hated Tiny
Tim. She changes the channel. Now it's a Christmas special with
folk singers in Austin, where it's not snowing.

It seems disrespectful to Willa, to sing winter songs in a place
where the sun is shining. It was probably taped in daylight. The
singer has an earnest face. She's playing the piano. Is she even
alive? This Christmas special looks 1975.

"Chopsticks" from the music room. Da da da. DADADA-
DADADDDAAAAAA. Then a tumult of notes, hammering
on the keys.

"Stop it, Dilly!" she says, her voice sharper than she intends it to be. He's an hour past being sent to bed, and he's supposed to be sleeping. She wants to be sleeping too.

The piano stops, with the sound of complaint. She hears Dilly scuffling around, and she sighs. She'll go in, in a moment, and coax him back to where he belongs.

There's a small yelp she assumes to be Dilly slamming down the piano lid on his own fingers. Not the first time.

Roger's sitting at the table reading a medical journal. Willa eyes him from where she sits. He's rolled up his sleeves and his collar's undone.

It's Christmas Eve, the packages are already wrapped, and she takes her temperature every morning. There was a bad moment two years ago, but she managed to keep it secret. Willa wonders if she's like a rabbit who eats its young. What if her womb is a cave full of teeth? She turns off the television and walks toward Roger.

Her son's standing suddenly in the door of the living room, staring at her.

"You're supposed to be in bed," she tells him.

"I'm not sleepy," he says.

His pajamas look damp. His hair looks damp too. A nightmare? His lips are bluish.

"Why not?" she asks, weary of it, wanting to hold him, but he's getting too big for that, and she doesn't really want to, anyway. She wants to want to. What she really feels like doing is drinking in the kitchen with Roger. There he is, just out of reach, his foot in his slipper, tapping on the tile.

"I want my friend!" says Dylan, still standing there. She's forgotten him. "I want Gren!"

"What's that?" Willa says, looking down at him, hearing *grain*. Why would anyone want gluten?

"*My friend*," Dylan repeats. "He came to play. But he had to go home to his mommy."

Roger comes into the room. He bends to look at Dil. "He? Who's *he?*"

"I showed him my room," Dil says, and shrugs. Willa looks at Roger. Roger lifts his eyebrows.

"Is this person imaginary?" Roger says, and Willa shakes her head, knowing the answer. No child thinks his best friends are imaginary.

"Who?" Dil says. "Gren's real."

"And who's Gren?" Willa asks, kneeling to meet Dil's eyes. "You don't know anyone named Gren. That's not even anyone's name. You know a Benjy?"

Dylan writhes with irritation. "I'll show you."

He runs down the hall and, reluctant, Willa follows him. Roger gooses her from behind, but she's in control. She doesn't laugh. The pill she took in the kitchen is working.

Dil's gone into the music room, and when she arrives there, he's sitting at the open piano. Roger's behind her.

"Imaginary," Roger whispers, and almost laughs.

"What, Dilly?" she says. Roger has no idea what it takes to do this job every day. He's in the city, nipping and tucking, a gardener tidying the edges of labial hedges, while Willa's busy making Dylan into a miniature man.

She glances into the gold-framed mirror over the piano and sees a flaw on its surface. She steps forward to brush it away, but it's a scratch, like the ones on the kitchen door, and then she looks down at the piano keys and gasps.

"What happened here?" Roger says.

"I showed Gren our piano," Dil says, and sighs. "He didn't know how to play it. And then he saw himself in the mirror."

Willa puts her hand onto the keys and runs her fingers over the scratches, deep and wide. They make a sound as she touches them, a sound wrong for the moment, sudden chords, and she flinches.

"Who's Gren?" she asks again, in what she hopes is a casual tone.

"My friend," says Dil, and closes the piano lid again abruptly, nearly catching her fingers in it. "My friend who comes to play with me. Can he come again? Can you call his mommy? Can I have hot chocolate?"

"What friend?" she presses.

"*My friend*," says Dil again. He's gone from the room now, leaving Roger and Willa standing in front of the piano looking at each other.

"I don't know," Willa says. "Maybe he got a knife?"

"How could our son possibly *get a knife*?" Roger's looking at her with more blame than she could ever deserve.

"From the kitchen?" she says cautiously.

Roger gives her the look he gives her when she's failed in any small way.

The pill overtakes her now, filling her with gloom. He is ruining its proper effect, which should be cloudless calm.

"You'll have to lock them up from now on. Our son? Access to knives? No, Willa. That is a no."

"It wasn't—"

She looks up, and into the mirror again. There's no one reflecting there, no one but herself and Roger.

Something tumbles in the kitchen, and they both run in, but it's only Dylan scaling the cupboard, hunting marshmallows.

She sways. *My friend. My friend came to play.* In the morning she'll call her mother.

"Time for bed," Willa says. "No exceptions. Let me see your teeth."

Dilly bares them.

"Brush them again."

Yes, the mothers. All of them, Roger's too. What if the housekeeper's bringing a dog? Maybe it's a pit bull.

The pill is working. She's falling, but she's upright. The window, the dark outside and the light inside. There should be curtains. For a moment she sees something flashing, out beyond the house.

Roger has his hand on Willa's thigh, pushing up her white gown. Dylan's back in his bedroom, having drunk the hot chocolate she doesn't remember making, but there's the dirty pot on the stove.

Sometimes, she tucks her son into bed and she feels like she's tucking a wild animal beneath the covers. It's always been that way.

Willa shuts the kitchen door and locks it, twisting the little metal clasp that brings the bar across. There are locks on all the interior doors here.

She turns and looks at her husband.

"Well, I don't know what all that was, Roger!" she says, her voice puppeted by the pill, using his name so he knows she knows it.

"Just Dylan inventing something," Roger says. "He has a big imagination. The knives, though? We'll get locks for a cabinet and shut them inside it. That can't happen."

Willa looks at the clock and changes the subject.

"Merry Christmas," she says.

She pushes her hips up over the lip of the countertop. She's tall enough to hop up without being awkward. She crosses and then uncrosses her legs.

Long and pink, like fronds, she thinks. Under the nightgown, which isn't for sleeping in, everything is cream-colored lace, trimmed in red for the holidays. The lingerie saleswoman advised her on what men want.

It was nice to be naked in that room, watched by the saleslady, appreciated. "That suits you," the lady said, clapping her hands. "That's perfect."

Roger's mouth is on her hip bone, and she's arching and pushing herself up. The counters are clean. She sterilized them with a spray bottle.

She looks out the windows as Roger pulls her nightgown off her shoulders, and she thinks, *There, look at that if you're looking.* But she doesn't see them, whoever they might be. All she sees are her breasts in their lacy half cups, falling out of the dress, hard and pale, and as Roger unties the tiny bows at the sides of her hips, the triangle of red-gold hair between her legs.

The windows are like a mirror, light reflecting her own face, and Roger's, the two of them in their white kitchen glowing like they're a lighthouse, calling whatever ship, any ship. Lighthouses don't speak only to the ships of their own country, Willa thinks, and then no.

It's Christmas.

Everything is bright.

If anyone's watching from out there, let them watch.

6

Listen! It's time for church! Bells are ringing from below, this fat homesick sound that makes me think about everything I've ever seen at this time of year, good and bad: a skinny little plastic tree in a parking lot when I was thirteen, a red nose in the desert when I was twenty-three, a rose on a motel sign when I was twenty-four, and I'm confused for a moment before I remember that it must be Christmas.

It snowed during the night, and everything is blanketed. The world feels safer, against logic, and I feel summoned, like I might get up and run down the mountain, now, after all I've been and done. I haven't been to church since I was seventeen, and the church I went to then is gone, underneath Herot Hall like everything else.

Instead, I check traps, the ones in the darkest part of the trees, where no one can see me from below. Nothing in them. I need a bird or a rabbit.

Gren's still fast asleep, and so I watch Herot through the scope on my weapon. I'm not aiming at them. I'm just looking. I haven't killed a human since Gren was born. Before that, I killed ten. That was my count. Maybe someone else's is different.

Seven years ago, I woke up in a hospital that wasn't really a hospital. My guns were gone, but when I got out of there, running,

I climbed into my friend Bobby's parents' barn in Nebraska. Hollow hoarding under a plank. Couple hundred bucks, some naked pictures of women I didn't know, some MREs, Bobby's M4 carbine and Beretta M9. Man was ready for any just in case. Bless you, Bobby, rest in peace. They're up high on a ledge, originally out of reach of Gren, except now he's tall enough to touch anything he wants. I've tried to teach him about danger, but he also knows how to load and fire. I needed him to know. There are emergency weapons in a situation like this. I don't use either of them to shoot, but I keep them clean.

I'm trying to figure out what Gren sees in the people below us, and it's obvious. They have so many things. Everything down there is brightly colored and bountiful. Up here? Rocks, sticks, rabbits.

The wall-sized TV is on. There are balloon animals parading down the middle of an avenue somewhere. Is there a Christmas parade now? I don't see a child and I don't see a husband. Just the wife, dressed, making coffee.

The parade she's watching is a parade of grinning giants. I saw a parade once that was all puppets with bloody mouths. That seemed more right to me, the way sticks moved them, the way they cast long shadows on the sand, and beneath the shadows little creatures scrambled, trying to get out of the sun.

She brings a bird out of the refrigerator. A goose, plucked by someone else. I watch her at the counter with a knife, opening it up, putting her hands into it, blood in the sink. She's stuffing this bird, and I'm up here, with my son, feeding him what tonight? The cat is turning on the spit, and no fat is dripping. There's a squirrel too, not safe in its den, but roasting in ours.

There's the boy, in snow gear. He looks very small, but that's because I'm used to Gren.

I think about how a mother made him. I've been a house like that, for more than just my son. I've been a warm room for voices that shout and scream and tell me they're trying to surrender.

I saw a baby blow up in its mother's arms when I was over there. A soldier touched its face and the baby cooed and the soldier gave it a kiss. Everybody died, mother, child, soldier. All the soldier's guys died but one, and I watched that guy running crazy, out from a black and white place in the dirt.

I saw a lot of movies played in a tent. That thing, the bomb, the baby, the last guy running? It might have been in a movie. One time I threw a beer bottle at a sheet, stretched between two buildings, and cried during a preview for something stupid I figured I'd never live to see. That's the last time I remember watching anything on a screen.

I think about what Gren would know if his world weren't the size of our cave. He could see what the world really looks like. What the world really *is* like.

The fossil trees, the ones around this mountain? Those trees were never hung with ropes, but that's only because humans didn't exist when those trees were alive.

Down in the tunnels off the main station, there are things from a century back, people using it before us. People hid here. There's a trunk with a jacket with a high collar, something made of dark fabric, bloodstained. A dress made of calico covered in mud at the hem. A paisley shawl. A christening gown, embroidered with flowers for some baby gone now a hundred years. If you leave things long enough, they stop belonging to anyone but the place they're in. When I was little, I had a doll my mother found in the caves on this mountain, small bones, carved and strung together.

My son has a rock with a fossil inside it, and that came from someone else to me, and from me to him. Discarded things can get used again, sometimes for love.

When I get back to our cave, I find Gren's toys on the floor. Stick dolls, each one tied together with string, each one broken into twig bits. Men he's made. He's killed them and I don't know why. I don't know what game he was playing, who he was angry at.

"Mommy," he says. He's never said that before.

He has a doll in his hand. I watch him crush it, and then throw it off the edge of the cave lip, into the water we can't see. Something makes a sound down there.

I'm looking at his spine, the sleek bones beneath his skin. Made by my body, those bones, and sometimes I'm broken by that too, the idea that this person came from me. I feel toxic, mostly, but I brought him into this world, and here he is. We look down into the dark together and something large splashes, a heaving up out of water, a slopping onto stone.

"Gren," I say. "All is well and will be well."

"No." He looks up at me, and his eyes flash in the dark. "I'm not right," Gren says. "I don't look right."

"What do you look like?" I ask him. "You look like yourself."

He shakes his head. He crushes another stick man in his fist, and it cuts his palm. Drops of blood fall from Gren's hand and down into the dark water. The creatures keen.

"Stop that," I say.

"They're hungry," Gren says, and flings another drop of blood down. He had thirty men here made out of sticks. Now there are only twenty-eight. "I played with the boy from down there," my son says, not looking at me. "You said they were monsters."

My heart starts pounding and I calm it as quickly as I can. I can't scare him. I have to get him to tell me.

"Only one person?" I say, my voice even. Calm. "Just him? Did you go down the mountain?"

"I played in the snow with him," he says. "He's not a monster."

"Did anyone else see you?"

There's something else in his hand. I've been seeing it glittering, not thinking about it, and finally I know what it is. A Christmas bow, the kind that sticks onto a package. I'd forgotten something like that even existed. Gren brings out a box wrapped in colorful paper.

To: Dylan
From: Santa

"He gave me a present," Gren says, and his mood has changed. Now he's happy. He looks up at me. "Can I keep it?"

He thinks his loneliness is gone forever, but this is the thing that happens right before you learn that even though you love someone, they might not love you back.

Is this how it is in the world, for every parent? You follow your son. You wait outside your house when he doesn't come home, hoping there's a god out there paying attention to you. Or you wait for your daughter. You look in the windows of cars and houses, knowing you could lose your children in a second if you let down your guard at all. This is nothing new. The world is the world.

My world is worse than that one, but not by much.

I think of the little boy in his bear pajamas, the way he's running around his Christmas tree, his parents, the things he's going to tell them about my son.

I think about that little boy, and I feel my heart fill with grief, with end of the world, because now I know who I have to kill.

7

"So?" says Willa's mother, Diane, marching in with her matriarchal unit on Christmas morning. There are five women here, all wives and widows of Herot Hall, dressed in holiday casual, pale cashmere and pearls. The mothers travel as a pack. They station themselves on the kitchen stools. "We got up early for this."

"Coffee?" Willa asks, the silver tray already in her hands. This is a council of war, even though it's Christmas Day. War is always one cup, black, no sugar, and, sure enough, the mothers take their portion.

No one eats breakfast. If Willa offered, it would be a national scandal. The mothers count calories like kills. Beneath their sweater sleeves are arms made muscular by boxing. Three have become karate black belts out of boredom, and the rest train on the Pilates reformer daily.

Willa ties her own wrap sweater tighter around her middle. Beneath her eyes there is a light treatment of concealer, which her mother wipes off with a disdainful fingertip, reapplying something Dead Sea from her own purse.

"There are marks on the window," Willa tells them. "And the piano. On the mirror above it too."

The mothers march through the house to examine the

marks. They seem unimpressed. She'd expected more. A crew of fixers running from a van like something on television.

"I always thought it might be a mistake to leave the back of the houses unfenced," Willa says. "Who knows what's on the mountain? There was that bear attack last year, and—"

"Absolutely not," Tina interrupts. "My husband designed Herot for safety. It's a mountain, Willa, not a safari park."

"What are the marks from, then?" Willa asks, feeling slightly desperate.

"Claudia doesn't have a dog," says Diane, considering.

"Who's Claudia?" Willa asks.

"The woman who cleans," says Roger's mother, Tina, a faint edge of disapproval in her voice, which has taken on an accent. "*Claudia.* She's been cleaning your house for four years. She's from Mexico."

Implications. Willa feels like a candy thermometer, blood rising.

"I know her name," Willa says.

Roger's taken Dylan to build a snowman, specifically arranged by Willa so that the visit of the mothers could be a secret from him. Thank god. She doesn't need Roger seeing this. Dylan's vision of Christmas Day, gleaned from television, includes dawn. Willa plied him with treats, and now Roger will have reaped the rewards of sugar, Dil sobbing in the snow, irrational and bitey with his demands.

"The marks are too deep to be from a cat or raccoon," Willa says. "They're too deep to be from anything I can think of."

"Maybe you've forgotten," says Tina.

"A delivery?" says Diane.

"A guest with a dog?" says Tina, and gives Willa a look that feels like an ice pick to the soul.

What guest? What implication is this? Tina might as well call her an infidel. Is that what it's called? Tina's never liked Willa.

Tina puts a questioning hand on one of the two fragile balloon wineglasses on the counter, left over from last night. Both have a bloody rime of red in the bottom.

Tina smiles at Willa, whose pulse visits her eyeballs, though she has no reason to be guilty. She's done nothing wrong. Tina's own son drank that wine.

Willa knows, though. This is her own fault. She's not supposed to rely on the mothers. She spent the night considering the way dying attacked by a mystery animal would absolve her of every carpool, every cocktail hour, every day as a daughter and mother and wife. Would dying be worth it? No.

The mothers look around judgmentally, and at least two of them have fingers out, dragging for dust. Willa has a sudden fear that her lacy panties are on the kitchen floor.

She glances down, but there's only a broken gingerbread man. She tries to scoop it up before they notice, but now Willa's on her knees and all the mothers are craning down at her like ostriches.

"I think it was a bear," Willa hears herself say. "I really think it was a bear."

"Oh, for heaven's sake," says Diane, and gives Willa her own ice pick look, except that this one resurrects a dead marriage and reminds Willa who the hero here really is.

"Never mind," says Willa. "It was probably something that happened at Dilly's last playdate. Maybe I just didn't notice."

The mothers nod. That narrative is their preferred, Willa failing slightly, regularly. Roger is perfect. Willa is not. This is usual.

Christmas morning isn't for package-opening, because the mothers prefer Christmas evening. The light is better then; photos live forever. They leave a stack of presents. Too many, if you ask Willa.

"I'll wear my armor and bring my sword tonight," says Tina, and laughs. "It seems someone's imagined a monster."

"My daughter's not prone to imagining," says Diane.

"Of course she's not," Tina says. "She only needs to be her own lovely self, isn't that right? Why would she need to imagine anything?"

Willa tries to get between Tina and the fridge, but she's not quick enough. Tina opens the door, dodging and bobbing as though the crisper contains a criminal.

"I'd never do a goose," Tina says, and shudders.

"The fat," Diane says, and nods, realigned in sisterhood.

"I love how she doesn't care about calories," Tina says, and then both of them look at Willa's waist.

When Willa was seven months pregnant with Dylan, she and her mother went shopping, and a woman smiled at Willa. The woman was large in a way that enticed, gloriously enormous, and unapologetic. Willa smiled back, and turned to see her mother shaking a finger.

"That's what happens when you let yourself go," Willa's mother said, and glanced at the flesh on Willa's upper arm, the creamy way it poured from her sleeve.

"There's a warning in this for us all," said Diane, all but crossing herself.

Now she lives on protein bars. They all do.

When the mothers are finally gone, Willa puts her head inside the freezer. Of course it wasn't a bear. It was Dylan and a paring knife. She regrets calling in the troops.

She ordered the goose from a retailer that gave the goose's entire family tree. It's a heritage bird. She ordered heirloom onions and grains for stuffing. There was a ten-page photo spread in her mind, her Christmas dinner as photographed for the masses. Tagged, envied. Now the goose looks yellowish and nervous.

She has it all under control. She'll drain the fat. She won't drink it. She won't boil it and pour it over anyone. She'd never.

She looks down at the cookie kicked beneath the counter. Dylan running through the kitchen sneaking sugar, or Roger last night, pushing her against the counter. She walks into the pantry in search of the rest of the three dozen gingerbread men, baked yesterday afternoon. She'll decorate them. Usually she loves Christmas.

But each gingerbread man is missing its head, neatly bitten off.

Gren, she thinks, in spite of herself, and shivers.

All around her the windows open onto snow, and the sky is falling. The bells are ringing out for Christmas Day, and in the foyer she hears Dil and Roger stamping their feet, the gusting smell of weather.

She walks out into the foyer but no one's there.

Snow pants sprawl like a bisected corpse in the hallway. A red scarf dangles from the banister. A balaclava like a sucked dry head, skull and eyes missing, only skin left.

A snowball hits her in the back.

She turns and another snowball hits her hard in the face. She blinks, and tries to keep smiling.

"Coffee?" she says, clenching in turn her teeth, her vagina, her fists.

The men are laughing. Not men, no, she corrects. *Boys.* Dylan is doubled over in hilarity, and Roger's laughing too, HAHA-HAHA, DADADADA Da DA da Da Dada DADADA!

Willa thinks about the chef's knives in the kitchen, her brain glancing over them, the way they stand in the block like soldiers.

"Did you eat the heads off the cookies?" she asks them. "Do you think that's funny?"

The white lights on the Christmas tree twinkle in staccato seizures.

"Someone had too much wine last night," Roger says, and then laughs. "It's just snow, Wills. Don't be so grumpy. It's Christmas!"

She flexes her muscles again, and then blows air out her nostrils like she's a horse. She's never had a horse. Some girls are horse girls. Willa's a walker. Suddenly she wants a stallion, and she wants to ride into battle on it, swinging her own sword.

Dil's standing beside her, his hands out for the mittens to be removed. For a moment, she sees claws poking through the fingertips, and a tail whipping up behind her son, but then that's gone.

"I showed Daddy where I played with Gren!"

She looks over Dil's head at Roger, who shrugs. "Snow angels," he says. "He went out to run around. There were some tracks, but it wasn't anything. I'll get Mark to come out with me and have a look."

"There are bears here," she reminds him. One got into the trash and made a mess of turkey legs and gullets last Thanksgiving.

"Bear tracks don't look like that," he says. "Also, it's winter. This is just kids. Don't worry. Enjoy Christmas. And your mother. We saw her car leaving, and my mother's car too, and who else, Margaret, and Alice? Patricia? The entire club, actually, which seems a little much, if you ask me. But you didn't."

Willa studies Roger, who is losing his hair as he stands before her. She drifts back to the kitchen and stares up the misty mountain. The slope is smooth as vanilla ice cream. The bells ring again.

From the living room there's the sound of the piano, not "Chopsticks" but something else, a tune she's never heard before. It makes her stomach tilt, her ears prickle, and bile rise in the back of her throat. It's not beautiful. It's strange.

Willa listens for a moment, then yanks a chef's knife from the block, but when she gets to the room, only Dylan's there, sitting on the bench. She puts the knife behind her back.

"What was that?"

"Gren taught me a song," Dil says, and smiles giddily, his tiny pale self, milk teeth.

Willa is reminded of an X-ray photo she saw once, of a little boy's skull, the way the adult teeth were lodged high up near the nasal cavity and deep in the chin, hidden above and below the pointed, pliable baby teeth, double rows, like those in a shark's mouth.

She goes back toward the kitchen, boiling. Why did she say she'd cook this goose? There's supposed to be some sort of archaic feast and packages, and everyone singing around the tree, in seven hours and thirty-seven minutes.

She's walking barefoot across the soft pile of the rugs, when her heel catches on something. She drops to her knees and crawls, her face an inch from the floor.

There are snags all along the passageway. She blinks, feeling dizzy.

She unlatches something sharp from the carpet fibers.

It's the sheathing of a claw, hooked as a tiger's, pearlescent white.

8

"So it fucking goes, man," one of the other officers laments as Ben Woolf picks up a phone that's not supposed to be ringing. It's Christmas Day. Then again, why are there officers in the police station at all, if possibility's on pause?

Ben Woolf's been up since five in any case, doing what a man of a certain age needs to do to stay combat-ready. Bodies want to crumble.

Fifteen miles on the stationary bike. Four hundred sit-ups, bench press, elliptical, pecs, speed bag, stairs, high school bleachers, up them, down them, chin-ups, yoga plank cooldown. Shower in ice water (circulation), jerk off while showering, why not, though the cold water makes that a challenge, dress in uniform, comb hair neatly, and out of there by 6:45. Steak tartare. Raw egg.

Ben Woolf may be forty (face it, forty-four), but he's in the best shape of his life. He's never off-duty, despite the drowsy nature of this situation. Trees fall on houses and he has to be there, nature committing crimes against property. People collapse in the middle of the grocery store, or end up driving while dead. Crime doesn't sleep and Ben doesn't either.

Now it's nine, and Ben's been sitting in the station, alert for hours, waiting for anything at all to happen. Chief is midway through his third piece of fruitcake. Ben watches as he brings a bite to his mouth. He's an old man with years of service. His hand shakes as he lifts his coffee mug. Ben sets his face in the expression he'd show his dad, good men united in a fight for justice, and lifts the phone to his ear.

"Ben Woolf here," he says. He doesn't know how to answer the phone. The receptionist is off.

"Hello?" It's a woman on the other end. "Is this the police?"

"This is Officer Woolf," Ben says, and she laughs, which catches him off guard entirely.

"That's funny," she says, and then, "No, it's not funny. I'm sorry, it's not funny."

"What seems to be the problem, ma'am?" he asks.

"It's just that there's been an animal," she says. "A wild animal. In my house. That's why I laughed. Wolf. I mean, it's probably not a wolf."

She's on speaker, and the other officers look at him. Chief twirls a finger beside his ear and Ross makes a gesture that causes Ben to avert his eyes.

"What kind of animal is it?"

She pauses, clearly thinking.

"No, not a wolf. It might be a tiger. I know how that sounds."

"Miss," Ben says.

"Mrs.," says the woman. "Willa Herot."

Ben sees Chief mouthing obscenities. He finds the mute button.

"Even if she's calling about an imaginary tiger stuck in a powder room, you're still going out to Herot Hall, Woolf, Merry Christmas to you. They donate."

"They should have their own police," another officer mutters. "They have all the money in the world."

Ben gets the particulars and hangs up.

"Got enough calories in you?" asks Chief. "My wife made cookies."

He pushes a dish of Christmas at Ben, who shudders in revulsion and longing. There are no carbohydrates worth it.

"Suit yourself," Chief says. "Wear your snow gear. Like as not they'll send you hiking up that damn mountain, treat you like some kind of neighborhood watch. Any trouble with them, tell them it's Fish & Game's job, and you're there on a mercy mission because of the holiday. Don't do anything that might get you rabies."

"And don't get eaten by a tiger, buddy," one of the officers says as Ben heads out. Ben almost turns to see what's got him going, but it's not worth it. People sometimes hate Ben. They take one look and think, *Fuck that guy.* Nobody's fault but their own.

It's a commuter town, but the commute isn't complete to Herot. The train stops near the police station, and then it's a forty-minute drive through forest to the mountain. Up and down the river there's nothing but trees. There's not a lot in the way of local employment either, couple cafés, couple gas stations, a general store. They've gated themselves in up there. The place is like a fortress.

Woolf doesn't understand it. Why isolate yourself? He likes to hear his neighbors. His childhood was orphanage to foster home, and when at last he was adopted he went quickly from being a beautiful boy into an awkward adolescent with acne-spackled skin, thin as a chopstick. He grew twelve inches in a summer, swam instead of talking, and almost made the Olympic team. His life was a series of almosts, until he joined the Marines and went to war, where the almosts became certainties.

It's been a long time since he's killed anyone. He drives fast, and, as usual, his brain's full of the dead. He counts them like sheep. Some were killed by bombs, some by drones, some by Ben's gun. He did okay. Better there than here.

This job in the shadow of the mountain, at the edge of the lake, isn't much of a killing job. This is a slip-and-fall, shoplifter-busting job. There are better jobs, though, and Herot, maybe, is the ladder to them. The money and the backers. Some jobs are elected. It's Ben's job to make nice until he gets himself to the chief position, or higher yet, maybe, running all the stations on this side of the river. State politics, even national. Not today. Animal roaming a suburb. It'll be a stray dog, maybe a raccoon, at best a possum.

He pulls through the gate in his cruiser, rings the bell, and waits for them to let him in. The house is mostly glass. There's nothing wrong here. He can see all the way through, from the front door to the mountain behind it. It's tight as a bedsheet.

Nobody's dead in this house. Nobody needs to be killed either. He misses the war. What kind of heroics are possible? Cats in trees and old ladies on floors. It's enough to make a man fall into ruin, and plenty of men do. Ben sucks in his gut preemptively.

The wife opens the door and stares at him, as though he's a surprise. Tall, blond, he doesn't notice the rest.

"You called the police?" he says to her. "I'm Officer Woolf."

It's his height she's reacting to, probably, greater than her own. She puts out her hand and waves it at the world, holding a full cup of coffee, then brings it back in just as he reaches out his own hand to take the handle. He sees her lipstick on the rim and realizes his mistake. Embarrassing.

"There's a tiger," she says. "Or a lion. Or a bear!"

He looks at her. Drugs?

"Welcome to Herot Hall," she says, correcting her tone. "There's no hall, though. Only walls and fences."

"Fish & Game's off today, or you'd be getting a man with a truck," Ben says. "Instead, you get me. I'll take a look around."

"There were claw marks in the window," she says. "And in the door. There were claw marks in the carpet. I wasn't going to call, but—"

Ben makes sure his eyes are kind. He is thinking about the likelihood this woman is entirely crazy. It wouldn't be the first time. He's had women wriggle their fingers and walk in the direction of the bedroom.

"—but then, we started to think about how whatever it was, it was in the house with our son. What could have happened. What almost *did* happen, and—"

"We had to call," says the husband, arriving behind her. "There are children here, for God's sake."

Ben reassesses. She's not inviting him in for that purpose, then. Or at least not obviously.

He tries not to look at the lace he sees under her sweater. Wrap sweaters always make him want to untie things and then double knot them. It's a failing.

"This is my husband, Roger Herot," she says. "Roger, this is Officer Woolf. Come in."

Into the house, then, all waxed wood floor and stainless appliances. The dining room contains a table for more people than could possibly ever eat dinner here, and there are tremendously high ceilings, cathedral, that's the word for them. They're almost high enough to make Ben feel he doesn't need to stoop to walk politely.

"Can I offer you anything?" the wife asks.

"Water, thank you," says Ben, and she brings him something not from the tap, but a bottle with a European label.

"It tastes like sulfur," she says, noticing his hesitation. "The tap water. Roger likes it, but I think it's disgusting. People used to come here to soak in it, can you imagine? People used to think this mountain was haunted, but now it's just a mountain."

Woolf sits down on the couch. At any moment they'll offer him carbs.

The child runs through, making his way from end to end of the room chanting a singsong.

"Gren, Gren, Gren," the child sings. "Gren, Gren, Gren!"

Imaginary friend, the husband mouths.

"Well," says the wife.

Woolf feels a button on his uniform beginning to detach, and makes a mental note to stitch it back on, tighter this time.

"It was Gren," says the child, planting himself on the couch, looking like an ancient and weary king. "And me. We played."

The wife holds out her hand. In it, there's a claw sheathing.

So, he revises. It's something large, an illegal seller, someone with a stash locked behind a barbed-wire fence. Some people like to pretend they're still fighting a great battle against the creatures of Earth, that the world remains wild around them. Other people like to think they're building Noah's trailer park.

The wife breathes in, a shuddering little breath.

"See?" she says. "I didn't make it up. You thought I was exaggerating."

"No one was here but the three of us, Dylan's grandmothers, and a couple of their friends," the husband says.

"*Someone* was here," she says sharply.

"Only if you left the door open," her husband says. "Those doors are secure."

"Glass is the opposite of secure," says the wife, and looks at Ben.

Ben looks away. Marital discord isn't his business.

"You said there were marks?" he asks, and they show him, leading him around the house.

He glimpses the wife's reflection in the mirror over the piano, her sweater still falling slightly open, the curve of her breast.

Other men are seized with lust in the middle of Walmart, following women down the aisles, imagining best-case scenarios. Woolf is made of self-control. His job comes first. Her mouth, though, is like a spatter of blood on a plaster wall, that's what Ben Woolf thinks. Then he carefully removes his thoughts from that part of his memory. Nothing is there, nothing but a stippled white surface and a man marching past it, nothing but an enemy captured and a door locked on a history of violence.

All he knows is that he's one of the few good men. He is the front line against the nightmare.

He gets himself outside. He'll walk the mountain himself. Someone up north filled a swimming pool with alligators, and someone else got busted with an elephant in the garage, bought fuck knows where.

His job at present is a performance, standing at the bottom of the slope and looking up toward the mist at the top, keeping the suburbs safe.

He can feel the wife watching him from the kitchen windows. He squares his shoulders. There are tracks in the snow, yes, but nothing more than those of kids playing. Half a snowman, footprints and snow angels, and then the tracks are lost in undergrowth, brushed over with weather and wind like all things eventually are. No paws. No bears. No monsters. Just kids. The only oddity is that some of the tracks are from bare feet, but Ben would have done that himself at that age. Might do it now, for that matter.

Ben marches up the mountain, fading himself purposefully to white.

He feels her the whole time, standing in that window, watching him rise.

So, this is what I have to do. I don't know how to do it. I load the M4, but there's nothing good in this. No silencer. More gun than this task, but I'm not close. I fumble as I load it. The saint sits beside me, raises her finger to her temple, and suicides with her own invisible weapon.

"Somebody painted a picture of my face on the cave wall over there once. That man lived here for a while, when they built the station. He found a bunch of bones. When I was alive, we thought those bones were dragons, but nobody ever saw a dragon in the real world."

"Nobody ever saw a girl with a candle lit in her tits either," I say.

"Sure they did," she says. "I'm just keeping it bright in here for you. Who likes the dark? Do you?"

I edge myself out of the cave entrance and blink in the light of the world.

Gren's behind me suddenly, and she's gone.

"No," I tell him. "Back into the cave, and down the stairs. Stay there. Don't come out until I say you can."

Gren backs away, and I wait for him to disappear before I resume surveillance. Windows look impermeable, but they're

made of glass. Houses are made of straw. There's always someone waiting to blow the whole thing down.

The boy in the house looks like he's been worried since he
was born, but maybe that's just the look of a little boy watching a
parade. There's a pile of wrapped presents, and lights on the tree.

He's maybe half Gren's size, wearing a Christmas Day suit,
with a tie, and shined shoes. He's as pale as his mother, blond
hair, pink and white skin. His hair's a sticking-up mess of yellow
curls.

He hasn't done anything wrong. All he has is a secret, and
the secret is us.

I think about how some mothers over there watched their
tiny sons talking to soldiers. I offered candy to the little boys, telling their mothers they'd be safe with me. By then I'd memorized
a few phrases.

"What are you doing?" Gren asks me. He's back, moving so
quietly I had no warning. When did he learn to move that way?

"Watching," I say. "Go in."

"Are you hunting?"

This startles me. I turn away from the scope.

"No," I say. "I'm not hunting. This isn't hunting."

You have to be vigilant and keep track of your mind, if you've
been out awhile, in any war on Earth, at any time on Earth. I put
the M4 away, back in the cave, back on the shelf. This isn't the
weapon for this. I don't know what I was thinking.

Once, in the desert, on the edge of the ring of campfire light,
I saw a black gleam. Ants carrying a body across the sand, sharing
the weight, millions upon millions of them, the corpse levitated a
fraction of an inch above the earth. I blinked and that vision
was a shadow, no ants, no body. A hallucination.

Anything could be like that. Shooting at them from up here
won't save us. It will bring them hunting us. This is no solution.
What has to be done is quieter. I have to get closer.

Gren grabs my hand and tugs it, like he's much younger than he is. "Don't hunt, Mama. I'm not hungry."

He's using the voice he'd use to ask for a story. He's scared of what I might be about to do.

I have a flash of Gren's body being carried down a long slope on the backs of those ants, and then brought to a river. I see him being ferried away from me.

"I'm keeping you safe," I say.

He looks at me, and his eyes are huge.

"I *am* safe, Mama," he says. "We're safe in our cave."

But who's ever safe? Down below us are the kind of people who walk armed into churches and movie theaters and through libraries, blast fevers into federal buildings, and build bombs out of things they bought cheap at a hardware store. What kind of myth is it, that people like them are keeping the rest of us safe?

Some people must be safe on this planet, but I've seen houses with thick walls blown up, kids walking down the street, cross-fire. *Crossfire.* Flaming in front yards, hoods in white, hoods on sweatshirts, and who's safe?

No one's ever found me. I think I got lost in a file of forgotten soldiers. I hadn't done anything wrong. I wasn't guilty of anything. Maybe they decided I was innocent. That's what I've been telling myself, but I look out over the slope, and my heart stops.

There's a cruiser speeding down the one road that comes here, circling around the mountain and through the front gate of Herot Hall.

The cruiser pulls into the driveway of the house I've been watching. Out of it comes a Viking-looking man in uniform, very tall and very blond, exactly the kind of man I know to watch out for. He was a soldier. I can see his march from here.

"If you hear anyone coming up the mountain," I tell Gren, trying to control my voice, trying not to scare him, "you have to hide."

"Why?" he asks.

"If you hear the sounds of dogs, or if you hear clicks or shots, or voices, run into the cave and go all the way down," I tell him. "Go into the station, and, if you have to, into the tunnel that comes out of it."

This is a last resort. If I die, he's still too young to make it on his own. Where would he go?

I see the places in the dark beneath the mountain, the bones of my family buried beneath Herot, and no one to bury us, so we'll be burned, maybe, and put in a box in some police file room, ashes to ashes, dust to done.

When Gren was tiny, I tried to teach him about death. We buried a soldier made of twigs and a plastic woman he'd found on the mountain.

"This is what you do when someone you love dies," I told him.

"Okay, Mama," he said, and his eyes welled up. "Don't die."

"I won't," I said, and I knew even then I was a liar. "I'll never leave you."

Now I wonder why I taught him to do any of the things people do: burial, grief, any of it. I don't know why I didn't just tell him to run as fast as he could, as far as he could, into the woods or ocean, away from people, away from guns and soldiers. I'm not ready for this.

"I promise I'll find you," I tell him. "All is well and will be well."

He hesitates. "Mama?"

The officer's out of the house, sniffing the air like he's a tracker.

"Go now!"

He's talking to himself, talking to nothing, and men who talk to nothing are men you can't trust. They yell into the dark, causing the rest of their company to spin in a weapon-drawn panic and catch some poor bastard taking a piss, one of your own, not whoever the enemy is, just one of your buddies, hidden by midnight. It happens all the time. Half of the dead are killed by their friends. Maybe that's the history of everything.

I take myself back inside the entrance of the cave, where I can still see the officer, and bring the Beretta down, aim at him, stare at his face and his hands and the way his face moves. I center on his skull, but what I see is a man who's been to war just like I've been to war. He's a boy with a badge and I'm a fugitive in the line of bullet fire if I don't get him first. We were on the same side. Not anymore.

The officer makes his way up the slope like a fire spreading from a cigarette. He's coming toward me, up the whiteness, straight up the center of the mountain.

The saint is back. She looks at me, approving of all of this. This man is my enemy, and I'm his. Maybe this is destiny. Maybe he's who I'm supposed to kill, out of all the people I've killed in war. Maybe I'm supposed to turn on a soldier who could've been beside me.

Finger on the trigger. Heart pounding.

The officer's in the trees, twenty feet from the hidden entrance of the cave, running hands over the rock, but I'm invisible to him. I keep the crack in the mountain covered with brush and wood, things I've made to look like nature made them. There are pine needles outside the entrance, and pebbles, things that keep our tracks from showing. I'm looking at him through a narrow opening, controlling my panic.

He's within a few feet of me, but now he's talking on his phone.

"There's nothing up here," he says. "I'm walking the mountain, but it's just snow, no animals, no people."

He looks around, sniffs the air.

"There's part of a claw, yeah, in the house," he tells the person on the other end. "Maybe the kid picked it up in the woods.

The wife thinks it's an invader, and the husband's humoring her. It's nothing. I'll close it up and head back in."

A bullet rolls off the ledge I keep the guns on, and across the rocks. I'm paralyzed.

He's alert, listening, but a bird sings out, and he looks up to the sky instead.

He's not looking for Gren. He's not looking for me. If he was, there'd be guns all over the mountain. They'd take Gren, tie him down, tear him open, look at his organs, map the way his heart beats. They'd count his breaths and call him a killer. I could tell them he's only a little boy, but it wouldn't matter.

They don't know.

They don't know about him, and that means they don't know about me. I watch the officer leave the mountain, walking down, still talking on the phone. I track his every move.

He turns once, feeling me looking.

"Hello?" he says.

I don't answer, and after a moment he keeps walking.

Death is one step in the wrong direction, a heartbeat losing its place. I know this much is true. Death returned me, and here I am. I watch until he's gone.

"Gren," I whisper into the dark of the cave, and he appears from out of the secret door, standing on the stairs, tears on his face.

✦

We have to leave this mountain. I was a fool to think we could stay here, not anymore, not now that Gren's older, but we can't leave today. The mountain's too busy. There'll be sleds on the slopes, carolers, Christmas lights. We'll go after New Year's, after everyone's stopped celebrating and the lights go off at night again.

We'll find somewhere else to hide then. Six days to think of where, six days to figure out how to get out without anyone seeing us. Six days to stay hidden here.

The saint sits down beside me. My companion, my hallucination, my dream.

"He's gonna die here, girl," she tells me. "He's gonna die on this ground."

She's been saying it awhile, but she isn't real and so I pretend it's possible to ignore her.

"Gren," I say. "Come here. Let me tell you a story."

He curls into my arms, and I tell him I can keep him safe forever.

WHAT

10

What will he do? We wait, watching, and the boy waits too, for his mother to leave him. He counts down, pretending to sleep, until she takes her nightly walk of the tunnels, the entrances and exits.

Then he slips out of the cave, as he always does, to watch the village below him, looking through the window of a house where a roasted goose is being pulled from the oven. The bird is steaming, and there's a dish of warm fat outside the kitchen door. The boy watches it solidify in the cold.

The houses are lit for the holidays. Cars drive a quarter mile across the subdivision, parking, the people in them walking up. Guests are dressed in red, green, and gold, and when they come into the houses, drinks are put into their hands, and bits of food too. Cocktail napkins. Olives.

The boy stands in the trees, banned from descending, looking down the mountain and longing for everything he sees below him.

A roomful of people, with piles of packages, the smell of meat and bread, and every house is the same, while he is up here, alone and different. Everything that happens rings in his ears, and calls to him. He pulls a cookie from out of a tree hollow, a spiced man, and eats it as he listens.

"Ho, ho, ho, Louisa!" someone whispers from the back door of one of the houses.

"Oh, Roger," she whispers back. "You're feisty tonight, aren't you?"

"Every night," Roger replies, and she laughs.

"Later?" she says.

"In the morning," he replies. "Meet me at four."

People call from around the neighborhood, heralding spouses and children and pets, shouting for grandparents and carolers:

"Punch bowl!"

"Little sausages!"

"Fred, did you let the dog out? Where's the dog?"

"Zip this, will you? That's why I'm turning my back, I can't get it, no, I need longer arms. It's not too tight."

"Oh, god, the poor thing! And her husband! What a catch. I know, but I just want to know if he's single?"

"Swizzle stick!"

"No, they're pretty, right? Colored sprinkles, don't eat the silver ball ones, they're poison."

In the house the boy is watching, there is a Christmas tree cut from the mountain's slope. The boy knows the tree. It sheltered an owl. Now it's covered in white lights and red orbs. The boy wonders if they're eggs, about to hatch some bird he doesn't know, but he knows all the creatures and things that live here. Every piece of this mountain. He talks to everything, and everything has a name. At night, he looks up at the sky and names the stars.

The boy watches his friend, sitting down at the table, eating dinner, people all around him, a cake, wine, laughter, and everyone raises their glass to the man at the head, the father, who then leaves the room.

Father is a new word for the boy, but he's learned it. Before this, he only knew *mother*. The boy's friend looks out toward the window, but the boy is invisible. The boy waves from out of the night at him, unseen.

The father returns, dressed in a red suit, a white beard gummed to his face. The boy flinches, startled, but then it is clear, a costume, for some reason, a new coat, a new fur to keep the father's face warm. The boy's friend sits in his father's lap.

Packages are brought, and the boy from Herot opens them. They contain things that bewilder the boy from the mountain, bright plastic items, shining ribbons, little animals made of soft cloth.

He watches.

When it's dark, when the boy from Herot is in bed, the boy from the mountain hunts for a present for his friend.

The rabbit's sleek and brown, fur speckled, long silken ears. Nostril with a little blood dribbling out. Eyes dull. Neck broken. Strong thigh muscles, soft fur. Meat for a night, enough to share.

The boy leaves it on the step outside the kitchen, then turns back and runs up the slope, quick over the snow and through the trees, avoiding the lights, the cameras, fast enough that he hardly touches the ground.

He slips through the crack in the stone and into the cave, then through the hidden door and down silently, into the old station.

The walls are already covered in his drawings, done in charcoal, a toy truck, a glass house, a piano. There are cats and birds in them, and spotted dogs with flapping ears, a sun, trees, cars.

Now he draws the boy from below, pale hair rendered in campfire ash, blue eyes set down in a stolen piece of wax from down the mountain. He has a whole box of colors.

He's already made a drawing of a woman with one eye, and beside her a blur. The blur holds his mother's hand.

Slowly, carefully, the boy from the mountain makes a line between the drawing of the boy from Herot Hall and his own portrait. An arm outstretched, pointed nails like little moons on the fingers of one of the boys.

Now two little boys hold hands in the dark beneath the mountain, on a wall of an abandoned station. Between them there's a package, a red bow, a tree, a rock. There's a rabbit.

The boy from Herot Hall is smiling, and so is the boy who has portraited himself in scribble, an obliteration.

He sits back on his heels and looks at the drawing he's made.

Carefully, carefully, he draws a star shining over the whole thing. He draws light as it falls from the sky, and another symbol he's learned from watching through windows, a heart of red wax, pressed onto the marble.

He goes over it twice with his crayon, tracing the outline, placing it in the center of the new world he's created.

||

What? Willa wakes up, heart pounding. It's five in the morning, and no one's awake but her. Did she hear something? Scratching, or soft feet padding away?

No. New locks are installed all over the house. There's been no sign of anything coming in. No bear. No intruder. There was no sign on the mountain either. No den, no nest, no lair.

Willa doesn't believe it. She doesn't believe anyone. Not the officer who swore it to her, not her husband, who seems to think the claw belonged to a creature that came through and then went.

"Maybe a mountain lion," said Roger, as though that was fine. "Or a panther. There are panthers no one ever sees out in daylight, but they found one in Florida, didn't you read that article? They thought they were extinct."

As though Willa should let giant cats sharpen their claws in the halls of Herot. As though there should be no feeling of betrayal. She's supposed to be safe. She's supposed to be protected. Isn't that why she married this man?

Previously, there's been only one moment in their entire marriage when Roger seemed likely to betray her. He began to pour himself scotch and sob at the dining table, using words like *existential* and *guitar*. Willa suffered for thirteen and one-half days, and then told her mother, who passed the omens to Roger's mother.

The next day, it was fixed. No one said anything about it ever again, and no one ever, ever will, certainly not Willa, who loves her husband, obviously.

Now, though . . .

Roger denies monsters exist, but Willa knows better.

"What about Dylan?" she asked him. "What if he'd been here?"

"He's fine," said Roger, and shrugged. "Nothing came near him. He didn't see it. If it was here, it's gone now."

She journals her dream in the book she's bought for this purpose. There are stickers for bad dreams and good ones too. It's like a scrapbook of nightmares.

Hundreds of people are at a party and I'm pouring red wine into plastic cups. I have a pitcher, but it has a leak, and so I'm spilling, drop by drop onto my dress until the whole front is red.

I bring wine to that police officer, but he's holding a goblet already, and it's big and ugly, the kind of thing you might get on a wedding registry from a relative, or maybe from a fraternity. If he was part of a fraternity. He probably was.

Just as I pour the wine into his goblet, something throws itself against the door—

There's a sound in the hall. She picks up the baseball bat she's started keeping beside the bed, but it's just Dylan.

"Dilly," she says, calming her heartbeat. "Did you have a nightmare?"

"*You* did," he says. "You screamed."

When Willa was little, and she came out of bed scared and crying, her mother told her that if she didn't stop waking up, she'd tie her into the bed every night, and how would Willa like that?

She stopped dreaming entirely. Only recently has she dreamed again, and these are dreams in which the world crushes down upon her. Dreams in which there is no place any longer for anyone like Willa, and everything she's earned has been taken away from her. In one dream, she clung to the knobs of her kitchen cabinets. In another, she was shrouded in cashmere and rolled into the sea.

She sits up, blurry, looks at the bedside table and sees red in the bottom of a glass. The whole thing suddenly looks like a hospital and the glass a transfusion.

"Back to bed," she says to Dylan, and looks to the other side of the mattress for Roger, who is apparently out for a run. She can see his clothes laid out on the chair, but his running shoes are gone. Who runs in snow?

She gets up. There's no point trying to sleep. She weighs herself for comfort. A hundred and fourteen pounds, but she feels like a dinosaur. Somewhere in one of Dylan's allegedly cute children's books there's a thing about dinosaurs, where it says humans couldn't grow that big because their brains would never catch up. There's a picture drawn with pastels, a human woman with tiny tyrannosaurus arms and a lobotomized expression. The book goes on to say that if humans were the size of dinosaurs, they'd just walk around with pea-sized minds, unable to talk, marry, or bury their dead.

She'd like to be a dinosaur sometimes, and thunder across Herot Hall all teeth, claws, and irresponsibility.

But no.

The neighbors will be coming later for champagne, caviar, toothpicked morsels, and "Auld Lang Syne." Willa thinks an evil thought: maybe she'll order pizza instead, the stress of the past few days. She could serve gluten, dairy, and fat on New Year's Eve. How would that be for monstrous?

Instead, when the sun's risen, she drives to the market and picks up the caviar in its little cooler. As she walks to the car, she imagines she's carrying two hearts on ice, each one suspended, but about to beat again. It's disappointing when she unloads the cooler at home and finds only implausibly expensive fish eggs.

By noon the house is full of workers, hanging garlands and fluffing pillows, and Willa follows them around, dictating their decoration. There are already luminarias lining the walk, each one a colored paper sack full of a battery candle.

Roger's home and showered by now, not particularly helpful. He's at the computer, diagramming a nose job. She's put his tuxedo out on the bed, with cuff links depicting Magic 8-Balls. Where'd he get those?

"Who's that?" she asks, leaning over his shoulder.

He's startled.

"You know," he says. "Louisa? From down the street? Mark's wife?"

Willa looks at the photo of Louisa, with lines all over her skin, a dot-to-dot of a new face appearing out of thin air, and feels ever-so-faintly something.

She goes back to the kitchen and makes blini the size of thumbnails, whips sour cream, slices baguettes. She hard-boils eggs and tries not to choke on the smell of sulfur. There is cake to bake and there are carrots to chop, and when she next looks up it's later than she thought, and the evening is twitching its way across the sky. She should be showered and dressed.

She turns on the faucet to wash her hands, and the coldness feels like fingers grasping hers. It's water from beneath the mountain, and it's full of the taste of bones and rocks. She's bought five cases of bottled to keep from having to serve this, even in ice-cube format. There's something awful about it. It feels full of ghosts.

She looks down into the sink and watches the water spin into the drain.

Willa thinks about when she was the wife of an about-to-be

rock star, who wrote a song about how she left him in bed the morning after she married him. He ended up with a gold record. She ended up the hostess of Herot Hall. She looks down at her thigh, where the once-upon-a-time tattoo of Richie's name is a white wriggle of invisible ink, raised up when she's cold, like a readable goose bump.

There's a long hair growing there, somehow missed by the waxer. She plucks it with her fingernails and throws it into the trash, then turns on the mixer to puree chickpea water into a vegan cocktail foam she read about on the Internet.

She thinks about the party, about how there might be flirting or fondling or fucking against the wall in the back hallway, where last year she glimpsed some hanky-pankying between a husband and wife, not to each other, and not to be named.

She swore secrecy, and told Roger.

While the mixer spins, she walks to the kitchen door to look at the view. There are tracks in the snow. But why shouldn't there be? Isn't the point of the mountain to climb it? That police officer went up there, of course, and who knows who else? The slope's been hammered down with sleds and discs, and it makes her feel strange, as though all of that is somehow against the mountain's will. *Stay off it*, she thinks, but she shakes that away. There are no voices up there. The mountain is only a mountain.

She can't help it, though. The snow makes the slope look like the pale crook of an elbow with blue and red marks in it. A man on a train in the city, years ago, nodding off, then sitting up, eyes wide, hands outstretched. He looked at Willa and said, out of nowhere, "*Listen to me.* What if we were the last two people on Earth? Would you listen to me then?"

Willa put on her headphones and raised the collar of her coat.

"WOULD YOU LOVE ME THEN?" he shouted. Willa felt scarred. *What if?* she thought. What if this was as good as it would ever get? A man shouting with passion on a train, telling her she was the one he wanted. Should she have surrendered? Sunk into it? Of course not. He was disgusting. But still, there's a part of Willa that wonders about every other life she might've had.

She starts to close the door, and sees the rabbit.

Dead on the doorstep, and dead for days. Frozen, eyeballs pecked out.

"Roger!" she calls. "*Roger!*"

Her husband comes into the kitchen, entirely too slowly for Willa's taste, half into his tux.

"How are you not dressed?" he says. "People will be here any minute."

She points and runs for the sink. There's no smell. It's the actuality of the death that makes her stomach churn.

"Shit," says Roger, who never says *shit*. He beckons Willa over. It's only when she bends closer that she notices what's tied around the rabbit's neck.

A bow from a package, shining foil, and a tag: *To: Dylan, From: Santa*, in Willa's own handwriting.

"Dylan!" Roger yells. "Down here, now!"

"Don't show him!" Willa says. "Why would you show him? Someone killed it and left it—"

"I'm not showing him something he hasn't already seen. He did this," says Roger. "The BB gun. I told Mother not to get it, but you left it on his list."

Willa remembers, belatedly. The entirety of the scenario that just played in her head—some disgusting stranger, bringing a rabbit, tying the tag gently on—was only a boy with a baby's bullet.

"The officer thought Dylan did the claw too," Roger says. "It seemed unlike him. Now I wonder."

"Therapist?" says Willa, queasy.

"We'll get a recommend," says Roger, and then looks at Willa with blame on his face. "I've said it before. You've been feminizing him."

Feminizing? How does feminizing make a boy kill rabbits?

"He needs sports."

"That's not my fault," Willa protests. "He just sits down in the middle of the field."

"Softball, rugby, tennis. He's trying to prove himself. He doesn't want to be treated like a child. This is a rebellion against you and those Santa tags. He knows there's no Santa."

Willa begs to differ. Dylan doesn't know that, even a little bit. He's a true believer in everything. Santa, tooth fairy, Easter bunny, which makes it all the more wrongful that he did this.

Roger's outside with a garbage bag, angling the stiff rabbit into it.

"We can't have your mother seeing this," he says. "She'll go ballistic. We'll deal when the holiday is over."

"*Your* mother's the one who gave him the gun," protests Willa, to deaf ears.

Dylan runs into the kitchen, and she thinks about how he never leaves prints on anything, at how he's perfect. A sudden horrible thought about the many cats that've disappeared from Herot Hall over the years. Just recently, the Moore's Siamese. What if? No. She decides not to allow that thought into her mind ever again.

Roger has the rabbit in the sack, but the gift tag is still on the step. Dylan beelines at it, grabs it, stares.

"Who brought this?" he asks. "Who left it?"

"We'll discuss it later," Roger says.

"What's in the bag?" Dylan howls, staring at the garbage bag on the ground, and his face begins to redden. "*Gren!*" he screams.

Then he's tantruming in earnest, red, white, and blue, a flag whipping in the wind, flung from his father's arms and raging in the snow.

Willa tries to get between them, but he's kicking, thrashing, screaming loss and rage. From the look Roger gives her, it might as well be Willa on her back, limbs akimbo, her mouth open so

wide that her tonsils are visible. It might as well be Willa screaming all the curses she knows, in every language she can find.

She drops to her knees, and slaps Dylan across the face, feeling the size of his head (tiny), the sharpness of his teeth (shards of
broken glass), the wetness of his face (slippery), and the sin she's
committing, all at once, even as he stares at her in shock, his eyes
enormous and liquid.

He lurches forward and opens the garbage bag, and then he's
crying, not in anger, but in relief. What did he think? What
imaginary friend lives in a rabbit skin?

The New Year walks heavily down the highway on its way
to Herot Hall, and there's a sound from the mountain.

Snow shuffles itself from branches and caves crackle, but it's
nothing awful, just a shiver in the century, and the three of them
crouched outside the kitchen door around a garbage bag full of a
dead thing.

Willa shuts her eyes and looks into the darkness inside herself, a room with doors that open onto nothing, a theater, and in
it red velvet seats and harnesses for flying, trapdoors that lead to
the secret chambers beneath the stage. She feels something in
there, something that can't be trusted. Her fingers sting with the
slap, and she feels the creature rising, horns and claws, a tail lashing, making its way through spotlight and shadow.

It feels good to be angry. It feels good to let go.

The doorbell rings.

"Oh, my god," says Willa, returning from going, going, gone.

"Your mother," says Roger. "Never not early."

"*All* the mothers," she says, inching aside a curtain. They're
standing on the front steps, stamping their feet.

Willa and Roger are briefly on the same side, as they scoop
Dylan out of the snow and mop his nose, as Roger, cursing, sprints
up the stairs carrying him, as Willa, also cursing, wraps herself
in a coat to get the door.

In the kitchen, something is on fire and she ushers the

mothers through the house as the smoke alarm goes off, lets them begin the party with the pouring of a bottle of champagne to douse a tray of devils on horseback, each date charred, and each piece of bacon sizzling and black.

"Happy New Year," says Willa, knowing she'll pay for this for at least twelve months, but who bought the baby a BB gun? Who caused him to kill a rabbit and tag it as a present?

And god, how quickly time is passing, whipping around her like a hurricane, Willa buffeted by flotsam. Old, older, drowning and withering at once. She'll be her mother in a moment.

Why isn't she sitting on a fire escape in the city? Why did she waste her youth? The peak of pretty, no wrinkles, no fat, no stretch marks anywhere. Why is she here at Herot Hall, where at any second something bad could come down the mountain, or tunnel up from below? Monsters. There's a whole world filled with monsters. They're everywhere.

Stop it, Willa. That's the nightmare, not the reality.

She shakes herself, then hides for a moment in the powder room and throws back a shot of vodka, not looking at her reflection. Why itemize the speckles on the bridge of her nose, the spiny cartilage of her ears, the tiny broken vessels in her cheeks? Why acknowledge the monster in the mirror?

Still swallowing, feeling the vodka burn its way through the frozen animal that's invaded her throat, she darts upstairs to the shower, blow-dryer, foundation, lipstick.

She'll conceal everything, and when she's done, no one will know what's there, just under the surface.

12

What kind of mess have we marched into? The matriarchs of Herot Hall arrive fifteen minutes early, as agreed, wearing silver and bearing bottles.

Kitchen full of smoke, grandson sobbing, Willa half dressed, Roger's tie not even tied. Well! We tie it.

Roger's clean-shaven, at least, his shirt pressed and starched. He's not much, but he's been made into a man with his daddy's money.

Oh, please, we knew his daddy. Died in a car wreck off the mountain road, yes, and could he hold his alcohol, no, but he could hold two women in each of his hands. Not one of us wasn't pinched by that man. Tina was his fourth choice. She was his secretary. This is the way it goes. Now Tina's having an affair with her personal trainer, Stu.

Diane's daughter stands before us, looking tipsy.

"Willa!" says Diane. "Upstairs! What's gotten into you?"

What's gotten into her is that she's a time bomb in yoga pants. We exchange a glance.

"Rough day," Willa says, as though that's an excuse.

Once, we had to have an emergency hysterectomy and we said nothing.

We tap our feet outside the shower, and then zip Willa into

the tightest sequined dress in her closet. Long sleeves and a high neckline, a dress that outlines her figure, semi-couture armor.

Diane stands back to consider her daughter. One can think one's own child is weak. One usually does. We turn away, polite, as Diane tugs Willa into Spanx.

We're commuter wives. These are our commuter lives. We're capable of carrying alcoholic husbands from the kitchen to the bedroom in a fireman's grip. Between trains, we train to fight with enemies we haven't met yet, battling against punching bags, leaping like the world is made of stone walls and we're storming them.

There's another version of commuting, of course, as in to commute a sentence.

This is our sentence, these suburbs, the train that does not stretch to meet them. We have not been commuted. We haven't slept in years. This is an advantage of menopause. Some nights, we meet for coffee at 4:00 a.m. We stand on the balcony of one of our homes, looking out over the river, itemizing betrayals, watching the fools of this place waking from their dull dreams. We see plenty of things at that hour of the morning.

We whip Dilly the Second into shape, washcloth and suit, and his fury is ignored. His face is red and his eyes are so dilated they've gone black. He's clutching a rock he refuses to surrender. When Tina tries to take it from him, he threatens to swallow it unless he can play with someone, some muttering about rabbits and bows, and then a truly inappropriate kick at a shin.

We lock him in his bedroom for a time-out.

One of us goes to the kitchen to plate appetizers and another fills ice buckets. Diane wedges Willa into silver heels like she's shoeing a horse. Tina looks into a garbage bag she finds on the floor, wrinkles her nose, and shoves it in the freezer.

The residents of Herot Hall are tromping toward the house for their feast, and as the doorbell rings, Tina raises a glass.

"To us," she says.

"And people like us," says Diane.

We clink and drink, answer the door, take the bottles, drape the coats over our arms. The party guests are not what we would've imagined ten years ago. Everyone's fleeing the city. This community used to be WASPs, is the joke, and now it's worker bees.

Here's that couple, the lawyer and his wife, the dancer-now-mother, and she's from India and he's from somewhere else. Another couple, both men! One from Japan, the particularly handsome one, and the other Moroccan! This is a diverse place now. The kids memorize all the countries in Africa on a big map, painted in pastels. The countries have changed their names since we were children, as though they all got married.

We make the rounds, passing appetizers, filling glasses. The TV is tuned to Times Square, where everyone's smashed together, looking frozen. Thank you, no.

Look at that fool who had triplets after his marriage to one of us. They were born when he was fifty-eight. No one wants a toddler of one's own at this age, let alone a trio. Look at his gaunt cheeks. Look at his wife. She's thirty-four.

Ha!

We swan past her, free as falcons, our muscles flexed. A baby has spit up on her shoulder, right into her hair. We offer her a wet wipe so she knows how much we care.

Where is Dylan? Forgotten in his room. Diane trots up the stairs with the key. We continue to walk the perimeter, seeking to confirm suspicions.

Yes, there.

Roger Herot is standing on the front steps with Louisa Bellow. The threads of heat spun cheater-to-cheater glow like dying elements in the winter cold. Louisa's a cup size up, a tightness to the zip at the back of her dress. We hand her a glass of champagne and an oyster. She pretends to drink one, and tries to hide the other in a luminaria. Roger Herot. A little boy with a dripping nose, the kind of boy who, sleepwalking, shits in the corner of the guest bedroom. It is against the law to cheat on one of the wives with another of the wives. If you cheat, you cheat in the city. Oh, Roger. We know your business now.

Did you know you could kill someone with a stiletto heel? Our daggers travel with us, underfoot, capable of being removed and jammed into an eye socket.

Do you think sixty-five-year-old women don't go to war? We are always at war. Our husbands spent their lives in comfortable chairs. Have we ever sat in comfortable chairs? No. Yoga balls, haunches tensed.

Our sympathies shift. All but Tina turn our heads slowly and look around the room. Is there a better man here for Willa? Is there a solution?

Diane beckons urgently from the landing, and we reverse-march upstairs, holding our champagne flutes, laughing as though there's nothing at all going on. Down to a science.

There's no Dylan in the bedroom, but GREN is written in red crayon on the wall, letters three feet tall, and he must have had to stretch to do it. There's a portrait too, a drawing of two figures. We get the Magic Eraser stick, but the more we scrub, the more they're there, crooked pink ghosts.

Window, open. We crane out, into the dark. Nothing visible. Third floor.

There are no crannies in Herot Hall, no crawl spaces. Where is he? Things are strewn all over the floor of the bedroom, bundles of twigs, a strange lace christening gown.

If you're the mother of a little boy, you never stop finding stolen objects in his pockets, or in the bottom of the washing machine. If you go to the grocery store with a little boy, you'll notice them dragging their hands along the bulk bins, stealing beans, thinking to grow a beanstalk. Go to the zoo and they're ready to leap in among the animals. Little boys are quick.

They get older and become criminals of suburbia. A contact lens stuck to the bed frame long after you've switched to bifocals, a tampon wrapper long after you've stopped bleeding. There are worse things to find than used condoms, and in truth, we're prepared to find them, looking at the loot on this boy's floor. A hatchet? Fishhooks?

Who's he been stealing from? What's he been doing?

And in the center of the bed, displayed on a black garbage bag, what is this?

A dead rabbit with a bow around its neck. Frozen solid. Last seen downstairs in the freezer.

Diane glances out the window and catches a glimpse of her delinquent grandson, running wild through the snow like a dog loose of his pen, and as one we make a sound of revulsion, not stopping to wonder how he got out. We see him duck into the downstairs through a door that should not be open.

Someone starts playing the piano, badly, weirdly, loudly, and we tilt our heads to listen. Is the party drunk already?

Tina steps on something. A set of dog tags?

We pick them up and read them.

Dana Mills.

13

What do we pack? Everything, which is almost nothing. We'll leave this mountain when Herot is sleeping, in the early hours of the first day of the year.

Two knives and my guns, a pack of food. Dried meat and berries from the summer. A pair of wool socks, a shirt made of blanket fabric, a thin windbreaker. Gren wears part of my old uniform, and part of his own. I came down the mountain three years ago, went across the highway to the surplus store, and tied a piece of cloth across most of my face. They gave me some blankets, some winter clothes, wool and synthetics, a sleeping bag, nothing Gren was born to wear, but I had to do something. He'd gotten too big, and everything we had was woven of broken thread.

Now I have all our possessions on my back, tested to make sure they're not too heavy.

We'll come off the mountain, through the tunnel, and up. A night journey. It's been a week of imagining north.

There's an island I heard of once, off Nova Scotia. It's a shipwreck island and nothing comes near it anymore. People've lost it on maps for centuries. It might not even exist. But maybe we could get to a place like that and stay. We can live on gulls and eggs, me and Gren, and when he's grown, we'll build a ship and sail off again.

Lots of parts of the world have nothing in them. There are places you could be a mother alone, trying to raise a boy into a man. There's no piano on a rock in the middle of the ocean, and there's no little boy to be his friend. There's no one who'll kill him instead of loving him. That's enough.

Four more hours in the dark, and then we move. I'm counting it down while walking the tunnel, thinking of my mother, my grandmother, my family. Thinking of climbing up this mountain when I was small. Did my family think this place was holy? I don't know. We thought it held our history. It's hard to leave that behind.

I kneel on the edge of the platform and try to say goodbye, then walk for a while, over the tracks where the train used to come, looking at the things in the walls and under the stream in the bottom of the passage. Something shines in the mud, a glint and point like an arrowhead, and that's what I think it is for a second, until I put my hand in the water and pull it up.

It's a sword, an old one, the hilt rough and crude, the blade as long as my arm. Civil War, maybe, that old? It feels that old.

I gasp, and then look at my finger, the cut I didn't feel happening. Sharp enough to slice.

Useful. I put it over my shoulder, into the pack I use for my guns, and climb back up toward our cave. Food, and then keeping Gren awake until it's time to go.

When I hear the sound of the piano drifting up the mountain, I don't think about it for a moment, but then I know the tune, played badly, played barely, but played. It's a lullaby. *My* lullaby, the one I sing at night. The song's quiet at first, and then louder. Someone's playing like they just learned what music is, not like they know how to play a piano, but like they know how to make song.

I open the door from the tunnel to the cave.

Gren's sleeping bag is empty. His things are gone, and mine are dumped out of my pack. A knife, my dog tags, his toys, missing.

He thinks he's running away from home, but he's running into an enemy camp.

I'm out of the cave and scrambling, rolling part of the way down the mountain. I crash into trees, bash against rocks, and I know I'm about to hear shots and arrive at blood. All I'll have left is vengeance and five seconds to take it before I'm dead.

I'm ten feet from the house, still in the trees, when I stop.

I can see his tracks in the snow. Up to the side of the house, and onto the roof outside the little boy's bedroom.

My heart's so loud I feel like anyone could hear it, but there's no sign of Gren.

Instead, there's a pack of women leaning out that bedroom window, looking into the dark. They're not screaming or pointing. They look curious, but not scared. No one else is either. The house is a party, not a panic.

Gren's inside it somewhere, or out here, with the boy.

I know where the security lights are. I don't trip them. I move through the trees toward the glass back wall, where I can see into the kitchen and music room.

The boy's mother is alone at the sink, dressed in silver, yellow hair, bright pink mouth, surrounded by bottles of champagne. She picks one up and drinks from it.

I scan the rooms looking for Gren, all the rooms I can see, but—

There. My son's creeping along the white-tiled wall of the kitchen, behind her. I make a sound that starts in my gut.

Nonononononono.

Trailing behind him is the boy he's come to see. The boy beckons my son over to a tray of food, and both of them take things from it.

Gren edges along the wall, toward the door. The woman doesn't see him. She's looking out the window over the sink. He's moving, secretly, quickly, like I taught him.

She looks up again, starts to turn like she's heard something, and so I throw a pebble at the window.

She looks out here instead. I scramble around the house. I'm not even thinking before I'm ringing the bell with my fist. *Look at me instead.*

The woman gasps when she opens the door, and then quickly corrects herself. Now she's just staring.

"Can I help you? Are you with the cleani . . ."

She trails off, and looks me up and down, my clothes, my hair.

"Sorry, but no," she says, and she starts to close the door. "We're all donated out this year."

But my foot's wedged in the jamb, and I'm into the party. No choice. No choice.

"Gren!" I'm shouting. "*Gren!*"

The older women are coming down the stairs from the little boy's bedroom, and I see things in their hands, things I recognize, a christening gown, a hatchet. What else? Things Gren took as gifts? Things he took so that he and his friend could run away together?

I'm shoving people in party clothes, food, wineglasses. Something spills. I trip over a cord and the music stops. Something crashes. I see the face of one of the people, and I see that person see my face too.

A lamp, light bouncing at us, flashing, and I'm starting to shake and fade, starting to feel like shooting into everything, or going flat to the floor, but I don't.

I hop a couch.

"Gren! Go home, Gren!"

A man runs toward me, and then a couple more, all big in the shoulders. They think they can take me? They think I'm some crazy woman, but I'm a soldier. I dodge and duck.

"Get out of here, Gren! *Now!*"

I don't see him, but I hear him wail with rage and sadness, and a door slams.

I run after the sound, into the whiteness of the kitchen, which throws me back in time. Bang, me waking up, blood on the tile, bang, stitches like ants crawling up my face, dizzy, blind in one eye, wait, no, eye gone—

No. I'm in a kitchen, not a hospital, not a prison. I stop. I breathe. No one has us captive. No one's taken us back to the police, or to the military prison. I'm surrounded by people in party clothes. They stare. I stop. I stand still, giving Gren time to get up the slope in the dark.

"Roger," says the blonde, her eyes wide. "Roger, do something."

"We have to ask you to leave," someone says, the man who lives here, tall and tuxedoed, the *host.* The word comes to me, now I can think again.

No one saw Gren. He's gone. He's safe. Where's his friend? I don't see him.

"Security's on the way, but you can go peacefully if you go now."

The host opens his jacket and takes out his wallet.

"This community supports the homeless. We donate every year. We collect food and supplies. There was a drive. We hate to see you in such a bad way."

"I'm sorry for the trouble. It was a mistake. I'm leaving," I say, with dignity, hunting the words from the back of my brain. I haven't spoken to anyone who isn't Gren in a long time.

I can see my reflection in the windows, my hair matted and filthy, my torn sweater over torn shirt, my jeans, my boots. Old uniform jacket, with the insignia ripped off. Tattoos still on me, but they're covered. Identifying marks. I'm already identifiable enough.

"I'm not homeless," I say. "I'm okay."

I feel them staring. The video of my execution was everywhere, but it's been a long time. I was on my way to being a dead woman in it, not a live one, and I have to think that's enough for them to forget me.

Someone pushes a plate into my hands, gently, gently, like I'm going to break. It's full of little fried things. They look like fingers. I walk out the front door, escorted by men, not screaming, though my legs want to bend out from under me.

I walk down the front steps and to the end of the street, out to where the bus stops. I don't run. Finally, I'm out of range of the cameras. I double, reverse, twist, turn, and make my way up the back of the mountain.

When Gren was tiny, I tried to find a way to keep him safe from this, all of it. I taught him his ABCs and numbers. I taught him how to add and subtract, how to make two from one. Maybe I made a mistake. Maybe I shouldn't have taught him any of the things of this world. I don't trust anyone here. I don't trust anyone anywhere.

"Here is a church," I told him. I moved my fingers, doing the lacings, the old game to keep children from fussing.

"Here is a steeple. Open the door and here's all the people," I told him, and he looked up at me, not sure if he had permission to laugh.

I did all the singsongs, all the games.

Here's an itsy bitsy spider, here's an alphabet, here's the sound
    a dog makes—
Here's the sound a hound makes
Here's the sound a round makes

I tried to teach him about danger. I tried to teach him about the things that might kill him, without scaring him so much he wouldn't be able to live.

I didn't do a good enough job.

"Mama," he said, and smiled at me, shining eyes. "You're silly."

He ran off into the trees, playing with a feather, and I stood watching him, trying not to think of the world as paper and him as ink, trying not to think of the way blood could redline the story of his life.

He'll be in our cave, angry and crying when I get there, but he never disobeys, not like this. He wouldn't. He knows we're leaving tonight. He won't run away from me. I'm all he has.

I hike up the side of the ice and snow, and I am so certain he'll be there, so sure I'm the only person he loves enough to listen to, that I don't notice there're no tracks ahead of me.

14

What happened? A crazy woman runs through a party, and afterward everything feels wrong. The television ticks down the seconds in the year and the ball wobbles and the announcers grin and there's confetti. No one's watching. No one's kissing. No one's singing.

Willa glances back toward the kitchen and the uneaten hors d'oeuvres. There's caviar, smoked salmon, and blini, all going to waste.

That woman, and her frightening face, her scars, her filth. Unclean. Beneath her shirt, hardly hidden, was something Willa only saw as she left.

A holster? And on her hip there was, Willa reconstructs it in her memory, a knife.

"Dylan!" she calls, suddenly realizing she hasn't seen him in hours. She spins into the living room. "Has anyone seen Dylan?"

She runs up the stairs and into Dylan's room, and there he is, toys all around him, his party suit looking worse for the wear. His hair is wet and his face is dirty. The room is a mess. It looks as though several people have been rummaging. All the drawers are open, and Dil's backpack is out on the bed, half packed. Willa sees a loaf of bread, apples, cookies, cans of soup. Every book is off the shelves.

Out of the corner of her eye she catches a flicker of movement in the hall. She spins. Nothing there. Paranoid. Adrenaline and champagne combined. She breathes twice, a mini-meditation usually done with an app.

"What?" Dylan asks. "What, Mommy?"

Willa doesn't know what. She has no answer at all.

"Did you see that woman?" she asks. "Was she in here with you?"

"Gren wanted to sleep over. He forgot to ask his mommy," Dylan says. "She got worried. It wasn't his fault."

Willa is at the end of her patience for imaginary friends. She sees some crayon on the wall, red stripes, and she reads them sidelong.

"Did you draw on the wall?" she asks her son.

"No," he says, clearly lying. "Gren did."

Willa bends over the bed and looks out at the room. Her son is flushed. She puts a hand on his forehead.

"No more of this, Dylan," says Willa. "No more Gren. Did you see anyone you don't know? Was she up here? She ran through the house—"

"Yes," Dylan says patiently. "She's Gren's mommy, like you're my mommy."

Roger's in the room. There's lipstick on the corner of his mouth, Willa notices, the same shade of red as the crayon that's ruined the wallpaper.

"Everything okay up here, bud?" Roger says, in his trademark jolly anesthetic tone. "Your grandma said you were outside in the snow. You know that's not allowed."

Willa wonders how Roger can call a rabbit slayer "bud." Has he forgotten? She's only just remembered about the rabbit, about the miserable next few months of therapists and family counselors making sure that their son is not on a path to becoming a serial killer. But what if there's nothing to be done?

And even as she thinks it, she sees, kicked under the bed, the black garbage bag, two limp ears, no eyes. She inhales raggedly and stands in front of it. She pokes it significantly with her toe, to let Roger know what's here.

"What do you think she wanted?" she asks Roger.

"Food, I imagine," says Roger, entirely too calmly, on the other side of several cocktails. "She looked hungry."

His bow tie is crooked.

"She was yelling for someone," Willa says. "Yelling a name, over and over again. She didn't seem like she wanted food."

"*Gren*," Dylan says.

"Gren," Willa repeats. It's true. That's exactly what she was yelling. Willa thinks about the woman some more, diagramming her face, remembering the look the woman gave her, the way she stared into her eyes. She envied everything. The house, Roger, Dylan, the party.

Where would someone like her come from? Not Herot Hall. No one like her lives here.

"It's fine, Wills," says Roger, and turns to leave. "Most of them are just mentally ill. Maybe the city put her on a bus and shipped her out for the holidays, keep the tourists from seeing her on the street. That happens."

"She had a knife *and* a gun," Willa blurts, her mouth getting the better of her.

This brings Roger to attention. "A gun? What kind?"

"I don't know what kind, but a gun. She showed me," Willa says, and instantly regrets it. Roger turns red and white. His ears look frostbitten.

"A gun," Roger says. "Are you sure?"

Willa isn't.

"Yes," she says. Better to be safe than—

Is there someone in the hall? She's seen it again, a movement, at the edge of the light, but no. She walks out and flips on the chandelier. Nothing. The windows reflect her own self, her dress a void filled with sequin stars.

"I'm calling the police," Roger says, already dialing.

"It was probably a toy gun?" offers Willa.

Once, years ago, in the city, a kid pointed a gun at Willa. She was dialing 911 when he shot her in the center of the chest. For days after, she felt that icy water, hitting her in the heart. She still feels it.

"She came into *our home*," Roger says. He was the rational one, but now he's switched. "*With a gun*. No. That is a no."

Willa's mother appears on the stairs, holding something. It dangles from her fingers, a necklace. Dog tags.

"These were in Dylan's room," Diane says.

✦

For the second time in a week, Willa opens the door to Officer Woolf. There are three more officers with him. Willa feels better already.

"This isn't supposed to happen here," Willa says. She might as well be back in the city, subway platforms and catcalls, dark hallways and elevator cages. Mysteries hidden in every stairwell. At least there she'd have been prepared for the intruder.

"It happens everywhere, ma'am," Officer Woolf replies. "There are people lost in every city in America. It's our job to make sure they don't hurt anyone else."

He looks into her eyes, and she feels herself quiver, an arrow notched into a bow. He must be seven feet tall, muscles visible through his sleeves. Roger's only five-foot-eleven, and that's enough, it is, but she can't wear heels.

"Everyone here saw her?"

She nods.

"Get statements," he says to the other officers.

The officers circle the room, viewing cell phone videos, taking notes. The party is improved. Willa makes the rounds, refilling champagne.

"Really," a neighbor says, "don't you think we're overreacting?"

It's Louisa from three doors down. Willa discovers herself about to pour champagne into Louisa's plumped-up cleavage.

"I know you'd be perfectly fine with guns and knives at *your* party," Willa says. "I guess Roger and I are just sensitive."

"Of course not," says Louisa. "I just wonder . . . I didn't see a gun. Do you think maybe you might have *misinterpreted* because of—"

Willa nearly crushes shrimp paste into her hair.

"She had a gun," says Willa, and walks away.

It's not racist to think that someone with a missing eye and a long vine of scar down her cheek might be a dangerous person.

"Drugs, I imagine," says Tina to one of the other mothers. "All I know is, I'm glad she didn't do more damage than she did."

"Thank god nothing worse happened," says Willa. "Have you tried the crab dip?"

"Hell of a New Year's party," says one of the Marks. There are too many Marks at Herot, and too many Sarahs and Matts and Michaels as well. Willa confuses them all with one another. Is this the Mark who's married to Louisa? He looks like he'd marry a woman with that nose, turned up at the tip.

"Where's that rum?"

"To Herot Hall! To adventures! Happy New Year!"

Willa glances at the officers, now talking among themselves. "What is it?" she asks.

"We've got a match. There's video," Officer Woolf says. "But it's graphic. You might want to—" He looks apologetically at Willa.

"I'll watch it," says Willa.

None of the people in the living room bat an eyelash. They're watching the screen like they're watching a wedding. Normally the TV is used for football, the players skittering across it like living dolls, but now it's New Year's Eve, and they're watching a woman on her knees.

It's not her, Willa thinks at first, looking at the woman, the way she tilts into frame, her long, elegant throat, her muscles visible. She stares into the camera, her eyes so dark there's no light in them, her cheekbones high.

"Can you identify her?" Officer Woolf asks. "This is Dana Mills. She grew up here, in the old town. Is she the woman who was at Herot tonight?"

The woman looks straight out from the screen. She has two eyes, not one.

"America, this is your doing," the woman says, and then holds up a piece of paper on which is written the same thing, in looping handwriting.

Her voice is the familiar part, the part that makes Willa take a second look.

"You might want to send your little fellow out of the room," Officer Woolf says, pausing the video.

Dylan's sitting in the middle of the floor. He's supposed to be in bed.

"Dilly?" Willa says. "Upstairs now."

He's fussing with something small and sharp, little plastic items, and a rock, from where, Willa doesn't know. Willa's already stepped on one of the blocks, a set meant to build a castle. Now she has to lug him up from the floor. She passes him to his grandmother, despite Roger's look. Diane lifts Dylan above her head with no effort at all. She's recently taken up boxing.

"I want to stay awake," Dylan cries, but up the stairs he goes. *You can't always get what you want*, Willa thinks, *even you*.

The video moves again, and the woman who ran through Willa's house turns her head slightly, looking up at someone. Then a blade slices through the edge of the screen, faster than Willa can see. There's a camera lurch, a blast, and black.

Willa retreats to the hall, nauseated, and hears some of the guests running out of the room, but her husband stays.

"I remember seeing that on Fox. I'm not convinced," Roger says. "The woman we saw didn't look like her."

Willa remembers this video. She never saw it when it was on the news, however many years ago that was. It feels like forever. There are some things a person never needs to see. It was released during those dark days during a long war she'd forgotten was even still happening. Sometimes there'd be a major boss killed or caught, and there'd be handheld cameras tilting into tunnels. It recharged the war, the beheading of a female soldier. Willa almost completely ceased watching television, and skipped like a flat stone into another decade.

She ventures back into the living room, where Roger is sitting, Louisa standing behind him. He leans slightly back, into breasts that give no territory to the hardness of his skull. On top of his head there's a circle like Stonehenge, the white center a place for sacrifices. *Oh*, Willa thinks, looking at Louisa's lipstick. *Oh*.

She returns to the circle. Officer Woolf smiles sympathetically at her.

"Everything all right, ma'am?"

"Call me Willa, of course," she says crisply. Roger doesn't even notice her speaking. His pulse is pounding in his neck. A second video is up, a woman walking down the steps of an airplane and onto the tarmac, soldiers all around her. She raises her head and there she is. Now with only one eye and scars down her face.

"That's her," Willa says.

Everyone agrees. The whole room is murmuring.

"Are you certain?" Officer Woolf asks. He's taking notes and looking only at Willa. "Corporal Dana Mills was in your kitchen?"

"That's her," Roger says, talking over Willa. "I should know. I gave her twenty bucks for food."

Somehow Dylan's at Willa's feet again, not in his room at all, and she wonders how long he's been there, what he's seen. He looks delicate, but maybe a beheading wouldn't be too much for a child with no other experiences in his life thus far. He has no context for horror.

There's a sound behind Willa in the hallway, something she can't translate, a creak on the floorboard, rattling, a strange muffled sob of a noise. The hair stands up on the back of her neck, and in the window she sees something reflected behind her, something from outside, something that—

She starts to turn, and so do Ben Woolf and his officers. Dylan's looking over her shoulder, his eyes wide.

"Look!" Dylan cries.

He raises his hand and puts the head of one of the little Lego kings between his teeth. What is he doing?

Even as Willa's rising out of her chair, he swallows. The king's head lodges in Dylan's throat, his face turning red.

A striped sweater. A glass of wine. Holy palmer's kiss. Thole. Palm to throat. Other palm to Dil's diaphragm. Willa lurches forward on her knees, and pries open his mouth. He fights her for control, but she made this mouth. She made these teeth. Had he refused birth he might have been found inside her years later, a tumor full of hair and fangs. *A teratoma*, her mind says, even as she bends him backward and feels his fingernails scratching her hands. She persists.

The urgency with which Willa shoves her hand into Dil's mouth, past all the rows of secret teeth, over his tongue, and into his throat, impresses her from afar.

She's a princess. She's a queen. She's a heroine.

She locates the point of the crown with her fingertip, and pushes it deeper into his throat, like she's pushing a toy train into a toy tunnel.

Deeper, deeper into the dark.

✦

Someone leaps onto Willa and shoves her aside. Woolf, she thinks, then, no, Roger, Diane, Tina? Confusion, screaming, someone dressed in camouflage, the smell of woodsmoke, the smell of pitch, and she's facedown, and her son has been torn from her arms.

She catches a glimpse of Dylan's head, over a shoulder and then fast movement, a candle tipped, fire on the carpet, champagne spilled and pooling, shouts—

The officers' guns are drawn, and there's a pop of gunfire, another, and then the sound of shatter, as the entire back wall of the house goes from glass to sand, and something, someone, rushes out and onto the mountain, into the trees.

Willa's alone on the floor and everyone's outside, screaming, and for a moment she stays there, flat on her stomach on the carpet, looking at the print beside her face, a bare human foot, not an animal track at all, impressed into the fibers.

She reviews the reflection in her memory, and then her mind covers it over with the worst case, the warring world climbing over the fences, home invasion, walls falling, no such thing as safety.

She runs her hand over the footprint and blurs it with her palm until it's obliterated, gone as her son, gone as her party, gone as any version of Willa that has ever lived a life she understood. Her hand is wounded. A drop of blood wells up and spills over onto the carpet.

Claws, she remembers. Fur. Monster, she remembers.

Monster.

15

What have I done? I've left him behind in the worst place he could ever be. I run out of the cave and look into the night, trees blocking me, half forest, half blowing snow, and there's shouting and then sirens bark out of silence like wolves. Oh, god—

"*Gren!*" I'm screaming, "*Gren!*" and something with no words, something that's coming up out of my arteries, like I'm bleeding screams.

I sprint through the trees, making all my existence into something that'll tear them from their wives and children, something that'll drag them into misery forever. My knife in my belt, my sword on my back, my pistol in my hand.

I call death onto those who don't know a child when they see a child. Men who think they made the world out of clay and turned it into their safe place, men who think a woman wouldn't flip the universe over and flatten them beneath it. I have enough bullets for all of them.

A window shatters and falls. Gunshots. The whole of Herot Hall is an alarm. The electric fence is flashing. The mountain's swarming with men in tuxedos and men in uniform.

I'm not here. I'm elsewhere, hearing bombs, tanks moving over a desert I never really left.

"Get the dogs!" yells a man, but I'm back in time, fighting, my team beside me. We were the ones with the dogs back then; we were the ones with the guns.

Someone thunders past me, and I scream Gren's name, but no one answers.

"*There it is!*" a man shouts, and I spin, looking into the dark, but I can't see Gren. There's a shot, up and out of the underbrush.

"*I see it!*" Another shot, another.

"*Here! Fuck! Get here! It's here! I just saw it!*"

The dogs are in one spot at a tree, moving out at all angles, screaming spokes of a Catherine wheel. The man in front of me raises a hunting rifle, blinking, and pulls the trigger into the air.

There's a crash as something heavy falls.

The police officer in charge shouts, "*We got it, goddammit!*"

A roar of triumph, from all the men at once.

I hear something different.

I hear the sound of my son crying for the first time after he was born, his voice telling me, wordless, that I'd brought him into the world, that he'd made it out of my body alive. I've only loved someone like that once. This love is the love that obliterates you. This is the love you die for.

I can't see Gren, but I can see his murderer lowering his rifle.

I draw the sword I found in the mountain in one clean motion, like I've been drawing swords my whole life. I swing it.

It whips through the air and hits him, the shock of his body. He falls, and an arc of blood spurts out, red letters in a white world, splattering into the ice and snow. We're alone for a moment, with only dark around us, and I'm gasping, choking on rage and tears, before I throw myself backward, out of sight and into the trees. The police officer with the blond hair runs in front of me.

I twist sideways, grab his hair in one hand, press my knife to his throat, the soft place below his ear. He's much taller than me, much stronger than me, but he still wants to be alive. I'm ready to die.

He's coming with me.

"Don't!" he cries, and I smell his piss.

The man I cut is down, and a bunch of others are kneeling over him, shouting, but none of them are in front of us. I'm the only one here, my enemy tight against me, and my ears are buzzing and I can hear my heart shouting. I force myself to turn my head now, to look at the other body on the ground. There's blood in the snow, and it belongs to Gren. There's blood in the snow, and it is the last of us, and—

It's not.

It's not my child, not anything like my child. Not human. It's a bear. Dead and covered in fur, dead and dark and part of the woods. Why was it even out? Bone skinny. I see ribs.

I still have this officer, his hot blood trickling down my fingers, and I hear branches breaking and dogs coming and then someone grabs me from behind, hard, and pulls me nearly off my feet.

There are shouts and dogs barking in a frenzy, and there's a shot and a bullet blasts into my arm.

Flashes of light go off in my skull, explosions happening inside me, and I'm no longer holding on to the police officer.

I'm rushing over a landscape that feels like I've dreamed it, and my son is dragging me across the high mountain rocks that boundary the lake.

There's a wall of water, the part of the mere that's outside the mountain, and I'm looking down at it, into the ice blocks and beyond them the hotspring, as we leap into the dark.

16

"What are you doing?" Willa's mother shouts.

The stretcher's too narrow and Willa's spilling over the sides. Her hips drape off the edge like a picnic cloth, and her arms fall. There's nowhere to put them. Willa looks down at her legs, bare, exposed, her dress rucked up. She wonders if she's wet herself. No, it's snow melting as it lands on her. How did she get outside?

It's beginning to look a lot like Christmas, sings something, a decoration, *everywhere you go*, and up on a roof a reindeer gallops back and forth in place. She should've taken it down. It's past the time for decorations.

For a moment the reindeer looks at Willa, and she sees its evil black and gleaming eyes. Then it's made of neon again.

Now she's in the back of an ambulance, but where are Dylan and Roger? They're carting her to a cemetery. She's about to be buried alive.

Willa sits up, but someone pushes her flat again, a mask on her face.

Where is he? she tries to say, but can't. The doors of the ambulance are open. It's not moving.

Tina's screaming into her phone. "It took him, some kind of animal, my grandson, and ran off, *some kind of animal my*

*grandson I said a bear I said a bear a bear rabies I said goddamn you
to hell I said a wild fucking animal."*

"It wasn't a bear," Willa says, very quietly, and looks at the
top of her hand where a tube has made its way into her vein like
a little red snake. "It was a monster."

*"A bear or some kind of wolverine how should I know? Do you
know who I am, do you know who you're talking to, do you know
anything at all? Because I want Fish & Game and I want every cop
and I want my goddamn senator if this isn't happening right this fucking second, get here, get your asses here, something took my grandson."*

Willa pulls the mask off. Everything is a watery haze and
Christmas lights are blinking on all the houses. On a neighbor's
roof, a man in a crimson suit with eight tiny reindeer is taking
flight.

Women are running around her, and the mothers are coming too, marching in, coming for Willa and for Roger. She looks
for Officer Woolf.

Willa's mother slaps her face.

"Stop making that sound! Stop it this second!"

Willa discovers that a moaning howl is coming from her
mouth. The lights of Herot Hall flicker. There's snow on her
tongue.

The hand wings across Willa's face again, *thwack*, and Willa
looks up, startled, hurting. On one of those fingers there's a rock
big enough that it could substitute for one of Willa's eyes.

Willa pushes herself off the stretcher and stands, wobbly,
tethered to the IV bag. She's the one in charge of this household,
not her mother.

"Officer Woolf!" Willa calls.

She hears dogs in the distance barking frantically. Gunshots
from the mountain.

Diane's hands are on Willa's shoulders, marrowing her bones.
"Pull yourself together!" She pinches Willa through her dress, in
the tender bit of flesh above her hip.

Willa can only point up the mountain, to the spot where the sky is turning purple—is it morning? The trees are saw blades stuck in the snow. The snake in her vein wriggles and turns to an earthworm, a pale pink shudder making its way in and out of her body.

She stares at it, remembering Dil's umbilical cord, which she never really saw. It was cut and bandaged, a tiny scroll of skin when the bandage came off. Now she's connected to a bag of fluid, or it's connected to her, and she can't tell who's feeding whom.

Everyone must be hungry. There are appetizers in the kitchen, fish eggs, flat champagne.

"Roger," Willa says, but her voice doesn't carry. Where is he? Where can he be?

Diane is talking to the police, pointing and shouting, and Tina is too, and there are more people coming.

At last, the man she needs is leaning over her. Willa presses both hands to his chest.

"Officer Woolf," she whispers.

"Mrs. Herot," he says, his voice breaking.

There's blood. Willa raises her hand to touch her own face, to see if she's wounded. Maybe something scratched her. There's a shining star pinned to him like he's the sky over Bethlehem.

"I let you down," he says. "I failed. I should've listened. I'll find Dylan. I'll find Dana Mills. I swear to you."

Willa's fingertips remember the feeling of the crown and her son's throat, the little head of the plastic king. Dylan's dead. He must be.

Tina is wailing suddenly, keening, running up the mountain, and everyone's looking at Willa.

There are medics carrying a stretcher down through the trees and over the snow, and there's a thin trail of blood coming from it, lit up under the lights of Herot, like the red sash on a dress bought for an opening night, or like blood on the floor of Willa's kitchen, the way it pooled after it ribboned down her thighs.

There are medics with a stretcher, yes, Willa recognizes that, and someone's on it, yes, not moving, covered in a sheet. It's Dylan, but why would there be blood?

Willa takes a step toward the medics as they pull the sheet off the body.

It's Roger.

Willa stands at the bottom of the mountain, watching medics tend to her husband in a way that tells her he's already dead. She tears out the IV and reaches his side in long steps, feeling like she's flown. No plastic surgeon can fix this. No one can draw new lines and reconnect the dots.

Her skin is hot and her entire history is illuminated. She's gotten what she deserves, after all this time on Earth, all these years of failure, all these tiny things dropped into boiling oil, the fried and forgotten pieces of her heart.

She's a marble statue, Mary in a cathedral, her dear one draped across her lap, her face a mask of tragedy.

"It wasn't Dana Mills who took my son," she says. "It was a monster. The monster killed Roger too."

Willa's mother is making frantic beheading gestures. Slicing her hand across her throat over and over again.

"It was a monster with a long tail, claws, and teeth, a huge monster with fur, but also not—like a bear, like a person, but also not like a person. The monster's name is Gren. He's Dana Mills's son."

Her hands touch her husband's body. A sob tangles in her teeth like thread. She's biting through a known tapestry to make a new story, a hunt unraveling and being re-woven in midair.

"Find Gren!" she shouts. It rings out in the frozen world. *"Kill the monster!"*

the mere

You could walk to their mere,

shaded by frostbitten trees, the surface a mangle of roots.

The waters are black, and every night,

a horrible wonder is visible in them, drowned flames

lolling beneath the surface like corpses.

They live in dark-unmarked, a place no one wants to go.

ATTEND

17

Attend to this, my brain tells me, *you're late, you're missing everything.*

I'm dropping through the mere, and it's deeper than I thought it could be, bottomless. I choke on lake water, and it fills me, a tide coming in.

I should've killed that officer, his neck under my knife. Everything's underneath the thinnest covering. All it takes is a puncture, a rusty nail, a bullet, and your history leaks out.

I should have killed him, because now he's killed me.

I feel like I'm still running down that mountain with a stranger's sword in my hand, but my arm isn't my own. It's an arm with poison in it. I didn't know I could breathe water. I didn't know I could live underneath the rest of everything, but it burns, it chills, it fills me—

Someone grabs me by the shoulders, pulls me out of the water and shakes me. Gren scrabbles at my jacket, pushing on my chest.

I'm looking at him from far away, but then I'm choking the dark up, and it's pooling around me.

"I thought you were dead," Gren says. He burrows in my arms and stays a minute, but I can't get any words out of my mouth. "I saw someone kill you, down there, on the screen. I was hiding and I saw you die."

I thought *you* were dead, I want to say.

The pain in my arm is real. Bullet wound. I feel it, a hard bore of light.

Gren crouches beside me, his worry vibrating him. Somewhere there are hospital beds and antibiotics, and somewhere soldiers are losing their limbs under anesthesia. We're here, again, in the old station, arrived from underneath instead of above. We're on the marble floor, in a pool of green water, and blood is draining from me into it, pink on the silvery tiles, a world gone Technicolor and then backward in time, into a silent film.

I have to try to keep myself alive.

"Is there a fire?" I ask Gren. "Can you make a fire?"

There are kindling and branches down here already, from the times we've been into the station during the coldest winters. I didn't know you could get in here from the mere, but Gren knew. How did he know? I can't think about him wandering off alone, but that's the only explanation.

Gren makes a spark, and soon there's a small blaze.

I put my knife into the flame, burn it until it's sterile and then cut into my wound.

I'm a blast of light, an explosion killing a whole city, and my body flies apart. Then, silently, it comes back together, everything centered around the bullet.

I push it out with my other hand.

I'm in the dark, walking through a black hallway, all around me doors, no knobs, and I don't know what's behind them. Ghosts.

I sear my arm with the hot blade, attempting to cauterize the wound, and I scream, and he screams too, and all I can say when I'm done screaming is, "You're keeping me alive, baby," and hope he believes me.

We smell my flesh cooking against the metal like I'm a witch. He's dragged me off into this cave to die, I think and then I think

I'll heal, but the bone is shattered, and all I've got are basic medic skills, nothing like what I need.

"People were burned at the stake later than you think," says my saint, appearing out of a corner, sitting on the case that used to house cakes. She walks in circles, periodically touching me with one of her frozen fingers, and Gren never sees her.

"Gren," I say.

My son turns his head.

"Mama," he says.

"Are they coming for us?"

"Who?" he asks.

"You know who," I say.

"They won't find us," he says.

I look up at the roof of the station, and it's like a whale's ribs. I wonder if we're sailing over the ocean, hiding inside the belly of this mountain, if we've taken off from where we were moored. Maybe we'll come out into the light, and there'll be the sound of birds, and all around us there'll be wolves and cougars and maybe there'll be my mother, alive again, her arms open for her grandson.

I look down at the water and see a rib cage in the wet. A spine as long as a bus. Starry worms hang from the ceiling, and bats chirr and rustle.

✦

"Mommy," Gren says some time later, hours, days. I move, gritting my teeth.

"Wake up!" he says, and tries to open my eyelids with his fingers.

"I'm fine. Let me tell you a story," I manage to say, but my voice is cracking, my throat dry and red.

"Let me tell you a story," I tell him again. "You were wanted," I say. "I wanted you."

I don't know how to explain love to this boy. He knows about love from falling for the music of a faraway piano, but maybe that's how I know about love too. Maybe that's how it is.

I'm hot and then frozen, delirious, seeing things I don't want to see, streaks slithering like red and black snakes up my arm.

Then I see something worse.

The little boy from Herot Hall is sitting on the floor across from me. He's pale in the firelight, his yellow hair sticking up, still in his suit. The boy's mouth is hanging open. He has a plastic truck in his hand, and bruises on his throat.

"Want to play?" he says.

He picks up the truck, and runs it up a ramp. Gren is beside him, with a truck of his own. Nothing I gave him. It's shiny and new.

"What's your name?" the boy asks me.

"Dana," I manage.

"My mommy calls me Dilly," he says, and smiles at me, gaps in his teeth. "But my whole name is Dylan Martin Herot the Second. I'm named after my grandpa, but he's dead."

Gren's holding the little boy's hand. He looks at me pleadingly. I open my mouth to say no, but nothing comes out.

Gren can't have a friend, but I lose my will to fight against it. All I can do is curl up in the corner of the cave and watch two little boys playing with toys I didn't buy for them. Only one of them is the son I gave birth to, but now I have them both.

18

Attend the social event of the season! Willa thinks, her brain filling in the tone of the announcer, TV, 1950s-style, and then stops that thought in its tracks, along with the luminarias and the hors d'oeuvres that want to come into her mind with it. Sour cream and lemons, caviar, or maybe stuffed mushrooms, the poisonous kind.

It's five days later. Police, Fish & Game, Animal Control, dogs, up and down the mountain, boats in the lake with dragging devices, but there is no sign of Dana Mills, no sign of Gren. No sign of Dylan.

Willa's dressed in black silk. She's wearing a hat with a veil. She can see herself as though from afar, her pale hair, her pale skin, like someone in a Hitchcock film, thinner and more beautiful than she was a week ago, more perfect, her body some sort of saintly relic, becoming lighter than air, because she hasn't eaten, no, because she hasn't slept, no, not since they brought her husband bloody and broken down the mountain.

Her dress holds her like Roger never did. Beneath it a black slip, and beneath that a garment made of strong elastic, something that squeezes every inch of her. She is made of obsidian, after all this time being made of marble. Marble isn't what she wanted. Marble shows every flaw. Obsidian is made of heat, stone melted into black glass. Willa is a pyre, except that her nipples are frozen, like buds on a tree that's about to be bitten down to the roots. Everything aches, but these are the clearest ones, the two lumps of ice in her chest, and she doesn't laugh, doesn't cry, she's colder than a witch's—

A camera flashes.

On the front steps of Willa Herot's house three dozen white roses appeared this morning, with a note. She's gotten emails of support from all over the country, people telling her they're sorry she's being blamed for something that's clearly not her fault. She was only speaking the truth. Monsters, yes. Thugs, yes. Shoot on sight, yes.

She wobbles. No? She's not a—

She runs through a screaming street in her head, because now she's under attack. How many times has she watched the video of Dana Mills? Too many times. No one got a video of Gren. Late at night she wonders what she saw. She has too many versions in her head. One of them is just a little boy—

No. It wasn't wrong for her to say monster. *Monster* is the right word. Some of the headlines say Willa was heavily medicated when she said what she said. Others say that she is someone other than the someone she knows herself to be.

Her hair is braided into a crown on top of her head. Later, she'll get the safety scissors and shear off all the inches she grew over the years of this marriage. She'll take handfuls of it and drop it outside the house and then they'll see.

The ground's been hacked into with some machine, carving into the mud-ice. There are hydraulics on the coffin, and it heaves up, then down, lowering like a storm over an unsuspecting world.

Roger Herot, she thinks, in strange wonder still. This was not the plan. Willa Herot is a widow and Roger Herot is dead.

There will never be any more kisses in public, never any more cocktails at 5:30, never any more of her dress bunching up against his belt as he lifts her onto the counter, never anyone ever again thinking they're the perfect couple.

You can't be the perfect couple when one of you is dead, killed by a woman with a sword—a sword!

Killed for no reason at all.

Willa turns her gold watch face in toward her skin, like time doesn't exist. It's a watch not to her taste, a strange watch for Cartier, a slender gold Chinesey dragon ticking the seconds, making its way in endless circles around the diamond-numbered face. A present from Roger in a moment when he couldn't remember which anniversary it was and bought her time instead of paper.

The photos are all over the Internet, happy marriage, wedding day, Christmas mornings, Tahiti, photos taken by the mothers. Looking at them, Willa even feels jealous of herself. There are cell phone photos too, taken by the neighbors and leaked, Roger, flayed, open at the throat, red and white as Santa Claus, but not.

The headlines are everywhere, translated into a thousand languages, the murderous missing woman who came to Herot Hall, killed a father, and stole a child. That's the news. The news is confusing, because it seems there was also a bear, or, at least, a bear died on the mountain. Dana Mills is nowhere, and neither is Dylan Herot, and neither is Gren, who doesn't exist as far as the story is concerned. There's only been this stupid bear, a big, dumb, dead body of a bear, fur and blood and glazed eyes.

Willa imagines Gren and his mother making their way through underground passages, a sword in one hand, a gun in another, and claws, claws.

Who knows what happened? Only Willa, as far as she can tell. *Gren*, she repeats to herself, because she's in danger of forgetting. *Hysterical*. She's not.

The mountain's been invaded, officers like ants over a hill, but no one's been brought down. No more bodies displayed. No hanging, no gun battle, no guillotine. No reckoning. No revenge. All five of the mothers surround Willa now, flanking her like crows. Tina Herot looks like a statue, but her hands are shaking. Willa has a mean and sudden thought about vodka.

As the coffin descends, Roger's mother makes a sound like nothing Willa's ever heard. Willa's own mother is behind her, elbows sharp as knives.

There are AMBER alerts and thumbprint alerts and every kind of alerts. Dylan's all over the news. His kindergarten picture, not the most attractive. Suspicious face, missing tooth. Why don't they clean the kids up before they photograph them? Smudge right down the middle of Dil's face in that photo, but it's the one they're running.

The mothers have done the requisite TV appearances. They formed a pastel pack and stood together, tearfully saying, "Bring him home," and announcing the cash reward, not with numbers, just with, "Substantial."

Willa has not been allowed on television.

Like he flew, people keep saying. *Like he just flew away.* But boys don't fly. Monsters fly. No one's saying what Willa knows, which is as follows: a monster took Dilly, and he's never coming back.

Willa imagines her son as a polished skull, stripped of everything that made him himself, his hair, his face, his brain, "Chopsticks."

Her son will soon be bones, and her husband too. She looks up at the mountain and wonders which god answered her prayers, wonders if she prayed them.

She looks down at the other mountain, this one made of flowers out of season. Where do they grow funeral flowers? Are they kept separate from wedding flowers? Are there greenhouses full of bouquets grown for the dead?

Louisa's weeping loudly and distractingly, her face covered in zebra stripes of mascara. Willa wants to hunt her, a safari for disallowed grief, and then it gets worse, because Louisa takes a ring off her engagement finger. The diamond glitters in the sun, larger than Willa's, as Louisa drops it into the grave. She puts both her hands on her stomach, which, Willa sees now, is rounder than it ought to be.

Louisa weeps louder, and louder, and someone takes her arms and removes her, people on either side, carrying on.

Roger has left Willa in charge of his entire fucked-up, secret-keeping world. This is what *Willa* should be doing. She should be taking off her own ring and then she should be climbing into the grave, the dirt around her.

"I don't know what to do," she says, to no one in particular, and her mother's the no one who answers.

"Keep yourself together," her mother says. "Don't fall apart. Don't let go. Stand up straight. This isn't your shame. It's Roger's."

Willa feels the mothers behind her, all of them clicking their heels in military posture. She doesn't climb down into the grave. No.

She does what he deserves. She throws a handful of dirt onto the place where Roger was. She throws another. She picks up a shovel, and starts heaving dirt onto the coffin, because all she wants to do is cover it all up.

Roger's in there on his little white pillow, sleeping through everything, just the way he always has, but this time he's sleeping underground. Willa will have to make certain the cemetery un-buries him and brings that engagement ring back to her. She'll sell it, take the money and use it to buy a pair of shoes, and then she'll walk all over these years she spent with him.

Her mother takes the shovel from her. Then Roger's mother. Then the other mothers. They cover him together, a small army of women sinking into the snow in their stilettos. This is a classic version.

The men marry. The women bury.

The earth is wet and water is welling up inside the grave,

water from the mere, Willa thinks, water from beneath the mountain. She sees it seeping into the place Roger is sleeping, like blood from a wound.

Willa thinks about Greek plays she performed in during college, the wailing chorus she was once a part of, but she has no wails left, no rending of garments. She has nothing but mud.

Under the ground, her husband, the favored son of Herot Hall, is enjoying every moment of this attention.

◆

Later, Willa stands in the kitchen, looking through windows replaced with bulletproof glass while she wasn't home. She's drinking vodka from the bottle, and wearing a kimono robe that belonged to her in the time before she was this Willa. It's ancient, tattered, faded, and comforting. It belongs in the garbage, and that's where she found it, in the housekeeper's—*Claudia's*—rag bag.

The bathtubs are full of flowers, and the refrigerator is full of macaroni, and Willa is full of something. She has never been alone here before, not for this long. Did she ever even want to be this person? Her phone rings and she nearly tips over.

"I'm sorry to be calling so late," says the man on the other end.

She comes out of the house to meet him, a hood to cover her hair, as though she's ever been invisible. She gets into his car, not the cruiser, a truck.

Willa looks at the man beside her. He has a beard he didn't have when she met him. He looks as though he hasn't slept in days.

She is the one in pain. Her son is a soccer-snack orange slice lost on the floor of a minivan, down in the wheelwell.

"I'll find him, Mrs. Herot," he says.

"Dylan's dead. I know that much. You don't have to pretend. And call me Willa. My husband's dead too. I'm not Mrs. Herot anymore."

He reaches out slowly, and runs his thumb over her mouth, leaving a print for later identification.

"Willa," he says, using her name like he's a man and she's not.

"Ben," she says, and lowers her face.

"I'm sorry," he says. "That was inappropriate."

She unfastens her seat belt and kisses Ben Woolf full on the mouth, taking the back of his skull in her hand and remembering how Dylan's skull felt in her hand when he was a newborn, that tempting triangle of detachment under her nail.

The whole world is a mess of blood and teeth. She can only angle for the things left. She looks at the man before her. She wonders who's watching, peering from behind curtains. Everyone. Monsters. Mothers.

When she leaves the car, she throws her empty bottle into the bushes, perfectly plotted, so perfectly that there's not even room for a bottle to break into them.

You can't fight nature, she thinks. You can't make it human. You can't even make *yourself* human. Everyone is an animal.

When she goes to bed, she doesn't dream anything at all. It's only silence, a black screen before a reboot.

HARK

19

Hark! We listen to the hunt. The same sort of hunt that's been conducted for centuries, though the people on this mountain are calling it something else, a search rather than an armed attack.

It's the same hunt no matter the monster, spears and swords and bullets in the side, blood on the rocks. Take the horn for a precious thing. Take the skin for fireproof armor. Take the blood. Poison enemies or heal beloveds. Harpoon the beast, capture the kraken, swimmers with spears, boats of the brave.

The mountain and the mere, like all old things, like all old places, protect those who live inside them.

There are boats with metal claws, motoring over our lake. They drop, dredge, and drag, but the woman from the cave never surfaces.

Maybe she's caught beneath the mere on a hook, or maybe she's gone backward into the flood. The water returns to being used for drinking.

There are crows and owls and rabbits. Everything burrows into the ground, and flies above the heads of Herot Hall, where the people look over their shoulders as they go from house to house. There are deer in the driveways, and ravens on the roofs. The houses are still lit up. Dogs, leashed to keep them safe. Groceries, put away quickly to avoid attracting more of the wild into the domestic. Countertops, clean; closets, closed. New locks and new windows installed.

The water from our mere rushes through pipes and into mouths, and ice cubes clank in glasses.

"There's a bear on the mountain!"

"A grizzly bear!"

"I bet someone had a cub as a pet in the city and didn't know what to do with it, I've actually heard of that before, I read an article—"

"But seriously, have you seen that movie about the, yeah, the Herzog movie, that one? He thought bears were his friends? Oh, my god."

"Did you see the video about the baby hedgehogs adopted by the orange stripy cat? Hang on, I'll send you the link."

"And poor Roger!" says a woman in one of the dining rooms. "Poor, poor Roger. And his wife, just—"

"I never liked her."

"But her son too."

"He's dead. There's no way he's not. A bear took him."

"Maybe it put him in a cave."

"This isn't *The Jungle Book*."

"Humans probably fed that bear and made it think it should eat humans—"

"Humans didn't feed it *people*! If anything, it'd have a taste for potato chips!"

"That Herot boy bit my Davis, did I tell you?"

"And scratched my Lisa too, but there's nothing to say about that to any of the Herots. What can you say? No, that's inappropriate. Tina Herot. She looks like the walking dead. She's just been going to the cemetery to sit at Roger's grave, like that's not morbid."

"I'm not drunk. I'm just a tiny bit tipsy—"

"I'm going to go out there, right out there and—"

"Stay inside, I'm making pot roast."

✦

News clips play from every television, every radio, every phone, and we listen.

"Reports say veteran soldier Dana Mills, missing for seven years, broke into a house on New Year's Eve, allegedly murdering a resident of a gated community, and kidnapping a child. Police officer Ben Woolf investigates."

An incongruous photo of a man swimming, naked chest, pectorals, biceps. And then a switch to a couple on-screen, cell phone video from the night of the catastrophe.

"The late Roger Herot," says the anchor, "and his wife, Willa Herot."

The residents of Herot Hall make a sound of recognition, a cross between sorrow and triumph. The man they knew has died, and some of them saw his body. Others saw the woman who must've killed him. Some of them hated him. Others loved him. Now he's a ghost on their screens.

The couple drifts through a party, beautiful, successful, certain, and there's laughter in the background. Glasses are raised. The camera freezes on the woman's face.

"I really could never stand her," says someone. "That fake accent."

"She thought she was the queen of this place," says another. "Look at her now."

"Did you hear what she said? About monsters?"

"Last year, she had a . . . well, we'll call it a miscarriage. I saw her standing in the kitchen, bleeding down her legs. I almost called the police. The police? I mean 911, of course. Only good thoughts to Willa."

One should know better than to live in a glass house at this point in human history. A neighbor goes anonymous on the news and talks curtly about uncurtained windows, an open invitation.

No one's saying *monster*. No one but Willa Herot.

And now she stands in her kitchen, scrolling through the photos on her dead husband's cell phone. A man playing guitar. A woman's freckled breasts, a video of two people naked in a bed, all of it radiant with 1970s light, a decade he didn't live, but only bought as a camera filter.

She drinks wine. She bathes in the mountain's water, boiling herself. In her heart, Herot Hall burns to the ground, melted windows and puddled tiles. Even a glittering green world can be reduced to a crumpled black cup in the campfire.

She walks down the street, and invites the woman from the cell phone photos over for a cup of tea.

Mere water, mountain herbs in it, and later, in an upstairs bathroom in her own house, the other woman bleeds until the heir she carried is gone.

A few days later the blonde stands outside her house with her mother and her mother's friends beside her, waving at the moving van as the other woman is packed into it, all her delicate wineglasses, all her low-cut sweaters. The other woman's husband stands at the window, watching her go.

Lamplight flickers on Willa Herot's wedding ring teetering on the edge of a bedside table. It rolls into the corner, where tomorrow the maid's vacuum will suck it into a whirling void of lint, dander, and dirt.

Time passes for lost objects, and it is not time at all. Centuries after a burial, bogs turn up the murdered, and foundations turn up the sacrificed, and beneath this very house, there are a thousand nights ending in tears, the salt of those tears part of the soil now. Not enough to ruin the possibility of crops, but enough to change things. We know it. We've been watching the world.

We look at what the vacuum does, taking that salt, that skin, that hair, those silk threads, and twisting them into a hoard, the ring at the center, swaddled like an infant.

We remember other hoards like this one, a place in the desert with another golden wedding ring, polished by sand, khaki threads knotted around it to keep it the right size for a slender finger. That ring. How old it is, how bright, how polished by recent wear.

Time passes slowly in this glass house. The alarm clock shakes itself, second to second, the kind of clock that can be thrown against the wall and not be broken. It has a glow face, better than a glow dial, no history of radium. Six hundred seconds, the clock shuddering.

The wedding ring becomes something other than a wedding ring. All its history of love is gone, and its history of hate too.

It has been worn for seven years (220,838,400 seconds), but now it belongs to us again, and to the gods of garbage.

20

Hark, Willa thinks, a few days after the funeral, Dylan still missing. *No heralds, no angels, no newborn king.*

There's no peace on Earth, either, but when has there ever been?

"Meet me," she says, gets into the car and drives to a roadhouse upriver from Herot.

Now, she's sitting on a cracked red vinyl bar stool, which she can feel pinching into her bottom, old germs, old disinfectant, old yellow foam bent to old yellow forms. No doubt most of the people who sat here before her are dead. They ate hamburgers and thought their lives were getting better. The wall behind the bar is postcarded with fifty years of peeling waterfalls, curled corners.

Willa's in a parka and beneath it a skirt cut to hug, kick pleat, and a sweater, V-neck, soft black cashmere.

She orders a gin and tonic with lime, gets lemon. The bartender's a woman with two red-and-gray braids, a face like a leather purse. No one else here has a playgroup or a Montessori cubby. No one else here has ever seen a monster.

She has a vision of Gren rampaging through Herot Hall, eating everyone there. She wants them shredded like seven-year-old taxes.

It's Clam Chowder day today. If she were home, she'd have Cornbread (Homemade) already in the oven. It's a mix from a box. It only takes twenty-five minutes: three active, twenty-two vodka + orange juice.

Willa orders another, hold the tonic and the lemon. It's still legal to find oneself, at the end of a perfect marriage, perfectly miserable. Roger is the one who lost his life like a set of car keys. She's doing nothing wrong.

2:00 when he sits down on the stool beside her and orders a beer.

2:05 when his hand is on her knee.

2:07 when his fingers pluck the elastic of her panties away from her skin.

2:09 when he puts those fingers into his mouth, and she's looking around the dark bar, wondering if they'll get arrested for public indecency, but he's the only officer here.

2:15 when they walk across the road to the motel with its sign on during the dark of the day. Snow falls down over the boy in a barrel and the girl in another barrel, both of them at the top of a blue neon waterfall that flickers because some of the strands of neon are from the fifties and some are from the eighties.

2:25 when she's underneath him. She winds her fingers into his hair, bright gold in the lamplight, and for a moment she's a queen with a hoard, before she's here again in a motel room fucking a man she barely knows.

2:31 when she's facedown on the mattress, the bed shaking like a ship, and he's inside her, his hands on her hips, steering.

2:36 when there's a shipwreck. There are so many clear explanations for icebergs and captains. It's never an accident. She envisions the *Titanic*.

Pillow between her teeth while he roars, no care for who might hear. So Willa, bruised biceps, scraped lips, spits out the pillow and screams, her body wracked, unexpectedly seized with something that isn't pleasure and isn't pain and isn't even human. She's fucking this man because her son is dead. She's fucking this man because her husband was fucking the neighbor. She's fucking this man because she's never gotten anything close to what she wants.

She holds on to that.

2:39 on their backs on the bed. Willa smokes a cigarette because one does. Badge on the bedside. Gun in its holster on the desk made of wood that's not even wood. It's walnut laminate. She looks out the gap in the curtains and there's the parking lot covered in new snow, no footprints at all.

Her watch is still on backward from the funeral. She flips it over and looks at the little golden dragon flying around the edge. It cost as much as a car.

3:15 when she runs a finger down his chest, over a scar like a rope. "Where did this come from?"

"I ran into a burning building to save a kid," he says. "There was an explosion as I brought him out."

She wonders. Something too humble in the tone. His breathing has changed. It's quicker, and when she puts her head down on his chest, she can feel his heart. She polygraphs his breath and beats, and finds him to be veering away from truth and into myth. She needs him to be a hero right now, but not historically. She'll change him into the man she wants. The past doesn't matter.

3:30 when she's on top of him, contracting herself into a Kegel vise. See what she can do if he looks at her the way he's looking at her now, as though she's the queen of the world, and not a widowed woman in a motel room near a pretty boring wonder of the continent?

"Let go," she whispers, because it is she who's in charge of everything, never mind what men think—

Let go. Feel your life disintegrate. Make a new one.

3:50 when they're in the shower, someone else's long hair in the drain, Officer Ben Woolf soaping the back of the woman with the missing son.

4:00 when she picks up his gun. Flirtatious, not flirtatious.

She points it at him. He's not even scared. Would Officer Ben Woolf really go to bed in a motel room with a near-stranger and leave the bullets in his gun? She's impressed, as impressed as she can be at this juncture. He's planned ahead. He's not the kind of man who gets killed by a woman.

"Dana Mills ruined everything," Willa says. "And now she's just free, out there somewhere. She can do whatever she wants, and no one else can."

He doesn't say anything, but she can feel his thoughts now. They're the thoughts men always have. She's spent her life anticipating those thoughts, working around them, pouring their drinks and patting their shoulders, sewing their buttons on tightly so that they can feel secure while they undo everything. No more of that.

"I need you to find her," Willa says. "I need you to keep us safe."

She feels a tremor in him, the agreement they're making, the handshake, the deal. She's no devil. She won't feel guilt.

"And him," she says.

"Who?" Ben asks.

"Gren. I need you to kill them both. I need them gone from here."

"I didn't see him," Ben says. "If anything, I saw a bear."

"It wasn't a bear," Willa tells him. "It was wearing clothes."

He looks at her, and finally, *finally* he nods. Does he believe her? Does she believe herself? She's no longer entirely sure. It was chaos. If she got it wrong, it's not her fault.

4:15 when Willa closes the motel room door behind them, when they both go to their cars. *Yes*, something hisses, and it's a yes to an abyss, Willa walking forward to put her hand in Roger's hand.

Do you take this man, *yes*, do you take his hand, *yes,* for rich, for poor, for sick, for health. *Yes*. She should have said, *I don't know*.

Willa Herot is up a flight of stairs from her history, and her last name is hardly Herot now. She imagines her third wedding.

21

Hark! We slap the bell on the front desk of the police station. Though it dings like a tiny church, no congregation comes. We stand alone, unheralded, and angry. There's been a murder, and we will have justice, even if we have to fight for it ourselves. We should be the police, that's the truth of the matter. We do everything else.

First thing, we'd sterilize this whole place. The station smells of dirty laundry, stale coffee, and dog. We consider spritzing with the sanitizer we carry in our handbags. Instead, we barge through the station until we find Officer Ben Woolf at his desk, staring into the middle distance. Alas, there is no distance, only us, all five of us, in front of him.

Our officer is a mask of masculine tragedy, days of stubble, bags beneath his eyes. He projects grief and guilt for failing. His uniform is no longer pressed.

But he's smiling absently, and what does he smell like? He smells like Willa Herot's perfume. We've mistaken his greed for grief and his gluttony for guilt. He doesn't even notice us. He seems to be screening a dirty movie in midair.

There's a long tradition that says women gossip, when in fact women are the memory of the world. We keep the family trees and the baby books. We manage the milk teeth. We keep the census of diseases, the records of divorces, battles, and medals. We witness the wills. We wash the weddings out of the bedsheets.

We know everything there is to know, and we keep it rolled into the newel posts, stuffed into the mattresses, smuggled inside our vaginas if it comes to that. Women's clothing is made without pockets, but we come into the world equipped.

We lean on his file folders, furies dressed in midday luncheon attire.

"Are you *sleeping*, Officer Woolf?"

He jolts and looks up at us.

"Ladies," he says, and blinks. "How can I help you?"

We have no illusions about men. They're all strong until they're skeletons. Tina brings out a string of photos. It seems we've hired an investigator to look through windows. It could be any blond woman and any blond man, but it isn't.

Don't climb our walls if you're afraid of boiling oil.

We pass one of the photos across the desk. Officer Woolf looks at it for a moment, and swallows hard. "That's clearly fake."

"We'd like you to focus on recovering our grandchild," says Diane. "And apprehending the killer of my son-in-law."

"Instead of focusing on the recovery of his mother," says Tina.

"I don't know what you're talking about," he says. "But whatever you're implying, it's disrespectful to both of us."

Does Officer Ben Woolf remind us of anyone we know? Of course he does. He reminds us of some of our husbands, the way they took us, unwilling, on trophy safaris, once-in-a-lifetime trips during which we rode in Jeeps, while they got too close to lions.

No one here has ever reached the limit of her patience. No one here's ever had an accident with her husband's prescriptions. The thing about erection pills is that they make the blood flow away from the brain. No one here has ever, ever stood at the top of a staircase, cocktail in one hand, looking down at an oopsy-daisy.

We know what kind of man he is. A lazy one. It is our task to get him back on track. We've been marching the perimeter of

Herot Hall since the kidnapping and murder. We've studied the photographs of Dana Mills before and after. Apparently we're the only ones who care. Herot Hall has been breached. We will have a body and a perpetrator, or we will have this officer's job.

"Ladies," he says. "Believe me, all of our resources have been dedicated to this, and only this—"

Tina Herot slams her fist down and spills Woolf's coffee.

"Don't you dare lie to me," she says. "You'll find my grandson, and you'll find Dana Mills. That's an order."

We spin as one and depart the police station. We walk to our cars, and lean on our horns. We will not surrender. We will not back down.

Soon, soon, the mountain will be covered with men in uniform, hounds, cars moving fast, people telling and yelling.

Soon, soon, we will have what is ours.

22

Hark! Yes! Dogs on duty! Criminals, teeth! Robberies, noses! Drugs! Bombs! Riding in cars with heads out the window, official vests! We're off with our agitated officer, ten dogs without leashes, the whole company met and released, inclined by right of nose.

Our officer blows a horn, and we sniff his secrets. He's taken a few things to keep himself awake, bulk illegal from India. Pure protein and adrenaline, chewable fear. He's been scanning a map of the mountain, an old one, and we smell that too, railroad, crumbling paper, oily fingerprints.

Hounds in a swarming pack, moving as one sleek body, leaping a wall made of stone, an interesting smell there. Four hundred years ago someone died on this rock, a hundred years ago someone hung from that tree, thirteen seconds ago there was a squirrel, run, run, *yes!*

Big mountain cat spray! Drop flat to the ground, creep, no, not above, look up, careful, branches? Oh, no, oh, no, silent slinking murdering cat, ah—

Never mind. Long gone. Housecat, tiny, fluff and flea powder. Scratch over that, dig a moment in disgust, show them your work, boys, show them.

Dogs can tell how many times a person's heart beats, how

many breaths they've taken, whether they're sick, whether they're dying. Dogs can find the secrets their people don't know, tip them over, spill them onto the ground, roll in them.

Dogs can feel this officer and his cowardice, making him miserable. He doesn't want to find the things we're looking to find. The world is full of secrets no one cares about, no one but dogs. Sniff it. He's scared of the woman in this mountain, but he has a long yellow hair stuck to his jacket. Fur of a different beast. We sniff it. Officer has been roaming.

We huff the target sweater again. Boy, chocolate, poison divine, lick, yanked back! Dirt, bloodied knee, soap?

Sometimes we're in a cage for days. Sometimes we're at a café for days, waiting, biding time, eating clandestine crumbs with tongue out, casually tasting toddlers. We are rarely used to our full sniffing capacity.

"Rub his nose in it, there you go, get him the scent good."

We already got the scent. We had the scent before you knew there was a scent, from three towns away we had the scent!

We've been hunting this boy for two weeks. We travel on perfume lines, drink them out of the air like you listen to the radio. Put our heads out the window of the speeding car and smell someone touching someone else five lanes over, blow job, string cheese, tequila, and a new wedding ring. Respect. Ears back, grin on, yip.

"Rub his nose in it again, yeah, he's lost the scent, there's a good boy."

We never lose the scent. Scents don't disappear the way you think they do. We tug them like ropes.

Hounds running uphill, a wall of the correct smell. That sweater again. We know it by now, don't we, and every day it smells more interesting. Now it's coffee, doughnut, plastic sack, car keys, sexual lubricant, vodka, yellow-haired woman who smells like—

She smells like the boy we're tracking. Where is that boy? All over the mountain.

Oh, yes! It's the smell of the sweater, it's the smell of the lost boy, making his way up the slope!

Highest leap, over fallen trees, over icy creek, snow to the chest! Cold paws, trip trap trop, snow ruins the smells.

Who needs to shit? Stop, paw the snow, look busy.

Oh, the horn again, RRRRWWWWAAAAAAAAAA, and it breaks the snow off branches. One of us is military, retired, brought back on a flight, misery forever. Mostly he only points for tobacco.

But. He stands over a crack in the snow, pawing, a gap in the story of Earth, a wriggle. It's a scent he knows! Sand. Desert. Someone made of war. Bomb and bright and night and birds screeching overhead.

What's in here, shall we? Yes, we shall.

A skinny spiral of smoke coming from a fire, a chimney under the mountain. We think about the underground, because our officer thinks about the underground. Caves, railways, trains, tracks. Where are they? A rail tie there, a barricade there. An old crack in the old earth.

Point, boys. All at once, every hound here. Paw down, nose down, show him where the scent went.

Our officer kneels.

A tiny crack, and through it, we smell the scent, of the missing, of the mother, of the other. All three, down there, out of reach, but that is not our business.

We thrust our noses into the dangling palms of police and bark our victory.

For our quest is complete!

Treats.

23

It hearkens back to the war, all of it, the mountain, the caves, and no visible villains in front of him. People hiding where they shouldn't be able to hide. The dogs insist they've found Dana Mills and Dylan Herot too, but all they've found is smoke.

Ben Woolf stands on top of the peak, and the whole thing might be a hive teeming with his enemies, but he can't see the evil for the trees. He's been given intel like this before, and he has no desire to die on this damn hill. In the war, he dodged bullets, hid in alleys, pressed himself back and away from the line of fire. He went to war to be a hero, and he failed at it, never mind the body count. None of that was glory. Glory should feel good.

Now's the time to change the course of his existence, find a murderer and bring her to justice, come back to applause from Herot Hall.

The smoke, though, is only a tendril, coming up out of the snow. There's no passage down into the center of the Earth from here, but the dogs orbit him, certain. No one with any sense dives into fire.

He doesn't want to go in, even if there was a way he could see to do it.

Dana Mills waits behind his eyelids, her face gaunt, her eyes shining with tears. He knows what kind of soldier she must have been. She was behind him on the slope, her knife at his jugular. She almost had him. She was tougher than he was, and the proof is in that video. Whatever happened to her, it's still happening.

He's watched her beheading a hundred times, and he knows that she is something unnatural. She needs to be burned, staked, any of those options. How else could she have taken him on? He outweighs her by at least a hundred pounds, and he's a foot and a half taller than she is. No normal person is willing to die, but she was willing.

His mind is full of blood spatter, white walls, cement, words written in red. He takes a piss in the snow and feels his future, the way his kidneys will fail and his cock will go limp, the way his stomach will increase in size as his legs become pins. He tosses his head, feeling his wound stretch, seeing Dana Mills's face. He's still shot full of antibiotics and painkillers, but if he lets himself pause, even for a moment, he feels his jaw locking, infection spreading through his body.

He needs to do chin-ups on a construction fence, go into a dive bar and punch someone in the face, push someone in front of a speeding train.

He needs to banish this coward crouching inside him. The coward has always been there, if he's honest. There's a reason he's a small town police officer. He looks down at his stomach and feels shame. One day without working out, and even his flesh turns against him.

Ben takes the dogs back to the station and takes himself to the gym. When he's done there, he shaves his face, the bristles dulling his razor. He draws the clippers down his body, shearing away half an inch of hair. He used to get his back waxed when he was a swimmer, but waxing an entire body is no pleasure, and lately he's taken to maintenance and laser hair removal. If his skin always feels prickly, mammals are not by nature smooth. He's done the Internet research. Even whales are sometimes born with fur.

Good man, he whispers to himself as he shaves, over and over, the cadence soothing. He stews in the shower, steaming, and then looks at himself in the mirror. He was wrong. There's no weight gain, no muscle loss. He's stronger than ever. He's strong enough to take her.

He flexes. He flexes again. He pours himself an ounce of caffeinated vitamins, throws it back like a shot. He touches the wound absently, feels it knitting, tugs the edges apart. It can wait to heal a little longer.

He returns to his house, eats a plate of beef and three egg yolks. He listens to inspirational voices, calling him from the speakers, pushing him onward, upward, Ben Woolf who's always been destined for greatness and never yet achieved it, Ben Woolf, who is a police officer in a place where nothing ever happens.

This is the answer to his ask, he knows. She's what he's been waiting for. Police have no business praying for peace.

Dana Mills will be the enemy he brings out of the mountain, slung over his shoulder. He goes over the body he'll dismantle, the way he'll take her apart, tendon by tendon, bone by bone, cell by cell, dividing her from her soul and tearing out her heart.

He looks at the geological survey maps, all of them disagreeing, but none of them disagree about the mountain. There's room inside it for anything the world might wish to hide. It's been blasted and shut down, covered over, mined, flooded. Haunted too, or so goes the bullshit. Plenty of dead in that ground, but there are plenty of dead everywhere.

The only way he can think to get under that ground quietly enough to surprise her is the same way she went in, and that is by swimming. A leap, a dive, a drop through water into stone.

Into the lake, he thinks, and down to the bottom. There must be a passage. If there's smoke, she's the fire.

Things that don't make sense are not things he thinks about. Dana Mills was presumed dead all these years, but that's not his business. It will be his job to return her to the proper category.

Later, when he's found her, and when he's found Dylan—the kid is likely dead, but maybe he isn't—all the men of the station, the chief, the rest of the officers, and Willa, her too, all of them will sing a song about someone being a very jolly good fellow.

He'll be the hero who saves Herot Hall.

TELL

24

Tell me I'm going to make it, I'm thinking, but no one knows to tell me. I'm in the dark. It's like I'm in a palace. Golden bathtubs and beheadings. There are too many things that happened in the dark, and too many things I can't remember. I open my eyes.

I don't know how many days we've been down here. I'm made of pain and heat, clammy skin, jaw tight, and I'm scared of tetanus, of gangrene, of every horrible way to go. Another thing war gives you. All soldiers are scared of bleeding to death, and all soldiers are scared of snagging themselves on old metal. It's better to blow up than to survive, halved. There are good deaths, and bad ones. Lockjaw is bad. Blood poisoning is bad. *Give me the cold*, every soldier thinks, even when they're not stationed in the ice. *Let me freeze to death. Let me not wake up.* This is cold, at least, the mountain, but not cold enough. The water's running.

Gren is on his knees beside the stream that pours over the tracks. He looks like a kid at Disneyland, not that my kid will ever go to Disneyland. Not that I've been there either. But that's what he looks like, the advertisement version, a kid on a dark ride.

Dylan's beside him, unafraid, because he's never had to be afraid, and because Gren is protecting him.

I'm afraid, though, of this boy's ability to break my baby's heart. Hasn't everyone had a best friend?

"Your parents need you at home," I tell Dylan. He shakes his head, but I've seen him in his footed pajamas, a child with everything he could ever want, spoiled and coddled.

Tenderness is dangerous.

And then I realize that I've said *parents*, and that the man I killed was his father. His face comes back to me, the man in the glass house, the same man who tucked this child into bed at night. The same man who told me to leave the party.

I killed Dylan's father because Dylan's father killed Gren, but Gren's not dead, and I—

Gren's made him a comfortable spot with leaves and a mattress of sticks. I don't know where he's gotten them, but I know he learned to make this mattress from me.

The two of them sleep curled up together, like halves of a whole.

"Yes. I got lost. Anything helps." I'm hearing myself whispering it now, endless repeat, my skin against the warm sand of memory, the knobs of my spine naked and water pouring over me. Someone returning me to the living. I'm remembering the desert, without anything to keep me from it. I don't want to remember it, but at night I feel the grit of sand in my fists.

Gren swims for fish, and through the dark for bats. He can press his body through narrow spaces, climb the walls, slip along rocks that have no handholds. He slides through places I couldn't come close to fitting into. He reaches his fingers into tunnels and finds the things inside them. Drops dead creatures at my feet and smiles. Gren's teaching Dylan to catch a fish with his fingers, but at night Dylan still sucks his thumb.

Gren makes a fire to cook a rabbit. I don't know where he found it. I don't ask. The other boy has been to camp. He speaks authoritatively about pyramids of twigs. Gren imitates him. The other boy knows nothing. Gren shows him how to crack rocks together to spark a flame.

I watch them play like the world doesn't exist. Imagined games, the games of every little boy everywhere.

I take a bite of meat. The taste of that is an old gamy taste, a good one, but I'm getting sicker.

I was a child born outside this mountain, a hospital, a house, a home, a mother, a father, grandmothers. I have vaccination records somewhere out there. I have a birth certificate. I was a citizen of this country, part of the world until I wasn't.

I hallucinate the house of my baby days back into existence, my bed, the kitchen cupboards, the peg rack for coats. The childhood phone number, a number I want to call. Maybe all of the dead will answer, come to the phone together, *It's Dana!*

I called it once from overseas, collect, and while it was ringing, I thought I was about to hear my mother speaking to me, telling me what to do.

I thought maybe she'd answer the phone, and I'd say the usual things, but then the disconnect came on, and the operator and I listened to it together before I hung up.

They'll find us. There's no way they won't, and I'm not strong enough to fight them.

It's five days, then ten. Then more. My arm is swollen, and hot to the touch. I wrap it in a sling, but I know what's coming. We ran without anything when we ran. No antibiotic, no alcohol, nothing to keep my life from turning into death.

"You're the one who gets away!" shouts the woman on the sidewalk inside my skull. I shake my head.

I look down at my hands, at my arms, at my body, and I'm just the woman who was Dana Mills, who was a soldier, who was killed, who died, who came back to bring Gren into the world.

Who am I now? I don't even know my own story.

Add it up. I hold my breath to keep from screaming out the

losses, tallying up the dead, all the people I've killed, all the family I can't find, all the rest of the lives no one got to live. Is this the guilt of being a soldier? Is this what you're left with after a war, when you follow orders, when you're not the one in charge? I see the dead all around me. The cave is full of them, and I'm full of them, and they're not just the ghosts I'm responsible for making. They're the ghosts of this place too, my ancestors and the people here before them.

There are two little boys running up and down the tracks, laughing, holding hands, leaving a trail of footprints in the muddy sides, Gren fast, Dylan slower, and then Gren carries his friend on his back. I hear them singing to each other, Gren singing our lullaby, the boy teaching him new ones. They're working on a project in the tunnel, bringing out the dirt.

I open my eyes to the light of my saint, examining my arm, holding the hand I'm about to lose. I'm grateful to see her this time, though usually I'm not. She's a reminder I'm still alive.

"Everyone, holy and not, good and not, ends up a series of relics in the end," she says, like it's nothing, like there are no big deals left on Earth. "People stick them in glass cases and look at them in churches, or they make a pile over them and call the spot a place touched by heaven. Shit," the saint says. "You didn't ask to be this, but I didn't either. Guess it's just the way things go."

"I guess so," I croak out.

"You could be a saint like me," she says.

"I don't want to be a saint like you," I tell her. "I don't want to be a saint at all."

"Somebody chose you," she says.

"I didn't want to be a martyr."

She smiles. "You're not. You're alive."

The saint smokes her cigarette, and inside her chest the candle is flickering.

"If anyone up there saw him, you'd be on the side of one of these already," she says, pointing. "People'd be praying to you to settle their accounts. Maybe you're the miracle one, not your boy."

"No," I say. "I was a normal person."

"Sometimes you get noticed," says the saint, "and then there's no accounting for it. What'd you do in the desert? Did you run into God out there?"

"I don't know," I say. "I ran into someone."

She walks out onto the water in the passage and it steams around her invisible feet, sizzling as she steps on it.

I think about riding a bus across the country, the way each hour on a bus feels like a hundred years, each mile, each marker, each state passed through like you're marching. Those buses are full of the dead. Everyone on them is on their way out. Once, I sat in the seat beside an old woman who didn't get off at the end of the line. She just died right there on the Greyhound, silently. We all tried to wake her up, but she was stiff and cold already. It doesn't take long for life to disappear.

"What saint are you, anyway?" I finally ask.

"Oh, I don't have a name anymore," she says. "I just died in a bad way and came back to Earth like this."

"But you had a name before?"

"So did you," she says. "But the name you'll get remembered by is his."

"What do you mean?"

"They'll call you Gren's mother."

✦

I'm surrounded by spinning dark. Gren and Dylan are bent over me.

"You were talking," Gren tells me.

"Sometimes I talk in my sleep too," says Dylan, and pats my forehead. "Sometimes I have nightmares."

Gren holds my arm like I'm the child, and I gasp with pain. It looks like something other than an arm, something more like a tree trunk cracking open in lightning. I feel it rotting, things boring through it, movement underneath.

I make a tourniquet of my shirt.

Everyone might be a monster underneath their skin, me included. Bring out the bones and see what's there. I look at my left hand, this hand that's been mine all these years, in charge of firing guns and of gutting animals, this hand that's been the one that held Gren's skull when he was sleeping.

I think about the girl in the hospital bed next to me, her legs gone, this girl I made into my saint, and I wonder if the ghosts of all lost limbs travel the world, pulling themselves along.

Gren's crying, but listening to me, and I tell him how hard he has to swing to make this work.

"Cut it clean," I tell him.

He's wavering, not sure if he trusts me to know what's good for me. The other boy is standing there too. There's nowhere for him to go, no way for me to protect anyone from this.

I shut my eyes and breathe, and all around us, in the dark, I feel the place, the things of this mere, skeletons reassembled. There's my mother, watching, and her mother, and ten generations of mothers before them. Here are all the years of my family on this mountain. Here are all the years I've been running from something I didn't do wrong, trying to get away from pain, trying to start over.

"Do it," I say to Gren. "Do it now. It's okay. Just do it quick."

He's a soldier too, just like his mother, and this is what a soldier does. You sacrifice the weak to keep the strong marching. You bury the dead by the side of the road if you have to, and you keep walking until you get to where you're going.

Then you fight.

He raises the sword higher, higher, and it whistles through the air, making a sound I've heard once before.

Listen. In some countries, you kill a monster when it's born—

My baby brings the blade down.

25

Tell the story. There is only one star in it, if you ask Willa. That star is the sun. If anything else glows, it's secondary.

Willa's never been the sun before. Years in the shadow of everyone else, child, husband, mother, Herot Hall itself, and this goddamned mountain.

Now, now, she is rising, flying through the space of her future. The years spent on eradicating uncertainties, pouring cocktails, cooking dinner—those years are over. She's free.

Her mother comes to visit her late, the night before Ben Woolf plans to go into the water.

"Willa," she says, in a tone.

"What?" Willa asks.

For a moment, the two of them stare at each other across the table.

"You know exactly what I mean," Diane says. "Don't pretend. Well, it's not the worst thing you've ever done. He could run for office. He looks like a politician. You were pretty enough for a doctor, I always said that, but that's spilt milk now. Let's make him a chief of police, and from there, something better. Herot Hall's yours now, except for Tina's share, which it wouldn't have been in a divorce, there's that."

As though Willa meant for Roger to be murdered.

Willa wonders if her mother has plans for everyone she's ever met, graphing their futures on some invisible chart. Her mother and women like her are the reason men can live at all, running corporations, announcing wars. Every man has a woman at home, and every woman plots the course of the universe, putting it into his breast pocket, like a note attached to a kindergartner, sending him out into his day.

Diane's already called reporters, planned the arc of events, and nothing about Ben Woolf's dive in pursuit of Dana Mills and the missing child will be invisible. There'll be cameras, lights, words. He'll be a hero, and Willa will be alongside him, the bereaved.

Willa wonders if anyone is actually grieving Dylan. Everyone else seems to think he's somehow lived through this, but he barely lived through being born. He's always been delicate. Willa feels the grief in public. In private, she remembers the feeling of the crown against her fingertip.

It's time to keep pushing.

Willa, she thinks, this *is what happens when you let yourself go. You don't die. You float, relieved of the chains around your ankles. You float, higher, and you leave the rest of the world behind. You are not a monster, but an angel. You're not a nightmare, but a dream.*

She runs a thin line of pink lip pencil just beneath her eyes. She brushes a powdery blue shadow into the hollows of her cheeks, a little, enough.

With her shorn hair, she looks like a figure on the wall of a tomb, her face without vanity. She's paint-by-number, but the cameras will erase what she said about the monster, and see her as Willa the Widowed, Willa the Wounded, Willa Whose Poor Son Is Missing.

Black boots, black jeans, black sweater. Black coat, long and lean, made of the fur of a sheep dead on a slope ten thousand miles away.

She is her own creation, a pearl in mourning, and she walks

out the door just before sunup for the first appearance of her new existence. She tightens her gloved hands around the steering wheel as she drives, moving in her mind from the Willa she once was, her stinging, freshly tattooed thigh, her wedding dress wadded up in the bottom of her purse, her newly minted husband picking her up and carrying her to bed, to the Willa after that, the second husband, the meals and potty training, Tahiti and waiting for the train, to the Willa she will be. She digs a pit for her marriages and kicks sand over the faces of her former men; she waits for their skeletons to reveal themselves.

She glances at herself in the rearview mirror, checking her makeup, and catches a glimpse of something else.

A girl in a white dress, running down the highway behind Willa's car, barefoot, and then suddenly she's in the road, right there.

Willa swerves, but the girl's against the dash, her claw-tipped fingers spread as starfish, and her mouth a sealing wax rose, her long blond hair, her white dress, the red trim on her lace underwear, and a wedding veil over her face—

Her mouth behind that lace, opening too wide, revealing sharp teeth, as blood spatters all over the glass.

And then it's over and gone and Willa's still driving in the darkish dawn, panting.

Nothing.

The dash isn't cracked, and out there is only snow. Willa squints because a white deer is bounding, just on the edge of the light, but no, it's the lake, and even as she approaches, she can see news vans.

She pulls herself together. She's good at that. It's like suturing a wound, stitching together all the Willas.

Her neighbors are there, and at the center of them is Ben Woolf, dressed in winter diving gear. His voice booms out.

"I'm doing this for Roger Herot and for his family, for his wife, Willa, who has more cause than anyone to call for justice.

If no one else can find Dana Mills, I will. She's my responsibility. I'm the one who let her escape."

Willa allows a single tear to slide down her cheek.

"If you haven't been to war, you don't understand. Dana Mills does. I do. She came into Herot with slaughter on her mind."

The sun is rising behind him.

"I was with Roger Herot when he died. I heard his last words. 'Take care of my family,' he said. 'Keep them safe. My son. My wife. Tell them I love them.'"

Willa feels her mother behind her, nodding with Ben, and this reminds Willa to nod with him too.

"Roger Herot is dead, his son is missing, and Dana Mills is on the loose. She wants to destroy everything Herot Hall stands for. I won't let her. I can't."

Ben Woolf bows his head. He struggles to get the words out. A handsome man with tears in his eyes, and everyone is crying with him. He looks to Willa.

"With your blessing," he says, and she feels the crowd exhale.

"You have it," she says, perfect pitch.

Ben Woolf eases himself into the mere and plunges below the surface, lower, lower, tethered with a thin line of air to his diving tanks.

As he dives into the hole in the ice, the place where the hot springs merge with the cold, Willa looks down into the water, and for an instant she sees him swimming into fire, a burning city, the world blazing and coming apart at the seams.

Then he's gone and it's only darkness, a hero dropping through a mountain lake toward a sunken villain, a soldier, a dead-body-to-be.

26

Tell the depth of the mere in inches, in feet, in fathoms. How deep he dives!

How long will it take us to drown him? Water wraps around his limbs and tangles in his fingers. He falters, struggles, continues to swim.

We're used to being infiltrated by things, tin cans, rabbits, birds, lost cats. Our water's nothing pure, though it pretends to be, and neither is the man. He's hot blood pumping through a cold heart.

He swims, a headlamp lighting his way down. He swims until he reaches a space between rocks, and when he finds it, he presses himself through it and swims deeper, deeper, until there is nothing left to swim in.

He's inside the mountain. He takes off his mask, and passes through a tunnel. The bats can smell him, and so can the worms under the soil. There are blind things and they stay still as he passes.

"Dana Mills! Tell me where you are!" he calls into the dark of the tunnel, and then, experimentally, "Gren?"

There is no response from any of us. We have nothing to say to him.

He keeps walking.

At last, there are rail tracks beneath his feet, and the walls of the tunnel are paved. He's come through a slender entrance, a service passage, and into the main tunnel. There are footprints here from the ones who came before him.

One of our birds flies past his face, a clutter of black wings, and he looks back in the direction it came from.

We've seen this kind of man before. We've felt atomic explosions, undersea tests, fireworks, and bridge buildings. Meteors have fallen and hit hard, delving out cracks in the surface of the Earth. This man is only a body, not a bomb.

Boulders shove him and gravel presses upon him. There is sand beneath his feet that shudders. We give him the feeling of a songbird in a mine, making him gasp, running a trickle of water over his feet.

He doesn't stop. He climbs from the track into a chamber, and only then does he pause, panting.

A station, abandoned. He looks around in surprise. This station isn't on his maps. It's a closed place, forgotten on purpose.

There are reasons for that. There were accidents on the rail line, conductors confused, passengers wandering into the tunnel and struck by the train. Tourists from the city loathing the smell of the water in the lake. Other tourists loving it too much. Swimmers disappearing, bodies floating up, lace dresses and eyes shut in pleasure. Deer leaping over crevices, mist from the darkness.

We are nothing new.

Evidence of a fire, and of inhabitants, empty cans of food. There are toys on the floor, plastic trucks and dolls made of sticks. The walls of the station are painted with children's work, a boy and a house, trees, a mother, another child. There are words written all over the marble surfaces, crayoned and charcoaled.

Light from the beam of the man's headlamp, and from the filthy skylight a fractured sun, dust motes.

There's a sound, and the man peers into the shadows, but

there's nothing there. Campfire ashes, and ankle-deep swamp around the rock floor, a dark underground river feeding the lake.

There's a pile of bloody cloth and a little mound of dirt in the center of the room.

The man kneels over it and plunges his hands in, scrabbling, moving aside wet clumps of mud. There is something beneath the mound, and it begins to be revealed, curled fingertips, rising out of no body. There is no grave here, but we feel the man's memories of violence, places he's been in the past, bodies he's buried, sand he's scraped over secrets.

He moves the dirt aside, choking as he does, his face contorting. An arm, from bicep to fingertips, given hasty burial. It's swollen, scabrous, and pus is dried on the stump. The fibers of the muscles are sad flesh now, red, white, and unraveled.

The man looks around the station, but he can see no one here but us. No sounds except the trickling of water seeping into the station from every corner.

We consider a flood. The mountain quivers and material falls from above him, fine dirt hourglassing down over his face. He places the arm inside his diving bag and thinks.

He looks at the bag again, the way the fingers stretch, open-handed against the fabric. He stares into the dark of the tunnel he hasn't been through. There's something there, a large form, but he doesn't go toward it. A dead train. He can see it ahead of him, a silent dark body, ten cars, maybe less, painted red.

He looks around, suspicious, sounds, storms rushing from somewhere, far away, a howl of a wolf or dog, something, something.

He takes a step in the other direction, to the opposite end of the platform, where there's only a whistling wind, then returns to the safe, still spot.

He wets his hand in the mere and obliterates the paintings on the walls, the faces of monsters and women, the smiling child, the blur of joy that stands beside him. He blackens his hand removing all of this, erasing it until there is nothing left but gray, but he pauses over a name written low on the tiles.

Dylan, in tilted letters.

He looks up toward the skylight, considering a climb out into day, straight up from this station and into the sun. In the mound of dirt, there are only maggots and blood and rags, someone wounded passing this way once, someone dying, someone dead.

Even if she's still alive, there's nothing that could make her return to the surface, and he decides that this is all he needs to know. His enemy can only be dying of infection, if she's still alive. There's a pool of dried blood on the floor, likely too much to survive, and the blood tracks to the water, and into it. Her corpse will surface eventually, and the taste of death will plunder the spring water of Herot Hall. It won't be the first time.

He looks at the mess, thinks better of leaving it, and sweeps the mound of dirt and disaster into our water.

Something cries out from the wet, and he jolts. No.

The sound is coming from behind the counter of the café. A whimper. The man kneels, looking at the floor, tracks in the dust leading away from the place where he found the arm.

He stands, silent, stalking, and then leaps at the counter, and pulls a boy from beneath it.

The boy kicks, bites, screams, and manages to get his teeth into the man's arm. The man winces, and tugs his arm back, bleeding.

"Let go! They left and I'm waiting for them! They're coming back for me!" the boy screams.

The man holds the struggling boy out from his own body, and assesses him. This is the consideration of a pillager. Kill the child and the story with him, or swear the boy to secrecy. Or—

"Listen to me. Dana Mills is dead," the man tells the boy.

The boy stares at him, eyes wild.

"Liar," he says.

"In the tunnel," the man tells him, and inclines his head

toward the dark. "I found her hiding there. She came after me. It was self-defense. Go look if you don't believe me."

The boy stares at him, his lip wobbling.

"Gren?" he asks.

"I killed Gren too," says the man. "I killed them to save you."

"I'm not saved," the boy screams. "*I'm not saved! Gren! Help! Help me!*"

But no one comes for him, and eventually the man begins to move dirt and rocks away from the tunnel entrance, the side that faces away from the train. He pushes them out from the station, and back toward the world they came from.

BEHOLD

27

Behold the one-armed woman! Why do I find it funny? Why am I laughing? I can't stop. There's something bleeding, something searing, something departing, and it's mine, all of it, but back in the old days your losses could get you set up in a tent being a monster. Watch the armless girl play piano with her toes. Watch the legless boy dance on his hands and I'm laughing but then I'm—

I'm on a marble floor looking down into a lake, and up from the waters of the mere are rising the faces of people I used to know. The world is bent branches, cracking wood. I smell pine needles broken underfoot. The mere twists and turns, and it's full of my family, clawing up into the roots of the trees and toppling them, and I'm—

I'm swimming through a lake made of blood and salt. My brain blazes fluorescent and my body is a forest fire. It's a dark red day, a dark red night, a dark red life.

The world is full of voices, and the sound of the water beneath the mountain is inside me, the sound of the last trains running before I was born, sounds I never heard.

The sound of the wind in the winter rushing through the house I grew up in, the voices of the birds taking flight, and my mother's voice at last, my mother saying, "Listen, Dana, listen—"

"Mama?" I ask, but she doesn't answer. "Are you there?"

No. She's diving into the depths where there are things glittering. Gold and stones. Somebody's grave gifts, somebody's hoarding, somebody's weapons and bribes for the land of the dead.

Gone things aren't gone forever.

They float up.

They rise. I'm not gone, I'm—

No, God, I'm facedown in a truck bed, getting ready to be dead. There's a sack over my face. I think about praying, but I've never been any good at asking for help.

I try to sing, but there aren't songs for this. All I have is a line I read in a library book. I liked it. I memorized it.

All shall be well and all shall be well and all manner of thing shall be well.

I'm on my knees in the sand. They give me words, and I repeat them.

"My name is Dana Mills," I say. "America, this is your doing."

My neck bends backward for the blade. I feel the wind of it swinging back, and I'm in a thousand cities at once, and in the blackness there's a bright star, and it gets bigger, and bigger, and—

Did I see this in a movie I don't remember watching? Is this a true story or a story my mind made to convince me I was safe? I don't know what real is, I don't know what alive is, but—

I'm on my knees on a mosaic made of stone.

I touch my throat and find a scratch. There's a sandstorm moving across the desert toward me, a rising cloud of blur, shining and shifting.

I run up a flight of stairs to get out of the way of the storm, and there's someone in the upper room of the house I've tried to hide in. When I come through the door, he doesn't move, though I feel his attention turn to me. I get ready in case I have to kill him.

Am I dead? I ask.

Maybe, he says.

Is this where everyone goes when they die?

He laughs. *No.*

Are you some kind of god?

He turns around and I see his face. I don't know if he's a man or a monster, or something made of fire. I don't know about me either. I could be all of that too, a woman, a monster, someone made of flames.

Is this home? I ask him.

He holds out his hands.

Are you something I've never seen before?

I don't know, he says. *Are you?*

Now it's later and I'm wearing a ring on my finger, and the ring is wrapped in thread from my uniform to make it fit. He's smiling at me, my hands in his hands, my body against his body, and my heart is pounding with joy. There's a room with a bed, curtained, lanterns, and he is waiting for me in it and I'm home—

No. I'm sitting in a tent and there's a sheet stretched, and pictures flicker and fade. Some movie, some desert, some dream. Some story. A burning world. Someone is crying in the distance, but out here, someone always is.

I look to my right, and Lynn Graven is beside me, drinking a Coke. I look to my left, and it's Raul Honrez, focused on the screen, chewing gum. In front of me, there's Renee, but then she flickers too, and then she's bright with bullet wounds, and then she's gone.

I hold on to the edge of my folding chair, and out in the dark there's shouting, and in here, in the dark, I'm alone with my heartbeat, trying to tell myself I'm safe, as the whole world shudders apart like confetti.

I whisper the things I remember.

Home is me and my guys. Home is eating my meal, home is marching, home is the sound of breathing around me, the others asleep on cots. I try to remember my family. I'm standing in a desert alone, looking out over sand. Everyone's dead but me. Somehow I'm still here.

Am I the last one, trying to bury them, trying to keep their possessions together? Maybe one soldier stands away from the battle to send word if it goes wrong. Maybe it goes so wrong so quickly that she ends up walking down a cliff after the bones are stripped and the fires are out, writing down the names, trying to make a song about great things done in the name of nothing.

There isn't enough earth for everyone, she writes. *Parts of the world are sweet and parts are sour. Parts are drenched and parts are dust—*

I have no hand to write. I have no pen. I'm bleeding, listening to falcons shrieking, feeling the sun heating my skin and my blood boiling, and I'm hearing song from everything, even as my body is aching and wounded, even as I should be so long gone I'm not even my own memory. Under the water, the sun is sinking.

My mother is singing. No, I'm the one singing, a lullaby to a newborn, and I watch him age, I watch him grow, I watch him want what he can't have.

Gren's on a roof outside a window, trying to get closer to the boy he let get away. The world has teeth and claws, and my baby thinks he can walk in it. Hotel balconies and back rooms, speeches given in public, children marching, fists up, nothing to shield their hearts from bullets.

They shoot, walk away, let him bleed. No flowers on the

curb, no pictures mourning him, no memorial on the fence. My son becomes a place where the sidewalk is stained.

A thousand holes in his flesh, punctured, deflated, gone.

And I'm back here in the dark, a marble floor, a skylight, my arm a stump on fire, my body screaming out in pain, and the place isn't safe anymore, it's not safe, Gren's not safe, and—

"Listen," someone whispers into my ear. I move, looking around, trying to find a way out of here.

"Listen to me. Listen. In some countries, you kill a monster when it's born. Other places, you kill it only when it kills someone else. Other places, you let it go, out into the forest or the sea, and it lives there forever, calling for others of its kind. Listen to me, it cries. Maybe it's just alone."

"What monster?" I ask. "Who's a monster?"

She's with me, my truck-stop saint, chest open, candle inside it lit for Jesus, Mary, Joseph, and anyone else.

She's smoking two cigarettes, flicking sparks, her stringy hair, her sweaty T-shirt, her skin so smooth it glows, like she's a thing on fire herself, like she can jump water and hit the other side.

The walls are black and the floors are slick, and moss grows on the edges of the river.

We walk out a long tunnel, from the mountain and into the mere, and it's drained of water. All along the inside of it, there are trees. Spreading branches, crowns of fern fronds, big enough to shade anything, deep green and leaves, flowers on them too, strange spiky things. The trunks of the trees are like scales.

The sky's orange and pink. The saint takes me walking through the woods, picking her way over thornbushes. I see a skeleton assembled, a sea monster like the one on the rock, but much larger.

The skeleton develops buds, fat swellings along the rib cage, and out of those come flowers, blooming suddenly, a riot of red.

I want my life back, unbroken. I want to start over, but that isn't a thing people can do. I breathe in, feel the chill of the wind and hear birds singing, all my selves together at once, soldier, daughter, wife, victim, mother, monster.

I want not to know about war and guns and stolen land, not to know about who dies and who lives, not to know who gets enough and who gets nothing.

I want to know that the one I love is going to live on after me, to know he'll be happy—

Someone calls my name, *Dana Mills!* a ringing call to surrender myself, and I sit up, start to stand up, but Gren won't let me. He snatches me off the ground and he's running, carrying me.

He's charging through the dark and into a train that can't exist, a train hidden inside the mountain, a train I've never seen before because it was buried, because he's delved into the dirt with his friend and brought it out again.

Velvet seats and wooden benches, spiderwebs and berths with old pillows, dishes, luggage racks and my son, leaning over me—

Is this what love is? That you can see each other, even in the dark?

"Mama," he whispers. "Listen! We're hiding. Shhh."

I reach out my hand to touch him, but I don't have a hand anymore. There it is, falling away from me, an arm I can feel, fingers I can grasp with, drifting down through silt and red darkness. Gone, and something else is gone too.

"Where's Dylan?"

He shakes his head, his face frozen with loss.

My eyes are open and I'm looking at everything at once, brightness and dark, pain and joy, and in the near distance, someone is roaring a victory, but I'm still here, hidden.

I'm not the one the monster found. I'm not the one who's captured. I'm not the one who's dead.

28

Behold. Be held. Be whole. Thole. There are prescriptions willy-nilly, purse dust and childproof bottles. Willa opens them up, holds the pills in her palms, blue, white, red, and yellow. A rainbow of reactions. Five days. Six days. Seven days since Ben Woolf dove into the lake.

She didn't really know him; now he's dead. And what was he, really? A one-night stand? She won him as a door prize, but he wasn't her man. Not her husband. Not her partner. Not her crime.

She watches the golden dragon on her watch, ticking away the seconds remaining in her life. She's been a perfect daughter and a perfect wife, and now she's just a clock.

She'll have to move away from here. Back to the city? But the city, alone, and the stairs and the stairwells and the men and the knives and the—

Willa maintains a vigil. Certain tasks are relegated to women. Mourning, staring into the water, waiting for no one to surface.

It's a white man who's missing. Usually, that would be enough to keep it in the news, but eight days in, the police release their grief in an official report. The art of blame-casting is a lesser sorcery. History is written in sand, and a broom changes everything. Every woman knows the art of covering up a mess: a carpet, a dustpan, bleach on the boards. What do you do with the cleaning supplies of the world? Use them to wash the blood away, and grind the bones into bread. Swallow the confessions whispered in bed.

If events don't make sense, a story grows to cover up the confusion. Motives and mistakes.

Dana Mills, the report says, was a coincidence, a homeless veteran begging at a party, nothing to do with the rest of the disaster, and exonerated anyway, crimeless, a victim of a kidnapping a long time ago, and that is all.

Dylan Herot was grabbed by a bear, female, hungry, and nursing an out-of-season cub. There is a photo on the news, the dead bear's belly studded with pink nipples.

Roger Herot's autopsy says he fell on a chef's knife. He shouldn't have been running up a mountain in pursuit of a bear, holding not only something sharp, but a rifle he'd never before fired, a weapon belonging to his father. *Death by Misadventure*, says the report.

Ben Woolf, at last, is blamed for being too good, too loyal to the people he'd signed up to protect.

This, it follows, means everything is the fault of Willa Herot, temptress, and everyone understands that. It's a thing that happens, even to good men, even to the best of men.

Willa sits in the driver's seat, edge of the lake, drinking a thermos of coffee, which isn't coffee. She paints her fingernails red every day, and by nightfall all the scarlet is chipped off.

It's international news, then national, then local. Tragedies happen every minute of every hour. The world is full of worse than anyone has yet imagined, and there's only so much room.

Willa Herot told herself a story about a hero, and now she has to clean up her own life.

She imagines Ben Woolf floating underground in a lake of blood, Dana Mills standing over him, Gren sharpening a knife. She imagines him chopped, blistered in a fire pit, eaten. She imagines his body, that flammable hair, the scars he got doing things other than being a hero. Flesh to meat to bone to ash.

The mothers put on parkas, ski pants, and cashmere turtle-necks, and march up the mountain daily to sit with Willa, all the while discussing what it might feel like to die by drowning. They agree it would not be as bad as dying by shark. Something awful happened, but something awful always happens. The mothers sit in Willa's car, and list for her all the awful things that have happened since the beginning of time.

Willa's clothes look like armor gone limp in the wash. She's failed in every direction at once. She can feel a muscle twitching in her jaw, and one beneath her left eye. Her starvation is showing.

The mothers start planning a funeral for Dylan.

"Take this," they say to Willa, and open the bottles in their purses. There's every kind of sleep inside them. These prescriptions can make a person sleep for a hundred years if necessary, until everything is different.

They put Willa to bed in her own bed, and she sleeps, dreaming a history she doesn't remember. She walks the deck of a ship, silk and cotton petticoats, corsets made of whalebone, and under those boards, decks down, there are voices, screams—

Willa's mother pulls the sheets off, and Willa snatches at the blankets.

"That tattoo," Diane says, looking with wrinkled nose at the white scar on Willa's thigh. Willa feels spatchcocked, like a chicken on a slab, pink and raw, heart exposed. Diane looks at her with the gaze of a coat-hanger abortionist.

"Are you pregnant again?" Diane says.

"No!" Willa says, but then wonders. Her body feels buoyant as a seal's.

"Get dressed," Diane says. "He's back, and he's got Dylan."

"What?" Willa says.

"Don't you dare make that face," says Diane. "This is your moment. Take it. Get dressed and take it. You only get so many moments in a life, and you've had more than your fair share."

✦

On the ninth day, every news van in the world is already on the mountain, and the mothers are holding Willa's undead son in their arms when Willa, reeling, dressed in winter white, arrives.

Dylan looks like an innocent child rather than like someone who'd purposefully ruin the life of his mother by living through the impossible. He's wrapped in blankets. There are bruises on his throat, yellow and blue mottlings, beginning to fade. There is a mark on his cheek, a healing wound, a scar in the shape of a star. Willa looks at it. A star? No. It must be a claw mark.

"They dug their way out," Diane whispers. "It took days. There's an old tunnel from when the train used to come here. I thought it was gone, but they were inside it."

Willa reaches out her arms. Her son looks at her like he doesn't know her.

"You're not my mommy anymore," says her son. "I want to go home! To Gren! To Gren's mommy! He killed her! *He killed her!*"

He's pointing, and Willa turns.

Ben Woolf, frost on his hair like he's been crowned by some god, flash, flash. He nods at Willa, and she feels a rush of heat, melting the mountainside, melting the universe.

He's standing in what she now sees is a hole in the mountain. There's a black crack in the snow, and stones pushed out onto the slope. A photographer kneels to get the shot for the front pages tomorrow. News crews move their microphones closer.

"Dana Mills is dead!" Ben shouts, a proclamation, and Willa jolts. "I tracked her to the old train station beneath this mountain. I found little Dilly inside it, terrified. Dana Mills was a highly qualified soldier, but trust me when I say that something in her had snapped. She had a sword. In the end, I got lucky. We learned that in the war, Dana Mills and me both. Living is luck."

He bows his head. "I managed to turn that luck back on her at the last moment."

He shows his arm, the small mark of teeth on it, inflamed, and then looks around to make certain the cameras are pointing at him.

"Her body slipped into the water and sank before I could reach it. This is all I could recover," he says.

He lifts a black bag, full of something heavy. Willa steps forward, expecting a head, hoping not.

"Gren?" Willa whispers, and Ben raises a hand, silencing her. He opens the bag.

Inside it is a woman's arm, but there is no woman attached to it. He lifts it out, as though anyone wants to look at the fingers, as though anyone wants to look at the clean cut at the shoulder, her arm a piece of poisonous meat, and her blood no longer her possession.

Everyone wants to look.

Everyone wants to photograph it.

Everyone wants to cringe in horror and make proclamations. Willa averts her eyes, and fixes them on her mother, who takes Dylan and bundles him away, the boy protesting, but he is nothing compared to his grandmother, whatever feral demon he is.

✦

When all of it is finally done, when the story is written and the videos are taken, Willa takes Ben Woolf home.

She unlocks the front door of her house, yes, she does it in front of all of Herot Hall, and she holds Ben's hand.

She walks into the house with him, he still carrying a bag in which there is a piece of flesh—how much, she wonders for a moment, a pound? No, more.

Willa puts the bag into the freezer—it smells like death. The maid hasn't been in this week for obvious reasons, and Willa's not sure where the foil is. She settles on recycling sacks, blue and scented with lavender.

She pours two glasses of red wine.

"She's dead?" she asks him at last. "Are you sure?"

"She's dead," he confirms. He says it with grief in his voice, and with ownership, and she appreciates that.

"And Gren?" she asks. "Tell me how."

"Dead too," Ben Woolf says, and exhales slowly, showing Willa that it's been hard, his life, his dive, his journey down. Willa wants to know everything, but he has no more story to give her.

"I killed both of them. That's all you need to know. You're safe," he says to Willa, and only then does he hesitate, looking at her. "We're safe."

And the floor beneath her melts, the stairs melt, the entirety of the glass house melts, because Willa will not have to wander any desperate desert alone. She will not have to take herself back to the city and stand in the center of the sidewalk, signing herself up once again for hunger, guitars, tattooed signatures, matchmakers, aging eggs, hair salons, Kegels, Pilates, falling off a stepladder and getting eaten by rats.

✦

The investigation confirms Dana Mills's DNA and the lawyers confirm Willa's inheritance. Herot Hall, marital property, a controlling interest, and she can't be ousted. Tina Herot holds the rest. For the first time, Willa is the queen *and* the king. She's the woman in charge of the gates, the windows, the roads, and no one can say differently.

Do the neighbors talk? They do.

She stands opposite Ben, and it's a public wedding in a church. Dylan is there, as the ring bearer, though the ring he carries is the second one, because the first one he's swallowed, literally.

Who can get angry at such a little boy, a boy who has been through so much?

Willa breathes through her nose, hard, and then tells Ben what has happened, and they get a replacement. It's Dylan who'll have to shit a wedding ring. This is how all this trouble started, a child swallowing the head of a king, and now?

Now that Roger's gone, Willa can see exactly where Dylan got all his tendencies. He'll grow up to be someone's cheating husband.

"Do you take this man?"

She takes him.

Her new husband, who comes from no one, born to some mother entirely unknown, his adoptive parents bringing him out into the shine of the world. Ben's swimming medals are hung under glass in the room where the piano is, and Willa leaves the scratches in the piano keys as reminders of the horror that brought them together.

There are always horrors in the world. There are always upsides.

The wedding photos of Willa and Roger remain in the house, in the back hallway, for Dylan's sake, and for the sake of reminding Ben Woolf that he hasn't always had Willa's heart. This is something men need reminding about. She makes sure he knows it, even if she doesn't say it directly. Their wedding vows have had the sickness/health portion excised. Also the *till death do us* bit.

Then it's summer. Then fall, and twins are born, Willa in the hospital, Ben beside her, counting her down, counting her up, wiping sweat from her brow like they're two soldiers bunkered together waiting for an enemy, but this time, when she gives birth, she feels she's repopulating the world with heroes.

Ben's beside her, a newborn son in each arm, handsome, proud, happy at last, and don't they deserve it? Willa's wearing makeup that looks like it isn't. She smiles for the camera. She posts the photos, tags them. Blessed.

Goodbye to that old life, Willa thinks, clenches every muscle, one by one, stretches every nerve, one by one, and looks down at her breasts, which are pale as marble, veined with silver. The babies at her breasts are perfect too, wrapped in their little blankets. She feels she could found Rome, but wait. That was a wolf.

She stands up, walks down the hospital hall, and makes a

sound that bewilders even her own ears. It's a sound of some kind of triumph, a warbling rattle of vindication over gold records, and plastic surgery, and mothers.

She looks into her husband's eyes, and sees something in them she doesn't recognize. He's looking down at the babies, and touching their little faces, and she notices, on each of their spines, a thin strip of hair.

"What's that?" she asks. "Did the doctor say?"

"It's nothing," he says. "It'll fall out. It's only because they were born a little early."

There was a time this would have horrified her. Now Ben kisses Willa, and she kisses him back.

She has a nightmare, in which all her dead are around a dinner table, the baby she didn't have with Richie, the baby she didn't have with Roger, along with Dylan and Gren, all of them seated together.

Willa stands there, hostess to all these sons, but her goblet is full of blood. There's Ben, standing opposite her, drawing a sword as she offers him the loving cup.

She gets out of bed and finds Ben between the two cribs, sitting up, a hand on each son, the babies perfectly still, their eyes open.

Upstairs is Dylan, who will not speak to her. He sleeps beneath the window, curled like an animal under the sill, though he's been reprimanded. Willa's given up. If he wants to sleep on the floor, let him. If he insists on looking out at that mountain, let him. Maybe rabies is the explanation, some kind of emotional rabies no one knows about. If he insists on letting himself go, let him. Everyone has a child they wish they hadn't had. Willa knows that from her own mother.

She moves forward with her life, a wife, living at last in the sun.

the dragon

They saw there a wrathful wonder.
The dragon become ground-ghost, close enough to bruise
a devil, dead. This flame-spitter had been
scathed and sooted by her own song.
She was fifty feet long, and she'd
ruled in riving-rapture over the dreaming hours,
diving through dawns to nest with her treasure.
Now death had won her heart.
The worm would no longer writhe with coins, but with dirt.

AH

29

Ah, yes, we were there! We spend the next years telling the story to newspapers, to television, to neighbors, at the grocery store, to anyone who asks, and some who don't.

All around the world, conspiracies are discussed in back rooms, and officers fume at their failure to find Dana Mills, when this lowly police officer somehow managed it, out of nowhere, in the dark. The president himself declares Dana Mills dead, and our mere her grave.

There is a funeral. We attend.

Not at Arlington, with those white aisles of stones, but at the cemetery two towns away from Herot. There is a small head-stone. There are no speeches. There's a certificate of gone for good. There's a burial of what's left of her.

Where's the rest of her? we wonder.

We stand next to Ben Woolf. We won't forget him coming out of the water. He was holding hands with a murdered woman. We know what kind of man does that. Shortly thereafter, he held hands with Willa Herot.

There is a wedding. We attend.

White crepe. How pregnant? Showing. You don't wear a long dress when that happens. Not when your own much-grieved husband is only a few months dead. No, no, cocktail-length, with a nice lace bolero. Hide the lines with shadows. Who's the father? She's the mother.

Ben Woolf may be our officer, but we're watching him. There he is, putting a ring on her finger, and there she is putting one on his.

We wonder.

Tina Herot dies for the next few years, piece by piece. A lump the size of a plum, an orange, a grapefruit. The slow deaths are reserved for women.

We ask if she wants our assistance. No one here has ever swallowed a bottle of barbiturates chased with Château Lafite. No one has ever closed her garage door with her engine running and sat in the driver's seat, considering. No one's ever stood in the train station waiting for the weekend train her husband was on, wondering if time would stop if she leapt.

Please. Everyone knows none of us would attempt suicide after sixty, no matter the circumstances. At sixty-five, husbands begin to die like flies. Flies, we all know, do not die quickly enough. They hover around the room, crashing into things for years before they drop, little shriveled bodies with missing bits of wing.

They do die, though. We remain.

Tina doesn't. Look at her: hospital room, tubing. Look at her: a building falling. She shuts her eyes one day after a visit from Diane. Then she's dead all the way. She's excavated, demolished, and carted away.

Tina Herot was ours. Diane Nowell is ours as well. Who is to say what happened to Tina Herot, Diane holding the cup to her lips, Diane alone with her own daughter's future in her hands? Diane, looking down at her helpfulness. Oopsy. Daisy.

Tina was never our favorite. Sometimes one of our husbands converts a secretary into wife, and she comes knocking, carrying a basket of muffins like she's Red Riding Hood, when really she's a wild animal. What are we supposed to do? Throw a cup of

blood from the lamb we've been roasting into her face and warn
her away from Herot Hall? No. We invite her to lunch.

Did we expect Tina Herot to be promoted to be our com-
mander? We did not. Did we appreciate it? We did not.

Willa inherits Herot Hall. We watch from our balconies.
Ben and Willa Woolf, in their living room, looking out over the
mountain.

We've never had a daughter bring in a wolf and call him her
husband. We have no procedure in place. He plants himself on
the living room sectional, and Willa refers to him as her hero. We
hold tissues to our lips.

They make a plan for a new station inside the mountain where
Ben Woolf killed Dana Mills, a new railway on the old bones,
classic and charming, commuting in the style of our forefathers.

We shake our heads in disapproval.

We invest our savings, obviously.

No one here is going to live forever. But some of us are going
to enjoy this version, traveling in a pack to fund-raisers, our photos
in the society pages, Diane in the center with her daughter on the
rise. We rise with her.

We've been waiting years for a train to stretch all the way to
Herot Hall, and until now we never knew that there was an old
station still hidden inside the mountain, and a train waiting inside
that station, capable of being upgraded.

The train's been inside a tomb since the 1920s, like Snow
White sleeping in her glass coffin, or perhaps like something
bigger, something worse than a princess. We're in charge of the
grandchildren. We sit on couches watching movies. Dragons,
castles, and women made of trouble. Dead does, girls with step-
mothers, and witches with long white hair.

We keep ours short.

There is a groundbreaking ceremony. We attend.

We stand on the side of the mountain wearing hard hats, and

watch a bulldozer bite into the rocks. Men at work. We've spent our lives watching men at work. We retire for a cocktail, but from our balconies we keep track of every cup of dirt, every bucket of water, every tree and every rock, every piece of bone.

We know some things about the mountain, about Herot Hall, about the way the first Dylan Herot built over the people who wouldn't go. Some of it was eminent domain. Some of it wasn't. Tina Herot's secrets were our secrets. We've picked the locks on the drawers of the desks of the dead. We know things our husbands never knew we knew.

We are standing on the mountainside when the bulldozer's claw rips up a section of earth that's been hiding graves, the bodies of a hundred people, thrown into a hole, coffins broken, gravestones crumbling, covered over and planted upon, familiar vegetation in this section of the hillside, the kind of plantings Dylan Herot Sr. commissioned, deciduous trees, hedges. Recent graves and old ones alike. Some of the stones list decades we remember.

We lead the charge to make certain the mountain isn't categorized a graveyard. Recent stones go directly back to gravel.

Enough time has passed that a hidden graveyard full of bodies on ground destined to be developed is something we've figured out how to spin.

We make a museum out of the problem. Plaques, glass cases and respect. We protect our investment.

We watch the construction, the permits, put money in the hands of the senators, make sure everyone knows who made this train happen. We attend land use and zoning meetings, dig up old diagrams, consult geologists, take meetings with conservators.

It's not Ben Woolf, nor is it Willa Woolf. It's us.

We're the ones who make the world, the warriors who stand watch, the women on whose wrong side you would not want to walk.

What do you get the women who have everything? You get them more.

30

Ah! The mountain is opened and everything that was hidden is revealed. We watch from the water, from the walls of the cave, from the roots and the burrows.

Trucks come and cart our dirt away. Saws chew at our trees. We're breached, and the water from the mere wells up to be made into coffee. It percolates, scenting the air of the old station, which is now to be the new station.

The station is built of the mountain's materials. The china beneath the counters is made of bones from a secret grave, and the glasses are made of sand from the bottom of the lake, and the silver was wrested from out of the earth by sweating miners. Or so their version of the story goes.

Ties are hammered into the earth and curving tracks swoop through the mountain and out again, so sun comes in from both sides, not just from the skylight. There are stained-glass windows beneath layers of soil, and they're scraped. A deer picks her way up the slope and over the colored glass, glowing red as she wanders. A robin plucks a worm, and flies, a writhing body in her beak.

A shower of fine dust falls onto Herot Hall, and rain falls after it, washing the mud of the mountain into every garden, every fence post, every place we haven't been.

Car wheels skid on slip, workers inhale mineral deposits, and a few struggle as the tunnel fills with water. We kill none of them.

The mountain is hollowed by progress: the old tunnel mouth is reopened and stabilized with cement, the ceiling tiles replaced so they look like the tail of a sea creature. Dust is moved and marble is polished, and bloodstains are bleached.

We were a mountain, but we were also a tunnel. We were a cave, but we were also a stopping point on a journey to elsewhere.

And the woman from the mountain? Her son? They are hidden deeper than this. There are still secrets in this old place, and the caverns run all the way down, beneath the lake and beneath the station, into the bedrock of the Earth and out again, through a passage, a hidden door from here to there, a tunnel slender and meant for one person at a time.

The antique train is rolled out onto the tracks, polished to a shine, the mud removed from the engine, the blood removed from the floor, the upholstery replaced. We let the rust flutter from it. We let the wooden seats creak. The places where white tablecloths were laid cough red particles.

The train is retrofitted. It's designed to speed to and from the city, while still looking like something from the past.

The station is plastered with posters showing old things becoming new ones: the Trans-Siberian, snow and black tracks ahead, the transcontinental lines obliterated by wars, the Hejaz Railway from Damascus to Medina, the steam locomotives turned to Shinkansen in Japan.

The events involving the boy from below and the boy from inside the mountain are forgotten but for a bench placed near the drinking fountains to honor a son of the suburbs.

The train will contain a bar full of cocktails that cost more than they should, and tables that will fold down from the walls over the laps of important men who've always traveled the back-and-forth route.

It'll be an all-day and all-night swarm of bees, whipping its way from the suburbs to the city, from the mountain to the masses.

We open ourselves up to the air and look out at the sun. We ready ourselves to be ticketed. We are the passage for passengers. We've seen canoes and rafts, we've seen waders and walkers, all coming up from the mere and into the shadows. We are the bones of the Earth, and we are still here, busy.

Years ago now, the boy from the mountain ran into the cave holding a boy who wasn't breathing. He ran down, into the wet and dark, into here, the mere, where we waited. There is no place on this mountain we do not watch over.

We watched our boy try to save his friend, on his back on the marble floor, breathless, blue, lips open, eyes shut. Fossil trees dripped ice on the dead boy's eyelids. The boy from the mountain brought his friend to be saved. We intervened, and the boy from below choked and spat out a king's head.

No one sees us unless we decide to be seen. We are the things that were, the things that are, the things that will be, and we have nothing to do with electricity, nothing to do with commuters. We love what we love and we kill what we kill.

The boy from the mountain is here still, safe in the dark, hidden, and we know what he imagines.

We know who haunts his dreams.

31

Ah! I gasp every time I open my eyes. Disbelief, belief. Days pass. Months pass. No one comes for us.

If people think you're dead, can you go out into the world like a ghost?

Gren and I have gone deeper into the mountain and the whole thing shakes with excavations, but they're not looking for us. Tunnels and caves, warm places in the dark, heated by the mountain's waters. There are passages below everything, older than the train, older than tourists. People went beneath this mountain before I was any kind of imagined person, before my mother was born, and her mother, and her mother. There were no sons in my family, not until Gren.

"I'm a monster," Gren tells me.

"No," I tell him. "You're a soldier's son."

He doesn't want to be a soldier's son. He wants to be someone else. I spend months healing, my missing arm haunting me with motion. When I can move again without screaming, I strip off my clothing, fold it neatly, and ease myself into the part of the mere that's under here. The mountain's all around me, a singing swell. In the pond, there's water from the center of the Earth coming up through the iciness, a hot current, and I immerse myself in it, my aching body, my arms and legs scarred, my face scarred. Who's ever managed to skin themselves without scars?

"They say you're dead," Gren tells me one day. "I climbed up. I listened."

He tells me I was killed by someone named Ben Woolf. I'm buried. There's a grave. If I have any family left, they think I'm gone. I'm the age my mother was when she died, and so I consider myself dead.

Some nights I wake up hearing the sounds of my boys around me, talking shit and playing cards. Other nights, my dreams are the same as they've ever been: falling, dying, flying, full of things that happened long before I hit the planet. It's war and ships and kitchens, running through forests trying to stay ahead of dogs, running down mountains with a torch in my hand, running at the house.

But now I know more than I knew. I drink the water down here, and maybe it heals me, maybe it does something else. I feel like my muscles have been wired for electricity, glass nodes, strong circuits.

I live on fish and rabbits, and the things Gren brings me, walnuts, windfall apples, pine needles, bark. Tins of vegetables, a peach with soft down, a loaf of bread. Sometimes I don't ask.

He's been out and wandering while I was sick, away from me and into garbage or grocery stores.

He sits on the other side of a coal fire, turning a fish, and offers me a can of apricots in syrup, which he's opened already, with a quick stab of the knife.

He's not grown, but he's no longer someone who sits down when I tell him to sit down. He's been in the world and lost it too.

He makes his way through the mountain, fearless, swims in the mere, fearless, while I sit deep underground. Who's the monster now?

◆

It's a cold morning when I finally come outside again, Gren insisting there's nothing to be afraid of. My hair's gone white and my face is older than it was. He's brought me a pair of plastic sunglasses. I tie up my jacket sleeve. I'm dead. A dead woman can't be seen. A dead woman who looks like I do? Invisible.

I look down into the water of the mere, and it reflects me back to myself, my mother and my grandmother, faces I know. I feel less lonely looking at them.

There's snow covering the ground. I take a breath of icy air, and feel my lungs freeze a little, smoke and crushed stone.

Years underground, years of training in the dark. This isn't what makes a monster. This is what makes a soldier. Battle drills, sword swinging, one-armed and merciless. I can fight better now than I could before. My reflexes are sharp. I can see in the dark.

Look at how transformation happens. I think of my mother, and I know she went the other way, thinner and thinner, weaker and weaker.

Gren brings me clothes and I walk to town, not Herot, but ten miles upriver, away from anyone who might have seen me here. I have my sword down my waistband, and so I walk like I have a fake leg. Young-old woman, hobbling.

No one even looks at me.

You don't really own anything. Nothing is yours forever, not your body, not your youth, not even your mind.

There are people on the ground once I get into the town proper, sidewalk sitters, and I'm not one of them. Maybe everyone who's ever disappeared has felt this way. Maybe the lights make them squint and the sounds of horns make them hurt. Some of them are veterans of the same war I was in. They have that look of permanent surprise.

I walk past them. No one grabs my ankle. No one makes me listen. A couple of people nod at me, and I nod back, like I haven't been gone what feels like a thousand years.

The first time I go looking for my own history, I panic all the way in, but no one notices. I stand in the center of the town library, which is small and understocked, but it's like a miracle.

There are stacks of books teaching a person how to live in the world with nothing, cabins built of fallen trees, traps made of thread, but I've done without them. Gren knows how to read. I taught him. Gren knows how to write. I taught him. Gren knows everything I know, and more.

"Miss?" says the librarian, and I flinch.

"Yes?" I ask, looking anywhere but at him, ready to have it all taken away. The smell of mint tea. Carpet lint, old books, flowers on the call desk, wool jackets, shampoo, bricks on the walls, a stuffed animal in the children's section, a dragon six feet long, balanced on top of the shelves. A castle made of sugar cubes. A pumpkin carved with a smiling face. It must be Halloween. There's a cat and I look at him, orange fur, fat belly, and I don't have to think anything else about cats, nothing about hunger.

I bend my knees. I put out my hand. I touch the cat's face, and it butts my fingers, trusting me.

"There are computers here," he says. "And newspapers. Or if you're looking for something in particular, you can ask me."

He doesn't pull at the strap of his bag, or look at a camera in a corner.

"Thank you," I manage to say. "I don't need help."

"If you do," he says, "I'm here to help you."

I don't lose myself. I don't sob. I don't scream.

I walk to the computer, sit in a chair, and learn that everything has changed since I went underground.

The war is officially over, no declaration of *mission accomplished* this time. I pore over the articles, learning what passes for history. Somebody's going to teach this in schools, and it will be full of lies. Slowly, slowly, de-escalation, slowly, slowly, the war ended, like a quiet divorce. Soldiers shipped home, strangers to their country. Their wives and husbands had installed cardboard replicas of them so that their children would feel raised by someone. One day the war itself was declared dead. No ticker-tape, no funeral flowers.

But like me, the war kept living after it was supposed to have been buried. There are monsters still out there, monsters I can name. The famous ones kept going, video, photos, headlines, and here they still are, running countries, pressing buttons, standing in offices insisting that all the money in the world belongs to them, pushing secrets through votes, starving the bottom so the top can feast.

Everything kept exploding, now unofficially, cities bombed to dust, and ancient pathways crumbling, so that there was no way to heaven from the desert anymore, and no way to any other place either. War's contagious. It spreads like a plague, reducing countries to catastrophes. I could've told them that.

Archaeologists and historians dusted the war away from the ancient world. Mostly, the discussion in print revolves around grief for extinctions, cities found and lost again, libraries burned, museums torched, animals poached.

I look at all the articles, all the possibilities, all the places on the map where I might have been when I disappeared.

Finally, I find something I recognize. I hover over the link for a moment before I can bear to click it, and then I do.

A buried city full of gold, jars, cloth, and books. This city was lost—they say—for two thousand years, and now it's found. Bones and books and treasure, and all around it, trip wires and bombs.

I'm sitting in the library, staring at the computer screen, and I know every street, every building, every fountain. Every staircase. Every square.

Every place I ran my fingers over a sculpture, every market stall, every dead corner full of every dead ghost, every scrap of silk, every scroll.

Every bedroom.

I sit in silence for a while, and then I close the window and let the computer sleep.

I look at the dark screen until it's dark outside too, and then I walk back to my cave beneath a mountain and an old mere, under stars that punch holes in the sky, blazing rays of frozen light.

◆

By the time Gren's thirteen, he's a foot and a half taller than I am. By fifteen, he looks like a man, but he's not. He's still a child, and only I know it, because only I've known him since the beginning.

Gren looks at me across the fire and asks me a question.

"Do you think he remembers us?"

I feel the world stop around me. It's the sound of the piano all over again, the sounds of the suburbs, people in them waiting to kill us, people waiting to turn us in to the police. Dylan would only remember us as nightmares. The woman who killed his father and the boy who left him in the station and ran away from him.

"No," I say. I'm lying. If he doesn't remember us, there's been a miracle. We've had some miracles, but not that one.

"I remember him," Gren says, very quietly, almost so quietly I don't hear him.

"Remember?" I ask. "You remember, or you went hunting?"

"I wasn't hunting," Gren says, but he won't make eye contact with me. I picture him running at night down the side of the highway, sprinting along, or climbing a mountain in order to look down on that boy he's never been able to forget.

In two years, if Gren were me, he'd be taking a bus across the country and signing up to be a Marine. I did it because my mother died. Will I be dead in two years? If he were me, he'd be getting sent over the ocean and put into whatever war was going. And there are wars going. There always are.

He's searching, and I know why.

Here's the truth of the world, here it is. You're never everything anyone else wants. In the end, it's going to be you, all alone, on a mountain, or you, all alone, in a hospital room. Love isn't enough, and you do it anyway. Love isn't enough, and it's still this thing that everyone wants. I see what he wants. I know him better than I know myself. I know his whole history, and I don't know my own.

"I'm going to find Dylan," Gren tells me at last, and his voice is both rebellious and apologetic. He isn't asking. He's telling me he's grown. He's done being my baby, and now he wants to be in the world. "You can't stop me."

"I won't," I say, for the first time in his life. I know well enough to know I have no choice in this.

A baby's born. He might have twelve years of safety, maybe less. You hope he'll stay small. Small is safer. Your son wants to go to a playground. He wants to run and climb and sing, he wants to leap fences and play. He falls asleep with his face in your neck, humming to himself.

How many other mothers' sons have died as a result of me? I have a count of those souls, but I also have a count of things I saw when I was looking up, missiles falling like stars, food packages containing explosives, poisons in the water.

"I just want to see if he's okay," he says.

"I know," I say.

"I'll look in a window."

He thinks I don't know what a liar looks like. I love him so much I don't care. *Lie to me,* I'm thinking now, *tell me lies. Tell me you'll be safe. Tell me you won't risk your life hunting for love.*

I don't know what he looks like to other people. He looks like me in the reflections I see in the mere. When I see him pass me in the dark, down a passage, or in the woods, he looks like a boy. He's not a man yet. That won't stop anything from happening to him.

I know we can't hide forever, but we've been hiding so long I don't know how to stop. He's hardly hiding, though. He's out in the very early mornings, before doors are open, before the world's awake. He brings home books, and more clothes, strange ones, from dumpsters maybe, or donation sacks. Once, a bottle of vodka, and I don't know where it came from, but I can guess.

I know that if I were him, I wouldn't choose to live my life this way, a boy inside a cave, in hiding with his mother. How much life do you get?

I know that if I didn't have him, I wouldn't choose this life either.

Gren doesn't know that a handful of years is a thousand years, is a hundred thousand years, that he'll be a memory of pain to Dylan.

Some nights I think about that city they found in the desert. Some nights I think about what it would be like not to be alone. I used to know. Now I've been alone too long to be anything else. But I don't know how to forget safety. I don't know how to forget arms around me.

Why should Gren?

I sharpen my sword. Sharper, sharper, bronze and steel. There are stones deep under the surface here, white quartz, yellow opal. Down in the dirt there are flints and spikes, old tentacles turned solid. There are fossilized fangs.

I sharpen my blades on all of it, everything I can find, until my knife and sword could kill someone without them even noticing they were dying.

The whole time I'm doing it, I'm wondering who I'm planning to protect. Myself? Him? Someone else entirely?

Keep them sharp, I think, because at least I can do that thing. The world is the world and my child wants it. The world is the world and my child will go into it, whether I like it or not. He doesn't have any magic. I don't have any either. I have metal. I have to think it's something, even if it's not enough.

32

Lo, out of nowhere, Willa's thirty-five, then forty. She disbelieves the narrative that ended her up here, but every morning it's still true, recited like a ballad by gossip columnists, blind items, chroniclers of power. She has her fans and her enemies.

She's as lovely as she's ever been, maybe lovelier. Now she has a team of beautifiers, and when she gets dressed, it is with input. She lets her hair hang free, blood-red lipstick and a little reminder to everyone, stabbed in over her heart, a brooch in the shape of the American flag.

Mayor? Governor? Senator? President?

A designer inserts a pin into her waist, and she has him arrested. That's a joke. She has him go down on his knees and pin each pleat by hand, carefully, his fingers spread on the silk, the top of his head visible to her, in case she wants to bring her wineglass down on his skull and stab him with the pieces. People in her position poison, they don't stab. Another joke.

The kitchen windows look out onto a mountain with a tunnel through the center, widening daily, and the tracks, extending daily.

Willa and Ben throw dinner parties where they tell the story of Dana Mills, Roger Herot, and the kidnapping of Dylan Herot, the story of how the abandoned station was discovered, how the train was unearthed, their personal mission for rehabilitating the mountain.

They talk until late in the evening, and donors nod along. Willa finishes the parts Ben finds difficult to discuss—the death of Dana Mills—and Ben finishes the parts Willa can't speak— the death of her perfect first (face it, second) husband, so innocent, so good.

It could kill a conversation, this discussion of a home invasion, a kidnapping, a murder, a criminal hidden in a cave, unexpected love found in the most terrible circumstances, but there is always someone curious enough to keep asking.

Willa brings out a tray of cordial glasses bordered with casual gold, and Ben clears the plates. Willa goes into the music room and puts on something to lighten the mood, walking slowly, her heels clicking.

"The moral is that you can survive anything, even the loss of the ones you love most," she'll add softly, returning, her earrings catching the light, tears in her eyes. "Sometimes there's a happy ending you couldn't have imagined, for more than just you. This is our happy ending. The Herot Heritage train line and station will offer jobs, employment for hundreds of people. It'll change the culture of the suburbs for the better. A return to the good old days, before the world became so cruel."

They tell the story often enough to get the Herot Heritage Station made legal, to get a hole properly cut in the side of the mountain, to get Ben promoted to chief.

Willa remodels the police station along with the train station. Ben sits at his new mahogany desk and oversees a growing center of commerce, culture, glamour.

Who wants to live in the city, anyway? The guns! The knives! The lack of human compassion! Come to this charming hamlet, safe and secure, just two hours from the whir.

"You're commuting to *your* community," says Willa, in the advertisement for Herot Hall and for the Herot Heritage train line.

There's a wine bar with wine made from biodynamic grapes. There's a bookstore. There are cobbled streets and wide sidewalks and Willa changes some of the perfectly plotted hedges to wild roses, to suggest romance. The white picket fences are replaced with sustainable wood, brass fittings, and the front doors are painted red.

Look at the people drinking cappuccino and eating sushi. Avocado toast, vegan cupcakes, and gluten-free pasta, and all that in addition to the Herot Heritage Station, a glorious relic full of cultural significance.

River views. Mountain views. A train designed to be silent when it travels, every hour on the hour gliding along sleek silver tracks. There are, it turns out, unused lines running all over, forgotten resort tracks and tourist destinations, and Willa's plan is to use them all, to fill them with trains to replace the ones that have stopped coming. This is just the beginning. There are platforms beneath the city where a person could stand forever without meeting anyone, parts of the underground where trees grow up through slanting funnels of light, where there are flowers in the damp and windows to old shoe shops with satin pumps on display, all these places where homeless people slept in the grime and dark.

At last, Willa is reclaiming them for the people they were meant to serve. The few people who've slept in the tunnels surrounding Herot for years are bought bus tickets to elsewhere. No one's been in the Heritage tunnel. That one, thank god, was closed off, safe from interlopers. Well, no one but Dana Mills, and Willa doesn't count her. She's long gone.

Willa Woolf's acquired rights to places beneath the earth.

Now houses at Herot sell moments after they hit the market, and the community ripples down from the mountain like a Christmas tree skirt.

And that's all anticipation! The station isn't even open yet! The train hasn't had her maiden voyage, though it's been tested, of course, in the middle of the night, whipping through the tunnel, fed by electric joy. The new Victorian-style bridge over the lake is ready, and the Edison bulbs are installed on either side. The bridge suits the train. It's shaped like a castle, tall and perfectly formed with crenellations. If there were no more humans, and everything went black, if the power went out and Earth lost its passengers, the train's bridge would remain for another thousand years, longer than a holy body kept in the basement of a church.

The lake bottom beneath it is a whirl of crushed boats and broken masts. There's a hidden metropolis of rust here, a lost and forgotten colony. This bridge arcs up like a bow. The train will cross it, rattling at speed, spitting sparks as it travels.

Willa spends her days talking about her train, and the heritage she's celebrating with it. Herot Heritage, yes, but more than that. She invokes both pilgrims and artisans, the beginnings of the wonderful world of America.

When someone questions her, she looks tearily down, and they remember why she'd feel strongly about this land, her pain, her loss of safety. They remember how she's personally honored the history of Herot, the old graves found in the land near the station entrance, the museum put in at the expense of both Willa and Ben. There was some criticism, from certain corners, inquiry into the nature of those graves, gentrification, eminent domain, but Willa and Ben handled it perfectly. Of course they did. Willa's own mother attended a fund-raiser for a state senator, shook his hand, patted his shoulder, brought him an envelope full of nothing at all.

At night, all night, every night Willa imagines riding her own train into the city, moving so quickly the world blurs around her, so quickly it feels like flying. She'll drink champagne in the dining car, sit against the window and look down on everything that's tried to keep her from getting what she deserves.

✦

On the day before the inaugural run, Willa's dressed in a suit of silver silk slub to match her train, drinking her coffee in a shining room, in a shining house.

She's looking across at the station entrance, planning the ride. There'll be music, champagne, a dinner in the dining car, and then, in the city, cake for the first commuters. Years of work coming to fruition.

The lake glitters like a sapphire, and the rail bridge is ruby red. The mountain has a snowy peak and the trees are decorated with fairy lights for the ceremony.

She's pouring another cup when a mouse runs across her kitchen floor.

She stands very still, her heels very high, and listens to the sound of the mouse's claws on the tile. The mouse, its teeth, its tail, this tiny thing in the center of perfection, gnawing.

She feels everything falter. She traps the mouse beneath a wineglass.

Ben walks into the room, and she's on the kitchen floor. She gives him a ridiculous can-you-believe-I'm-on-my-knees smile, while assessing him from below. Perhaps a tiny pad of fat at his belly, seen from this angle, and possibly in his chest hair she's found some white. She'd never mention it. He still carries her up two flights of stairs when the boys are at sleepaway camp. He still throws her onto the bed, and she still finds herself startled by desire when she runs a hand down his spine.

Her heroic husband is the envy of everyone, and sometimes she has him carry her purse through a crowded room, just so other women know she claims him.

"There's a mouse," she says.

He looks amused. "Are you going to eat it?"

She leaves the glass on the floor, unfolds herself from her crouch, and into Ben's arms.

"Yes," she whispers. "I'm going to eat it."

She lets him crumple her up in his hands like a cocktail napkin. Men will be men.

A pang of hunger again, as she's on her back on the countertop. She's denied herself food since last night, when she opened the refrigerator and found a raw steak. Ben's, of course. A fork into it, a failure, and then a knife, and then three bites in quick succession before she wrapped it up again imagining a tsunami of flesh. She wants to buy hamburgers from drive-through windows, creamy milkshakes, boxes of Girl Scout cookies to shake down her throat.

Her phone buzzes. Dylan's school. She doesn't pick up. They'll leave a message. The phone inches its way across the counter and falls off. Ben leaves for work, and Willa straightens herself.

Dylan's not coming to the ceremony. She doesn't need the stress, and Ben agrees. The little boys will be there, one on either side, but Dylan will be at school.

Last term he starred in a play, and she went to see it, hidden in the back of the auditorium. There he was, onstage, standing in the spotlight with an agonized face, a monologue. Tight black leather pants, tooled all over with peacock feathers—clearly purposeful. Eyeliner. Platform shoes. Mercutio as Freddie Mercury.

She stood in the dark, her heart full of something.

She hasn't seen him in months. There was plastic surgery to repair his face. There was a psychiatrist to repair his mind, but apparently he left parts of it shut. There are tens of thousands of dollars of therapy in his history, discussions about trauma, people coming up from underground, bunkers, basements, broken. It seems to be the reverse, though, the basement in Dylan's head. The cave beneath the mountain was Paradise, as far as he's concerned, and everything else, no matter how expensive, is inferno.

Eight years, three months: kicked out of private school for biting. Nine years, six weeks: screaming curses in the grocery store. Eleven years, eight months: roaring down the road having stolen Ben's car. Money to keep that quiet? Yes. Pulled over and brought home by police who are, thank god, loyal to Ben. Twelve years, birthday: Dylan wandering Herot Hall, somehow scarring all the neighbors' doors with fake claw marks. Twelve years, two months: boarding school, a relief. He's been there ever since.

Two years ago, he said to her, "I remember, you know."

"What do you remember?" she asked him.

"Everything," he said, and that was all, but she knew what he was talking about. She knew, and he wanted her to know.

"Murderer," he calls Ben, despite all evidence to the contrary. Ben's been a model stepfather, and Dylan's the one who's been a trial. Most recently he attended a protest in the city against police brutality, holding a sign that read I AM THE PROBLEM. He gave an interview, spouting a long string of something about witnessing illegal activity and injustice as a child. His stepfather, of course, treats him as though he's all in a day's work.

"Boys will be boys," said Ben, as he arm-wrestled Dylan at dinner and faked a loss.

Now Dil's fifteen and not speaking to anyone.

She dials his phone. She should make sure he knows he's not coming, though she can't imagine he'll care. He's waiting to graduate, and then to go forth in any embarrassing fashion he can find. No answer. She tries the school line.

"This is Dylan Herot's mother, returning your call," she says to the secretary.

"I'll transfer you to the headmaster."

This is unexpected. There's an ominous pause. Willa imagines:

1. *Suicide*
   a. Pills?
   b. Noose?
   c. Gun?

2. *Call to Ben*
   a. Grief, seven stages.
   b. What to tell the little boys?
   c. Their brother is gone to a better place?
3. *Press conference*
   a. "The worst that could happen to a parent."
   b. Ben or Willa. Probably Ben.
4. *Funeral*
   a. "A time for the family to reflect."
   b. Good photography, like JFK's funeral. The little boys in matching suits. She and Ben, in black, her face in her hands.

Willa's learned over the years that preparation saves suffering. She paws through her handbag, finds a granola bar. It's dry and crumbly as dirt.

"Mrs. Woolf," says the headmaster.

"Yes," she says, in a careful tone.

"Your son seems to have run away," the headmaster informs her. "He's been missing since last night."

She exhales. "Is there any reason to think he won't be found? Any sign of anything actually wrong?"

The headmaster seems nonplussed.

"He always runs away," Willa says. "He'll show up."

"He's not on the grounds," the headmaster insists. "Should we report this to the police?"

"No need," she says, realizing. "I know where he's headed."

Her son is still her son. One last chance to steal focus. It's Willa's big day, and he's coming to humiliate her.

Fine. She goes upstairs, and pulls an old suit of Roger's out of mothballs. At least if he shows up at the ceremony he'll be dressed like a son of hers, and not like the horribly tattooed attempt at a punk rock tragedian he is.

She goes to the pantry and looks in. She'd never fling her

entire body at any of this, her hands open for fistfuls of sugar cereal. Bottles of olive oil, wine by the liter, sitting on the floor in a heap of potato chips, her cheeks puffed around unchewed bites, her body plumbed at last with something other than desire.

She'd like to dissolve her maternal bond to Dylan like gelatin in hot water. Instead, she imagines her son stepping off the new platform in front of the train, a blazing spotlight, an ovation. Roses falling in every direction, and then motion, fast and brilliant, no brakes, nothing but an end to this story.

She bends over and picks the mouse up, tail between her nails. It dangles from her fingertips, moving like a toy, and she breaks its neck, places it on her tongue, chews, and swallows.

No.

She dangles it over the garbage disposal, flips the switch, and runs the water.

Back to the mere it goes, with the rest of the bones, and she's off, out to the last set of meetings before the gala opening tomorrow afternoon.

She runs her tongue over her teeth as she walks out the door, and feels an edge, something needing to be filed down before she bites her tongue. Dentist. Manicure. Makeup. Hair salon. She tastes blood, swallows it, pops a mint into her mouth. Small repairs. There's no woman alive who hasn't found the occasional hole in heaven, and carefully, meticulously, covered it back up.

33

Low ceilings and low tunnels, but none of that stops Gren from moving fast. I let my son think he's really alone, but he hasn't ever been. I let him think I'm not with him, but I've always been.

Listen to me, I want to say, but he's done listening. He's me at this age, and I am my mother, broken, injured, walking behind him.

I can see him from where I'm standing at the back of the trains he takes, ten miles from the mountain, the old commuter line. I'm between cars, and he's on the top, riding it like he's riding something living. He's not noticeable, because no one is expecting anyone to travel the way he travels. He moves at night, out of the mountain and into electricity. Risking everything, but maybe that's normal. Maybe that's what I did too.

I put my hand on the side of the train and feel it humming. The tunnel is tagged, gilded with spray paint by people willing to walk through the bones of the city into a territory of tin cans. The metal of the train beats a fast, cool heartbeat. The train's old. It's been signed by who knows how many names, people writing themselves into the future as the train sleeps in the station. I signed it myself back when I was his age.

Gren doesn't lead me to anywhere Dylan might be. He lets

me think he doesn't know I'm with him. I remember seeing my own mother waiting for me at night, in the window, looking out through the curtains. I remember seeing her car behind me, a block or two, as I made my way into town.

We go to a museum. I walk in the dark behind him as he touches sculptures. We go to a library. He sits in corners, reading. We go to an ice rink, and he spins in silence in the center. We aren't alone in the city, but it's late and cold and we make our way quietly, heads down. At first I'm ready every second for someone to stop, to stare, to see him as something he's not, to scream.

We pass an old man who moves aside for us.

We pass a woman who nods at me. A police cruiser slows, and I clench myself, but it moves on around the corner.

No one looks at him for more than a moment, and when they look, they look away. A very tall boy walking. A very tall boy with a beautiful face. A very tall boy with a beautiful face and hopeful hands. I try to compare him to other people, to other men and boys, and he looks like them. He looks like he belongs here, not hidden, not in the mountain fearing for his life. But I know things about the world, I—

I think about long ago, the woman in the Army surplus store, me bringing my baby to see her, and her reaction was—

Maybe her reaction wasn't. Maybe I read between the lines of her silence. Maybe she was scared that I had a child and that I looked so broken. Maybe she was pitying me.

Maybe I've been hiding for myself, not him. The buzz in the corners of my brain. The feeling of a bomb blowing up nearby, the ground shaking. My soul raked over my sins. My boys, dead. My mother, dead. Myself, dead.

Gren, alive. He walks like he knows every block.

We go to the main station, and he stands beneath a ceiling painted with stars. He stops, looks up, considers the points of light, the chandeliers, the golden ram and fish flying across some-one's version of heaven.

The stars glow, and we stare up at them together, two people gazing at a sky made of electricity. How many ghosts are here? This land, this city, this station. How many people have died here, in the dirt below us?

I haven't been here in twenty years, not since the war. The new century on its side, glass, metal, and paper drifting down, and then the videos of people leaping. The phone messages left by the leaving, both the ones in the airplanes and the ones in the buildings.

Listen to me now, people said. *Listen, I love you. Listen, this isn't the end of the story. Listen, I'm sorry. Listen, I wish I wasn't going this way. Listen, this is goodbye.*

Now I let myself think about places I could go. Out into the world. Away from here. Alone, and invisible, not taking care of him. I let myself imagine a life without this constant fear. Everything changes. He's almost old enough that he can take care of himself. Maybe he's almost old enough that gone won't be forever. Not every son dies before his mother. That isn't what has to happen.

After an hour under the sky, we go back where we came from. It's a snowy night and the windows fog over as the train shines its light into the gloom.

Two passengers. A boy and his mother. I ride between cars. He smiles at me as he climbs the ladder that leads him to the roof.

I know what this is. He's telling me he's leaving.

We leave the train where it stops, and walk back to the mountain, ten miles, first aboveground, and then through the old part of the tunnel.

It's been changed. I can smell the newness of it, cleaner than any tunnel has a right to be. It should smell like damp, like river, like old bones, but it smells like paint.

Everything changes.

We're back in our own station. I get a bad feeling in my stomach, because the station has changed too, no lights on, but the old broken chandelier unbroken, the windows replaced, the floor polished. The smashed crystal glasses have been replaced by glasses made in molds, and the soda fountain has a bar full of bottles behind it.

HEROT HERITAGE reads the banner across the entrance, waterproof fabric, bright colors.

I knew there was construction, but I thought they'd torn it out, made it modern. Instead, it looks like it looked the first time I saw it, before dirt got into it. I feel my thirteen-year-old self here, and my mother, looking out over the track and whispering. I hear her telling me this place belongs to me. It doesn't. It never did.

I feel that, and other times too, climbing down through the ceiling into safety, curling against the counter waiting to lose my arm. My history, here.

I stand for a moment inside the cavernous room, and then I see that there's a door leading off to the side. A sign that reads HEROT HERITAGE MUSEUM.

"What's that?" I ask Gren. He lifts his shoulders.

It's down a dark passage, not part of the station itself, hidden from everyone except those who choose to go in. I walk through the archway, and there's a glass wall, with skeletons behind it.

Gravestones. Artifacts. Dimly lit by filament lightbulbs, little plaques telling lies. *Unearthed*, they read, *unexpected*, *old*.

But I know this cemetery. I grew up going to the church that held this graveyard.

I look in for as long as I can stand it. It isn't an accident that these graves ended up here, two hundred years of graves, the people who lived and died in this place before Herot Hall came and took it.

They're here for decoration.

I look at names of the people who built this place, stones I know by heart. I look at the things found in their graves, rings and charms, funeral gowns, treasures they had buried with them.

They prayed here, on land that hissed and spit sulfur, on ground that shook, on a mountain known for ghosts. They prayed for safety here, just like I did. They prayed for their children to grow up, just like I did.

I put both my hands on the glass. I want to smash it. I want to break it all apart, and then I see—

There's a panel far along one wall of the display, and in it, there are bones marked as being from the 1880s. There's something else in there too, and I stare at it for a long time, trying to reconcile it.

It's the goblet I poured my mother's water into every night, the one she kept beside her bed, the one I polished over and over. It came down in our family, and it has our initials on it, embossed in the silver.

It was the last thing I put in her coffin before they closed it, and now it's out, with a light on it, making people feel like they aren't looking at a crime scene.

The sound I'm making isn't a sound I've ever made before. Those are her bones behind glass. This is what I'm left with, here, standing with my son. A museum. Heritage. Whose heritage?

"Who are they?" Gren asks me. "Do you know them?"

I told him stories about monsters below us, stories about how they eat people like us, stories about how you can't go down the mountain. I never told him any part of why. I told him lies.

"This is the cemetery from where I grew up."

"Where did you grow up?" he says, looking at me like I'm crazy. He's never asked. I've never said.

"Down there," I say. "Where the houses are. They took our land and built Herot Hall on top of it. I was overseas."

His eyes are wide, and I can see confusion rising inside him, betrayal.

"You told me you were a soldier," he says. "You said I was a soldier's son. You said you came from the cave."

"I came from down the mountain, where Herot is now. That was my family's land."

"Where did *I* come from, then?" he asks me. He used to ask all the time, and I used to tell him stories. I don't know what I'm telling him now, a story or the truth. I've never known what the truth about this is. I don't know his father's name.

"You came from the war," I tell him. "Your father came from a town in the desert, and all of it got destroyed by people like the people in Herot Hall. People like Dylan. He's one of them."

He's silent, but I can feel him. He's crying. I can't stop. I can't comfort him.

A wall of bones they stole from my family's graves, turned up to build those houses, those picket fences, those years we hid here, afraid of being found, afraid of being killed by them. There's something whipping up inside of me, something with teeth.

During the Civil War, there were accounts of a monster that came coursing over the battlefields on the Confederate side. A tsunami of transparent brown bodies, salt-drenched and cotton-worn, roaring up out of the fields, ghosts brought by blood, and suddenly the soldiers would see a line of them, and behind that line another line.

Except it's the reverse in my head right now, not the victims rising as ghosts, but their murderers. I'm seeing everyone from Herot Hall and everyone they came from. Thousands of them, stealing and stealing. Thousands of them breaking open graves and taking our bodies out of them. Thousands of them marching over land that should belong to us. I'm seeing my son, and all the years I've been afraid to let him walk in the world, not because I'm crazy, but because they are.

For the first time in my life, I'm praying. Not for salvation but for destruction.

Take it down.

Take it down and blow it apart.

Here they are, the people who stole my family's land, the people who've taken my arm, the world, my son's safety from me. I want them to know what it feels like to lose.

My saint is back, standing beside me.

"Sharpen your knives," the saint says. "Kill them all."

"I thought saints didn't kill people," I say, and she laughs, the candle in her chest flickering.

"Some of us killed hundreds, and others got killed."

"Why are you with me?"

"I'm not with you," she tells me. "I'm just your hurt walking."

Her fingernails are long and dirty, but her teeth are perfect. She has clear eyes and twisted hair, and that candle in her chest has been burning for years. There's a skull in her hand.

I graze my fingertip over that skull and then I'm pulling my knife out and turning myself toward the entrance to the station, toward the path, down the mountain to their houses. In through the back doors. Up the stairs and into their bedrooms—

"*Stop it! Stop talking to yourself!*" Gren yells. He's shaking me by the shoulders. "You're not a saint! You're not anyone!"

"I never said I was," I tell him.

"It's your fault we're in here," he says. "*You're* the one who killed Dylan's dad. No one down there has ever done anything to you. I played with him. That's all. The only person who's ever hurt me is you."

My son and I look into each other's eyes, and for the first time in our life together, we both see monsters.

"Nothing ever even happened to you," Gren spits. "Except that you're a coward."

I'm flashing into that goddamn white room, stitches crawling up my face, Gren in my womb, my body torn up, my brain torn up. Where was I? A good city? A bad city?

"Nothing happened to you," said the men when I woke up in the hospital. "Nothing happened to you that didn't happen to a hundred men. They were kidnapped, but they kept their mouths shut. You were a soldier. You were approached."

"I was taken."

"You sympathized with the enemy."

"Who are you, if you don't?"

They poured water into my face. They drowned me, baptized me in ice, resurrected me, drowned me again.

There are rules about torturing mothers, though not about torturing women. Always have been. You couldn't burn a pregnant witch, and you can't bend a pregnant soldier over backward and make her confess sins she doesn't remember. They went as far as they could, and then maybe someone stopped them. I was six months in, and I was carrying a light. I was a lit cigarette. Someone ground one out on my arm, but I don't know who, because my head was covered with a sack. I don't know if the things I remember are real or things I made up. I don't know if Gren's father was a kidnapper, or if he was a god, or just a normal man I met, someone I fell for in the middle of a war. I don't know anything.

"You should've killed me when I was born!" says Gren. "You should've just killed me, if you were going to make my life into this!"

My heart is a meteor hitting the ground.

"You made me think I was a monster," he says, and his voice shakes. "But I'm not a monster."

My son stands before me looking like a boy. Out there, I know it, I know it, my son running down a street would be my son confessing to a crime. My son shouting would be my son attacking. My son sleeping would be my son addicted. My son in love with the boy from down there would be my son hanging from a tree.

People say the world is changing, but it isn't changed enough.

"You don't know what it's like out there," I say.

"I don't know what it's like because you never let me outside! *I hate you*," yells Gren. He's my only reason for being here, my only reason for losing everything I could have had. "*You ruined my life!*"

I see white light, a blast radius. I see a city burning down. I see my own body burning and then I see myself walking out of the burn.

I'm wrapping my jacket around my fist. Gren's crying and raging and I'm done being careful.

"This is what they did to your family," I tell him.

I punch my fist through the glass, and it hurts, it hurts, but I don't care. I don't care about the sound it makes and I don't care about the consequences.

I take the goblet in my hand and hold it, feel my family initials, feel the warmth of my mother's hand on it, feel the way I'm back here again, with her again.

When I look up, Gren's gone, and I'm alone in the dark with the ghosts of the love I've lost.

YES

34

Yes: times are changing and we change with them. The mere is brimming over, deeper than it was, bitter water and heat, fury and fire. Excavations into our mountain spilling salt into sweet.

We are angry. We are breached and boiling. The center is darker now, and warmer than it was. It's not all heat. Some of the mere is ice, but a hot spring steams from the middle of the lake, wisps of white rising over the surface. The mountain shakes.

We are a white deer and we are a black raven and we are blood in the snow. We are a sword made of old metal and we are a gun filled with old bullets and we are a woman standing before her mother's bones, holding her family treasure, broken.

We wind around the mountain, looking into windows, gusting over the stars, covering the moon. The center of the mountain is open and inside it, the woman and her son look at each other and for the first time in their history, there is a war between them.

Then he's running through the snow, furious, wanting to flee her and save her at once. The boy from the mountain doesn't notice the cold.

He was raised to trust no one but her, to love no one but her, but he is made of longing. He dives into the mere and swims, sinking to the fish, rising to the ice.

Out of his sight, just, another boy is walking across the new rail bridge, a bag slung on his back. He's drunk on somebody's daddy's private stash of whiskey. He's been walking since he left the train station ten miles away.

We know this boy too, his mind, his heart, his hopes. We've known him since he was a child, and we know him still, though he has changed. In the gym, he bench-presses things that outweigh his imagination. In his pockets: a stone, a fossilized sea monster.

For years, he haunted us, collecting the nests in our corners, stealing a china cup, a crystal from the chandelier. He hiked alone and sat in the middle of the floor, arms wrapped around his knees. He left letters pressed into crevices, addresses, stories, and all of them were taken by his stepfather into black plastic sacks and to a dump, where they'll survive eternity.

He wrote on our walls with red paint. GREN. FIND ME.

We know his memory. We read his heart.

Earlier tonight, the boy was in the city, drunk on tequila. He was on his sixteenth bed, with his sixteenth girl, and he isn't even straight. Seventeen was on the bench at the back of a bar, vinyl opened with stuffing coming out, a mouse running by his foot, a girl with her legs wrapped around his waist, the wall behind her.

The boy from Herot's found plenty of things while looking for love: sweaters rucked up, zippers tugged nearly from stitching. How can love come from something as nothing as fucking? he wonders, even as he keeps doing it.

He still hasn't found what he's looking for.

"You seem high," said the girl. "Are you high? Can I have some?"

"I'm okay," he said.

"You aren't." She poked him in the chest. "You're pretty, though."

He wasn't planning to come to Herot. He was planning to spend the night in the city and then go back to school. Then, just before he packed up his bag and got on the train, she reminded him of everything he'd lost.

"You're the kid whose dad got killed by Dana Mills, aren't you?" she said. "I didn't even figure it out until now, but then I had this weird memory of seeing you on TV, like when we were super little."

His plan changed.

The boy from Herot has a tattoo on his arm, procured with a fake ID. It's a picture of the mountain, and inside the mountain are three figures. Once upon a time, he was the child of some other mother, and his beloved was a wonder of the world.

He got on the last train out of the city, and headed for the suburbs. Back to the house he used to stand in, looking through a glass wall at a mountain.

The last time he was dead, someone picked him up, took him home, and loved him. Maybe, he thinks, he should die again.

A ribbon-cutting ceremony, and an inaugural ride through a station he shouldn't have ever been inside, a place he helped destroy.

He's the murderer, not his stepfather. He's the reason anyone from out here went into the mountain, the reason anyone found the cave, and he's the one who tunneled out with his bare hands. He tried to go backward the whole time, until his stepfather held him to his chest, pinning him so tightly he was left with a star-shaped scar.

Now it's a series of white lines, almost invisible, a breached cheekbone.

The boy makes his way slowly across the bridge, considering a jump from the highest point. Get more rocks for the pockets. Or wait until morning, do it during the ceremony, the train and his mother, ruin his already ruined life, and hers too, and his stepfather's along with them.

He pauses. The water looks up at him. We are everywhere. We look out of the trees and the sky, out of the lake and the shore.

After a silent moment, we hear his heart pounding, his breath coming fast. He takes off his shoes, coat, backpack. He stands on our trestles barefoot, looking down.

◆

The boy from the mountain is below him. We've been watching him swim, his head up above the water.

He's talking to himself, telling himself how to live, how to run, how to leave his mother. He's telling himself he doesn't have to protect her, doesn't have to believe her about the world. The world, he is whispering, will take him.

I'm leaving, he's saying aloud, when the boy from Herot dives off the bridge and into the water beside him. He jolts, stunned at the splash.

The boy from the mountain dives, following the way the water trails from the other boy's fingertips.

They surface together, come apart, and stare.

We listen. Voices in the dark, carrying over water, whispers, uncertainty, hope. The mere counts the beats of their hearts through their skin. The mountain shakes, full of change.

A train, a tunnel, a woman in the cave looking at her own mother's bones, weeping over the things she's lost. We feel it all at once, the birth and death of the fossil trees, the gone dinosaurs, the bathers who used to come here, the passengers who used to walk through the station under blazing lights.

The boy from Herot presses something into the hand of the boy from the mountain. It's the fossilized monster, brought from his pocket.

The boy from the mountain pulls something up out of the water. There's a string around his neck, and on it is the head of a tiny plastic king.

And they hesitate, and the mere springs from the center of the Earth, and some of the lake is ice and the rest is boil.

They swim to the shore. They make their way into the old station. The world is sleeping. There's a grand piano in the middle of marble tiles and mosaics. One boy holds out a hand. The other boy takes it and leads him to the piano.

Maybe there's been a haunted sound in the past months, maybe someone's been playing these keys in the middle of the night, teaching himself how to make music. Maybe we've dampened the sound of song.

The boy from the mountain sits down and the other boy sits down beside him. The boy from the mountain opens the lid and puts his fingers on the keys. He plays.

We listen to it reverberating out from the building, and we move it through the dreams of Herot Hall.

This is the song he's playing from the dark, but nothing about it is hidden, nothing about it is secret.

Some of those who hear it dream of old stories, hunts and hungers, prey and riders, the unknown coming from under the hill, and others think of ice-cream trucks playing songs they shouldn't play, minstrel show songs selling cold to children.

The music fades and one boy takes the other's hand in his.

They look at each other. The boy from the mountain is too frightened to speak. He's talked to the train for years. There is only one train here, just as there is only one of him. He has talked to the birds, to the electric lights and to the fish. The two boys look at each other, silent, shaking.

I could leave again.

Don't leave me here.

I've been looking for you all this time.

There are two boys in this room now, for the first time in years, and the mountain watches. One boy puts his arms around the other, and feels his bones, his shoulders, his spine.

The boy from Herot Hall presses his palm to the palm of the boy from the mountain, comparing size.

"Do you remember?" says the boy from the mountain. "You taught me to play. We sat on the floor of your bedroom. We built a castle out of wooden blocks. You flew a little airplane over my head."

"Do *you* remember?" says the boy from Herot. "You brought

me here. You saved my life. You taught me to build a fire. You taught me to hunt. I slept beside you."

The boy from Herot lifts the other boy's chin, and looks into his eyes. "I thought you were dead. I thought I'd have to spend the rest of my life without you."

The boy from the mountain mumbles, stammering. Blood is rushing to his face, and his heart is pounding.

"I thought you wouldn't want me," says the boy from the mountain.

"I want you," says the boy from Herot. "You're the only one I want. Do you want me?"

"I want you," says the boy from the mountain, his eyes shining with tears.

"All is well," says the boy from Herot. "And will be well."

The boy from the mountain smiles.

"And the squirrels will be fed, and the trees will grow taller," he whispers.

"The snows will come and pile up, but we'll be warm," says the boy from Herot. "Like the animals. All in their dens."

"Like the fish sleeping beneath the frozen water," says the boy from the mountain.

"Like us, safe in bed together," says the boy from Herot.

What more do they say to each other as they make their way into the train, as they walk the cars? Nothing we are interested in listening to. Love is usual and rapturous, and nothing about it is new.

A cabin.

A wood, a river.

Another city.

A ship with a glass bottom, an ocean full of fish.

Let's run away together. Let's go somewhere else and stay.

Inside the mountain, inside the train, one boy kisses the other, and the other kisses him back, and there is nothing but history between them, and history is enough to make a future.

35

Yes: every soldier knows the dead return to walk your dreams. Ben Woolf wakes up with a start, the sound of piano music ringing in his ears, but it isn't real. His dreams are taking things over, and it's not because of the dead. It's because of the living. It's the ones he didn't kill.

He patrols early on purpose, his dogs beside him. He's been lying awake telling himself stories: the moment he put his hands around Gren's throat, the moment he felt Gren's fur and thorny claws, the way he tore Gren's head from his body, the sinews ripping, the skin shredding, the smell of blood.

He remembers it like it actually happened, but lately he's felt inclined to confess to everyone that it didn't. He wants to walk the streets shouting for Dana Mills again, and for her son. There's something in the air. The opening of the station, the public nature of it, the way old places will be lit and filled.

An arm in a heap of dirt does not guarantee a death. He knows that. He's always known. Soldiers lose limbs and live, just as they have done for centuries. And Gren? For all the screaming, all the years of Dylan's therapy paid for by Ben Woolf himself, there has never been a sign of any son of Dana Mills walking that mountain. The only place Gren exists these days is in Ben's head.

Maybe all good men feel this way sometimes, a yearning to give over all the wrongs they've done. Men, at least, have a code. Thousands of years of soldier's honor. Women and children have no rules. They've been allowed to do as they please, protected and full of secrets. If Woolf knows anything, he knows they're all stealth. At any moment a woman or child might come out of a doorway, holding something that looks like a flower, and isn't.

Gren walks Ben's dreams, and in them he's a blur, running, huge and strong, angry. Ben has never seen his face, and doesn't know what his enemy looks like. Big, he thinks, and that's all he can say.

The world isn't large enough for monsters and heroes at once. There's too much danger of confusion between the two categories. Ben Woolf's job is to defend this place against those from elsewhere. Every all-you-can-eat buffet eventually runs out of food, and it's his duty to serve his own. A man must have his chance to fight change. Borders are shifting and people are rushing across them. Herot Hall is safe for now, but Ben imagines what could happen, any moment, the place full of criminals from the world outside. The world is made of enemies. His own station house had bedbugs last year, and he fought them like he was fighting a ring of serial killers. He was forced to cook the whole goddamn precinct. Ben knew what to do. No mercy. No pause. Straight forward, and into the fire.

Never mind the dullness of that, the lack. Never mind the dearth of true heroics involved in extermination. His life has been quiet before. Surely he wants it quiet.

Ben opens the glove box, checks the weapons, locked there to keep them away from the twins, who are born warriors.

He's taught his sons to eat their meat bloody. He's taught them to pretend their eyesight is duller than it is, their strength less. He's taught them to respect their mother, and never to dive too deep. But once, a few months ago, both boys dove to the bottom of the swimming pool and stayed there, sitting on the bottom, their faces bright with rebellion. And once, a thing Willa doesn't know, he got a call from their school and picked them up midday, their faces flushed, and another boy beaten badly. An accident, they swore, and eventually the other boy swore it too.

There are no photos of Ben as a baby. There was no note in the basket. He was just left on the front steps of the orphanage.

When he thinks about it, he imagines his mother young, beautiful, a heroine, though he can't get beyond the point where she leaves him, the part where she looks around furtively, and then runs to a waiting car that contains his father. Ben Woolf doesn't judge them for running from him. Some days, he wants to run from his sons too. There's something about them that makes him uneasy. They might be criminals. They might be cowards. They might be both.

Beside him in the car, his hounds wait, a braided mass of fur, and that's comforting, though they're old. Who else would know the scent of Dana Mills if she came through a window?

Dana Mills is dead, he reminds himself. He can still feel her shoulder joint separating, the sword in his hand as he cleaved her arm away. He can almost see her slipping into the water, a pool of blood, the final bubbles of her last breath as she sank into the dark.

He's recounted the story so many times that it feels truer than any other part of his history. He dives after her, groping for her hair, but she's gone, disappeared like the nightmare she was.

Ben Woolf cracks his neck, thinking about how it feels to kill someone he didn't kill.

He thinks about the people he *did* kill too, of course, his own years making himself into this man. When he was fifteen, he started a fight with a kid who had a string of names inherited from his grandfathers. Something about that pissed Ben off, made him feel as though his own name was a broken thing, no lineage, no history. He isn't even Benjamin. He's just Ben, an orphan's name. It ended in the center of a river, two boys challenging each other to a contest. Together, they tried to swim against the current, and they ended up exhausted, in rapids. The other boy eventually went under. Luck was what Ben called it when he got to shore. *Luck* was what he said, when he knew that part of what had taken the other boy down was Ben's elbow.

Horrors are everywhere. They are none of Ben Woolf's business, those glitches in the narrative. He drives past the new train station, orbits it, parks, and takes a pass around the perimeter with the dogs, strolling proprietarily.

Sometimes Ben imagines a cave for himself, here in this mountain, a place he might hibernate through a winter, not on duty, but then he removes that thought. Who would he be if he wasn't defending? Desk, doughnuts, disaster. He's forty-eight (face it, fifty-two) and it takes more work than ever to keep himself in condition.

Suddenly the dogs are barking, pointing, and Ben looks around and sees no reason. The dogs hop and twist, and Ben still sees nothing.

"Heel," he tells the dogs. "Sit."

But they run into the station and bark, bounding from end to end of the platform, insisting. It's still night. There are decorations everywhere, and the Heritage train, polished and perfect, is parked in the tunnel, and wrapped in a giant bow, out of sight for the big reveal. It's already loaded with champagne.

Ben stands on the platform, looking once again into the darkness, but it's not darkness any longer. There's a sunrise beginning, purplish light.

He takes a step into the passage, and the dogs go wild, running up and down the tunnel. He has a bad feeling, but he's had bad feelings before. More officers for security today.

His toe touches something. A rock on the marble tile, some fossilized creature inside it. A step on the tracks, someone creaking away. No. He spins. The dogs are barking. Too loudly.

It's her.

It can only be her, even as he knows it's not. It's someone homeless, or an animal. Still. Better to draw the gun and walk.

He locks the dogs into the cruiser to keep them from barking too loudly. He doesn't need all of Herot up here.

He walks toward the entrance to the museum. He dodges out of direct view. Is there someone in the dark there? Is there a person in the passageway?

There's broken glass on the floor, in front of an empty case. It catches the light of the sunrise.

Step by step, he goes down the skinny set of stairs at the end of the platform. His knees crackle, but he doesn't have bad knees, because bad knees mean desk and desk means death. He steps into the undercarriage of the station, pursuing a phantom.

Because of an earlier incident, his head insists, preemptively cleaning up this mess. *Trains will be suspended, pending further notice.*

And what will the incident be? Who will he find? Who will find him?

Down, and into the tunnel Ben Woolf goes, pausing at every mark he sees, looking at every drag mark on the ground, everything that could be normal, and could also be an assassin lurking.

Footstep by footstep into a darkness that'd damn well better lead him to trouble with a solution, trouble he can cuff and question and take back to the station, trouble that lets him go to bed tonight in the arms of his perfect wife, back to his perfect life. There is no other version possible. Heroes don't die in the dark.

Yes, I'm whispering to her. *I'm the daughter you raised. I've grown into someone as tough as you were.* I'm telling her the last twenty-five years, telling her I'm sorry I wasn't with her when she went.

I'm telling her about my son when I hear dogs in the station. One moment I'm on my knees in front of my mother's bones, and then I'm out of the passage, away from the gravestones, into the dark.

I'm panting, sweating at the end of the tunnel, crushed into an alcove. I press my spine to the wall and shake, muscles screaming, body taken over by adrenaline.

A man walks in front of me, outside the cases full of my family. I see him in silhouette and I know who he is. I should have been gone by now, if I wanted to go.

He's the reason my mother's bones are here. He's the reason I'm still here, and have been here all these years. Uniform. Holster. A policeman walking slowly through the station.

Light bounces on the ceiling. Water trickles out of the walls, and it's not supposed to. I'm sure they thought they'd filled it all in. Behind me, there's a chorus of muffled howls. I've been invisible for a long time, and he's been walking the world with all the privilege of being a man.

He can't see me. He's looking the other way, toward the sun

rising, and then he turns and comes into the tunnel. He walks. I let him walk. He has a gun.

I have my mother's goblet in my hand.

I'm silent, but I can hear my own heart beating, and I can feel my own losses, shaking the walls of my body. When he turns, slowly, and looks at me, I see his eyes are as bright as something exploding and I know we're the same kind of thing, he and I. We carry the memory of death with us, deaths we avoided and deaths we caused.

He raises his gun and presses it to my chest, the muzzle against my heart. I can see my future, the bullet leaving the chamber and going through my body, the way my flesh will try to hold it, the way I'll sag, the way he'll drag me into the mere, weigh me down, drop me to the bottom of my own history. I hear him take the safety off. There have been so many clicks in my history, so many last seconds in my life.

I look into this man's eyes and he looks into mine, and I smile at him. I feel him waver.

"From the halls of Montezuma!" I shout, raise the goblet, and swing it hard, hitting him in the side of the skull, and he grunts and staggers against the wall, and goes down on his knees, holding his head. There's blood on silver.

After a moment, he looks up at me and blinks.

"Dana Mills," he slurs.

I drop the goblet, draw my sword. I know how to kill someone. I know how to be killed. I do it the way it's done. You say each other's names.

"Ben Woolf," I say.

There's a sound behind me, from the direction of the train. Enough distraction for Woolf to get on his feet and lunge at me.

Then we're face-to-face, stabbing and tearing. He's trying to turn me back into the dust of the desert we both fought in. We're both gasping, both choking. He's soft from the desk, and I'm hard from twenty years of war, but this is pain. This is two people no longer young, fighting to kill.

"You're dead!" he shouts. "I killed you! *Goddamn it!* I buried you!"

I twist and jab my elbow into his solar plexus.

We came from the same war. If I'm broken, he's broken too. If I killed, he killed too. He stood looking out at sunrises, just like I did, wondering how he'd die. He knows what it's like to say goodbye every time you say hello.

Listen, I'm saying to him. *I'm the one who lives.*

He gets a hand around my throat, another around my face, trying to break my nose. I find his hand with my teeth and wrench.

I tear a finger from him, and spit it out.

He swings at me with his other hand and hits me in the jaw. I slash him with the tip of my sword, straight across the face, a stripe like a clawing, and another, crossing the first. He's bleeding, his lip opened.

He jabs, tugging my knife loose and lurching across slippery rail ties. I can feel his fear, and I know, all at once, that he's not the man he pretends to be. Maybe he fought over there, but maybe he hid himself in alleys, up staircases, waiting for other soldiers to throw themselves out into the war and die for him.

I knew men like him. They're all dead now. Cowardice didn't save them.

I charge at Ben Woolf, sword out, and he levels his gun at me, finger on the trigger. I'm going to run him through at the same moment he shoots me.

There's another sound from out of the dark, a shout. He grabs me by the hair, twisting me around, holding the gun to my head, and then there are two boys in the tunnel with us, half naked, leaping out of the train. One is tall and one is small. One is tattooed with the other's image and is holding a Swiss Army knife.

One is my son and the other is the son of the suburbs.

I try to speak, try to get Gren to run, run, but it's not Gren who saves me.

Dylan Herot, T-shirt off, mouth bruised, motivated to murder by love, lifts his knife and plunges it into his stepfather's neck.

Then he takes Gren by the hand and runs with him. The gun falls out of Woolf's hand. I have it in my hand now.

Time slows down and speeds up and jerks into something other than time as I pull the trigger.

I shoot three times, but Woolf's gone into the brightness, the light I can't adjust to. Out of the tunnel and onto the slope, out of the mountain, into the blazing sunrise.

I follow the blood, follow the cries of birds and wolves, the songs of things from my mountain. All of us run the same way.

Snow's coming down hard, whiting them out. Blizzard weather, and I'm made of heat. My saint is here, with me. We burn.

There's a shout. Ben Woolf appears out of the white, bloodied and screaming. His eyes are the eyes from the photo I saw in newspapers from years ago, berserk, this man carrying my stolen arm, claiming he'd killed me.

He's chasing them into the house, my son and Dylan, sprinting into the white room, black room, red room, flashback, stitches crawling up the corners of the universe, sewing it all together, tearing me apart, and I'm running after them, to die or to kill.

37

Yes: the night before the ribbon-cutting, sleeping pills to ensure Willa's whole mind arriving at morning.

She's diving toward cold fire, the bottom of an ocean or a well, and all around her a chorus of other voices, voices Willa thinks maybe only *she* hears, because the water is suddenly filled with women in white, swimming around her, white deer, no, women, no, wolves, and she is bending into sleep, the bed chilling around her as a song twists into her lungs. She moves her own body in the dark and feels her tail lashing, and all around her are the rest of the wolves in her pack, their teeth sharpened on bone. No, not wolves, but women again, and all those things part of them, teeth and claws and tails, swimming toward some pale light.

Willa wakes to a loud noise, a—

A shot?

She's still foggy when she hears someone slam through the back door and into the house, screaming. The sound is animal, agonized, and she waits a moment, listening, the gun she keeps bedside, automatically in her hand.

"Ben?" she calls. She remembers Roger, his early mornings, and wonders, but no. She knows everything about Ben. She reads his email and his texts. She sets his passwords. He has no secrets left.

She pulls on jeans and boots in the kind of frenzy she doesn't usually allow herself. Her train. Her station. Her money. Her mountain. Her treasure. Out the window the sun is hardly rising, and there's snow, whiting out the view, spinning in circles, plastering itself to the glass.

Silence downstairs, but sounds, creaks, the floor that needs replacing, the stair where the tread is wrong. She runs to the landing, and suddenly Ben's in front of her on the spiral, protecting her from whatever's down there.

She takes a step toward him, her hand out to touch his shoulder, but he turns and she sees that his face is torn open. His neck is bleeding. She looks for bullet wounds, but no, nothing, only the slashes across the face, and a missing—

His ring finger is missing? What? Is he holding a sword?

He raises the mauled hand to his mouth to silence her. His pupils aren't the same size. The side of his head is bleeding.

She sees something at the bottom of the stairs, flashing past them, a shadow, a—

"I thought she was dead," he rasps. "She wasn't dead. *He* isn't dead."

Willa is still drugged. The world's half real and half dream. She feels the wrath of a woman about to strangle a man with her braided hair. There's a story about a woman coming to a conqueror's bed. The bed's draped in mosquito netting and wedding gold. The woman is a prize. The prize takes the man's head off with her sword. She puts his head in the sack she used to bring bread to the bedchamber. She leaves the bread in the bed, in place of his head, a feast she doesn't feel like eating.

Willa's eyes twitch over another shadow, light shifting in the room below.

A hundred bright red Herot Heritage balloons are loose in the house. They float from the living room and up the staircase, all around her and Ben, blocking her view.

She aims into the balloons with her gun, but Ben snatches it out of her hand.

In the hall, one of the twins starts crying.

Downstairs there are more sounds, and the back door slides on its track and Willa runs through the balloons, in front of the muzzle of the gun, down and into danger, protecting the children upstairs.

She darts into the kitchen, pulls a carving knife from the block and holds it. No one. Silence. A balloon pops. The kitchen door is open. The white mountain is covered in bloody prints.

Someone's here.

A sound. A breath. Willa spins. She's surrounded by balloons and they look like soldiers, each one the size of a head, milling around her, filling the room, red glow, mist. She can't see. Light is coming from everything, the floor, the countertops, the windows, and snow is blowing in from outside.

Gren. She knows it. He's in the room with her.

There are gift bags on the counter, upended, contents strewn across the floor, tiny plastic trains and skeletons to commemorate the museum, an aluminum goblet to replicate the antique silver piece in the case, older than you'd think, all over the floor, bare feet, and he's here, right beside her—

✦

Willa Woolf is sleeping when she stabs him in the back with a carving knife. It's harder to do it than she would've thought.

Here are shoulders. Here are ribs, stripes up the back, and the back of the neck, the knobs of vertebrae. Here is the place where the knife belongs, on the left, protected by shoulder blade—

Is this what shoulder blades are for? So that no one can stab you through the heart from behind?

Here is a hand spread in front of her face, and she can see claws protruding from the fingertips, long pearlescent claws, like sheathings found in the hallway carpet, so long ago now that she hardly remembers what they looked like. She knew what she was dealing with then, though everyone denied her. Not a bear. Not a tiger.

The claws are trying to catch her face, but she's faster, she's faster. Self-defense. She's saving her own life, and defending her husband and children, defending all of Herot.

Willa Woolf is a hero.

She grips the monster's elbow and pins it behind his back, and then she presses the point of her knife in along his spine, a butcher. Here is the reason for years of yoga and Pilates. She's fighting the reaper.

She hears herself, as though from far away, making a strangled sound as she pushes the knife in, grating on bones.

She's sleeping when her attacker's heart stops. Is she? She's sleeping when she cuts out the heart. Is she? Is this a mouse, is this her mouth? She licks her fingers.

Does she?

And is this her husband, who is not dead, only wounded, coming down the stairs, running at her?

Willa sees herself from above, floating in a sea of gore, her hair spread out, her skin stained, and all around are enemies, slain. She's defended the house. She's kept everyone safe.

Ben tears the knife from her fingers. He's screaming at her, but she doesn't hear him. She's dreaming.

Her hands are wet and warm. Her mouth is full. She clenches her fists and feels the points of her own fingernails piercing her palms. *Stigmata*, she thinks. *Holy, holy, thole.*

What if one night her husband finds himself on his back, reclining on soft cushions under a canopy of mosquito netting? What if he looks up into his wife's beautiful face, and sees the sword swing back, a silver slash across the remaining three seconds of his existence? Onto the bed will go a loaf of bread, and over this combination of loaf and corpse Willa will pull the coverlet. She'll walk out into the desert, her cloak around her shoulders, her hood up. She'll never be a wife again. She'll walk until the edge of the world, and she'll set villages on fire as she passes them.

Monster slayer, people will whisper.

She feels her body turning to metal, away from the marble and onyx she was. Maybe she's lost wax, a soft sculpture melted away in the forge, replaced by bronze.

Once upon a time, Willa thinks. She was rescued from this. On her finger is a diamond ring. On her skin is a name written in shining scar. It's not even her own name. Someone signed her as a piece of art. Everything that was Willa Woolf, that was Willa Herot, that was Willa Cotton, that was, first, back in the days before she was anyone's wife, Willa Nowell, all of that is gone.

She stretches her fingers and examines her nails. Her manicure is messy. It'll have to be redone. She squints at it, holding her hand closer to her face, but she can't focus.

Ben is over her, screaming at her, shaking her.

Willa looks at Ben through slitted eyes and a crack opens beneath him, erasing him from the face of the Earth. Maybe that's next. Cocaine. Errors in judgment. Drug habit. Who knew? Oopsy-daisy.

She'll have to call her mother to take him to the emergency room for stitches. He looks terrible. Little winged Band-Aids, antiseptic. That'll do it. Handsome men look better with scars. It's almost her responsibility to wound him.

Later, she'll do the train ceremony alone. She may end up on her own anyway. What woman doesn't? She thinks of her mother. She thinks of Roger's mother. She thinks of all the widows, and she thinks about herself.

It's 7:03 in the morning. Willa hears the sound of church bells, and a cell phone is ringing, but she's asleep again, curled on the floor, her pale hair a nest, and her husband running past her, his boots, his blood dripping on the white tile, all of it cooling as she stays there.

She's a dream dreamed by someone else, a network of scars and hidden wounds, a body made of hunger.

In her dreams she walks the aisles of the Herot supermarket, white linoleum, white walls, and she and her tiny son put their hands into the ice cream.

Look, she thinks, in wonder, the prints of beasts revealed, clear enough to be cast and displayed next to the bronzed baby shoes.

Her victory is so complete that she can sleep fully. Her body is hardly a body. She's bones falling through an ocean, a treasure in a shipwreck.

She dreams of audiences, theaters, ovations, her hands opening and spreading in bathtubs full of cream, bathing in milk, her body paler and paler as blood begins to pour out.

The milk is white.

The milk is pink.

The milk is red.

The house is quiet now, but for the sound of the radiators, and after a while there are sirens that aren't coming for anyone, because no one here has called for help.

SING

38

We sing the song we always knew we'd end up singing, ever since Willa married this man, ever since she trusted him with anything: her heart, her hand, her land.

We never trusted him. Our daughter dials us, her voice blurry, confused, murmuring frantically into the phone. We were waiting. We've been waiting for this day ever since we saw Ben Woolf.

Now we march into the house and stand in a row, seventy years old, tight and taut and *taught*.

"Where is he?" we roar.

We have learned every lesson, every horrible disappointment. Babies have died within us. Husbands have died beside us. We're the last ones standing.

Everything is covered in blood. Where are the little boys? Upstairs. Locked in their room, tearful, but uninjured. Heirs of Herot, unharmed. Check.

We put our palms flat on the kitchen counter. We control ourselves, but we are made of barbed wire.

"*Goddamn it!*" we shout. We knew what he was. The kitchen is smashed. He's written in absences: a blue fingerprint impressed on our daughter's throat, her hair torn out and scattered like the shed fur of a Persian cat.

Willa's on the floor, shaking, bloodied head to toe, arms covered in marks. We knew better than to trust him.

Monsters. Some people believe they're unusual. Others know that monsters are everywhere. We know one another's secrets, all of them. Confessions in bathrooms, collapses, emergencies. None of us have ever felt a shove from behind as we descended our front staircases. None of us have ever had a splintered jawbone reassembled. None of us have ever had the rest of us hold the straw to our lips as we healed.

Diane sets up business, sutures, antiseptic. We were doctors' wives. We keep hospitals in our purses.

We question Willa. She tells us that Dana Mills is back and Ben Woolf is deranged, and we believe her. Murderer not dead? Check. Monster not slain? Check. Hero not heroic? Check.

We take over.

Everyone thinks all we've been doing, for thirty years, is planting award-winning begonias. It's always the mothers who are hated. The fathers are too far away, home at 5:30, off the train, perfume on their jackets. The mothers are the clay pigeons children want to shoot out of the sky. Imagine being a target for fifty years, from your moments of first nubility to moments of humility, when your skin feels like paper and you stop sleeping forever, unacknowledged as being the armed guard of civilization.

There were times when we fought for perfection, for long carpeted halls full of family portraits, for scrapbooks.

Scrapbooks.

We've given all that up. Now we have PhDs in pain. We've watched the video of Dana Mills's original death, and imagined ourselves on both sides of it. We've seen the sword, the one taking Dana's head, flash through nothing. She managed to live through the first round of dying. It's no wonder she's done it again.

We who are survivors recognize her.

We've wanted to be like her, even, warriors with our swords, killing everyone who gets in our way, even as we know we wouldn't *really* be her. We'd hunt her, a pack of well-preserved women in boots, with our dogs and guns chasing her through the mountain. Well-preserved. Oh, we hate that phrase. Are we pickles or are we jam? Are we sour or are we sweet?

"Gren?" Willa asked Ben Woolf on the mountain that day, and we were listening. We filed that question away for later.

"What about Gren?" we ask Willa. Her face is agonized.

"There was someone in the house," she says. "*He* was in the house. Ben ran out the door after him. I don't know what happened then."

We take her into the bathroom. We turn the tap to scalding. She submits as we use the washcloth on her, looking for wounds.

"Stop flinching," we say, and tongue the cloth over her skin. We wash her clean.

She stares out the bathroom window, up at the Herot Heritage banner and the station.

Whose blood is this if it isn't Willa's? We hope it belongs to Ben Woolf. We hope he's discovered in the trees, flayed. Whatever he's done, it's criminal.

We go outside to take out the trash, step over the threshold and into the blowing snow, the back porch, the mountain. There's something—we take a step toward it, then leap back.

Look at how the porch rails are shining with a thin layer of ice and each tread of the stairs too, and look at how, just off the stoop, at the end of the trail of blood and footprints, right in the middle of the snow, there is—

A Dead Boy in the Snow
1. A pale shirtless boy with a knife wound in his back, facedown.
2. No, we won't look, we can't look, we—

3. The boy's arm is tattooed, and we know the tattoo. We know the back of this boy's neck and we know his hair.
4. We stand there for a moment. We breathe. We breathe.
5. We try to see the story. We piece it together from scratch. The past and the future. There is no such thing as a family tree without broken branches. The back pages of every Bible are corrected in white paint.

Willa comes out of the house behind us. She drops to her knees. We know the posture. She is Caesar's wife, Lady Macbeth, the chorus in a classical play. She's veiled by her platinum hair, and she's screaming and screaming, beating her breast.

She's letting go, letting everything go, letting her bladder go, letting her tear ducts go, letting her face, frozen without wrinkles, go, letting her voice go, out it comes.

We look at her. We know her. She's one of us.

The neighbors are summoned out of their houses. They're dialing the police. Nine-one-one bounces from satellite to satellite. She doesn't stop screaming.

There are sirens, and then more sirens, and then more, until the hamlet is ringing with them, like God has come down from heaven and called out for every church to pay tribute.

This is what the story of Herot Hall is now, revised from fairy tale into horror. The flip side of hero is monster.

No one ever knows what mothers do. We defend our children from themselves, tooth and claw, bending the admission boards and battling landlords, taking the extra set of keys and cleaning up evidence of wrongdoing. We save our daughters from disaster, over and over again.

We kneel beside our grandson. We calmly, slowly, remove our monogrammed scarf from the pocket of our coat, and use it to wipe the fingerprints from the handle of the knife protruding from his back.

We take care of the details, because the details are always the devil, and this is our story now. We write it. We scream it. We belt it out into the winter air.

"Ben Woolf!" we shout. *"Find the monster!"*

39

Sing on, normal world, even when everything in it is broken. Dishwashers and vacuum cleaners are humming from below. An announcer calls out over a radio, and Gren is with me. Sirens surround the mountain, and here we are deep inside it, my son, sobbing, sobbing.

No one has ever let me go. There's been no honorable discharge, nothing but dying, over and over, declarations that the war would never end, that my service would never finish. I curl around Gren and hold him. What is love but this dark, this cold, this child?

Hush, little baby, I sing to him. *Don't say a word.*

"He's dead," he whispers.

"He's dead," I say, and hold him tighter.

I saw Dylan in the snow, just outside the kitchen door, the boy who saved my life. His back and chest were torn open. I didn't look at his mother when I ran, but I remember what I saw of her now, sitting on the floor in that room, her eyes dilated, her hair stained red, her hands full of something wet, and I—

My knees gave and returned. We ran through weather, sliding, ice and blood and blackness, and Ben Woolf ran after us. We lost him in the trees, but we heard him shouting, running, stumbling, roaring with panic and frustration.

I burn for my child. For our mountain, stolen. For ropes on trees and for autopsies conducted in theaters with admission sold, for rebels charred at the stake. I burn for the women in the war whose sons and daughters were blown into the sky and left unburied.

Here I am, and my son with me, a product of a war that people thought was over. We manage, somehow, to be living. I think about how I felt, running through America, fifteen years ago, hoodie up, my face with my new scar, starting at the jaw and stretching to my hairline, walking dead with a swelling belly, guilty of no crime.

I didn't know what kind of baby Gren would be, but I could feel him while I was pregnant, a hand pressing hard to my insides. I tore my shirt off in truck stops as I made my way back here, sweating, my nipples darker daily, my belly button shifting, and Gren's little hand against me, showing through the ribbing of my undershirt, telling me that he was alive and growing, telling me that he was mine, and that when he was born, he would need me to keep him safe.

Maybe this has always been a job that mothers do. Raising them and protecting them, trying to get them out into the future still living, still loving, trying to defend them from all the things the fucked-up, broken world wants.

Maybe this has always been a job made for failure. This is the child I don't know how to hold. This is pain walking. There's no saint here now. There's only Gren and me, in the dark, and we are each other's hurt, and we are each other's only family.

"I want to kill Ben Woolf," Gren says. "And then the rest of them. Dylan's mother. Everyone down there. All of Herot Hall."

"I know," I say.

"He was my friend," he says, his voice breaking. "They killed him."

"I know," I say. "I know."

And he doesn't tell me, but I can see all the things he's not saying, an imaginary path into the future. A bridge made of red steel, a train taking them forward and away from here. I can't imagine Gren killing anyone for any reason but love. No one wants to live alone in the dark, not me, not him, no matter what we know about the world.

"I can't let them live if Dylan's dead," he says. "I can't be the one who gets away, not without doing something. Teach me what to do, Mama?"

He hasn't called me Mama in years. He hasn't used any name for me.

"Can you make me a soldier like you?"

I hesitate. I want to do it for him. I want to save him and keep the world away, but I've always wanted that, and that's never happened. The world is filled with pianos and people. Ben Woolf is out there, wandering the mountain, and Dylan's mother is in that kitchen, on the floor, and there is a dead child in the snow.

Gren and his mother. Dana Mills and her son. A man with a gun. All of us circling one another. I feel the walls of our cave move. I feel the trees and the bats and the dirt and the stars outside. I feel the mountain, the mere, the creatures that cry out from deep in the water.

He is here.

She is here.

"Yes," I tell my son. "I can teach you."

If this is the last lesson, it's the last one. The last line of every life story is the same. There's nothing precious about it.

I begin.

"Listen," I say to my son. "Listen."

4□

Now it is five days later, and Willa stands in the center of her station, beneath a chandelier and a hundred mirrors, all reflecting funeral candles. She blinks.

For a moment, the room is covered in handprints of blood and claws and the convex mirrors are skewed and broken. They reflect a battle. She looks up into one of the mirrors and she sees her own face, distorted. She's a queen wearing a crown of gilt and broken glass.

Then, no. Banners. A stack of funeral programs. A coffin wrapped in roses.

She goes to the catering table, where she eats and drinks everything she can find, bite after bite, sip after sip, feeling as though food is nothing relevant, as though she is made of infinite air. Her mouth tastes like chewing gum covering alcohol.

Every corner of the world could hold a mouse or a monster. She wants to slice Dana Mills into bites, make certain she's dead, and then consume her strength. Willa hears the back of her own mind insisting that if Willa is what she eats, given the right meal, she might become a revenant with a winged sword.

Down below, there are dogs being walked, a parrot on someone's shoulder, faces of people who know nothing about sacrifice, nothing about liars. There are people coming out of houses and going into cars, and Willa is no longer any of those sorts of people. She's painted her face into something saintly, gold leafing and pigmenting, sealing it all in, making herself holy.

She wipes her mouth and emerges, flanked by the mothers.

They stand behind her, welcoming witnesses to the funeral. Look at what they've survived. Look at how they've managed to live through everything. Willa brings out wine and serves it to the press gathered for grieving and for tribute.

This train is the memorial. Her son was the sacrifice. Her husband, the betrayer, the monster, is being hunted, FBI alerts, his own officers searching for him. Years of safety, now revoked. The fences and the windows and the gates, all irrelevant. Her enemy has been sleeping beside her, fathering her children, sharing her wealth, rising on her efforts. This is a performance of courage in the face of catastrophe.

If Ben is smart, he's fled. Gone to a cave to live there, where no one expects him to do anything. He could hunt deer, seals, whale, anything, as long as he never comes back to Herot Hall. Across the ocean, maybe, across the world. There are places men like him could hide, and it's not Willa's business.

He was always a mercenary, though he pretended to be a good man. He came to Willa, she knows now, because he saw money he might marry. All the secrets of her husband are Willa's secrets too. She's seen him melt like a crayon in the sun, and now she has to clean it up. It's disgusting, but typical. Her own mother did the same, and Roger's mother. Ben's mother would have done it too, but she abandoned him instead. Willa understands that now.

She imagines what will happen next, when Dylan's funeral is done, when she goes back into the mountain, this time with something stronger. She trusts only herself. How many years has she known there was something she didn't know? She has a gun, and she's a good shot. If Dana Mills is still in there, she'll find her. And Gren?

She imagines it as she's imagined it for years. Willa is going to be the one who kills him. She's going to murder him and his mother too.

She thinks for a moment about her own son. Dylan made his choices and left the world of humans behind. She was his mother, but he always took after the dead. His school sent his laptop and condolences after they got the news, and his files were full of poetry, all of it old-fashioned. She'd pictured him playing rock and roll and instead he was writing an opera. Who knew he'd learned to play piano? Not Willa. He never told her. The singer today will sing one of his compositions, picked by the mothers. Willa didn't have time to listen to them all. The singer, though, is nationally known. She was meant to sing at the ribbon-cutting, and she's singing at the funeral instead.

There's a crowd gathered now, all in black. They seat themselves in chairs that don't fold. Willa's spared no expense. There are reporters and donors, friends of the mothers, politicians, photographers.

"Ten years ago," Willa says—she has to talk about it; there's no way to keep it quiet, it's national news—"my husband encountered a woman who'd turned against the United States. She murdered my first husband, Roger Herot, and kidnapped my son, Dilly. In the process of saving us, Ben Woolf, then the officer in charge, was forced to end that woman's life. It scarred him. It broke him. And this, the horrible thing that happened to my son? It can be blamed on her as much as on him."

She doesn't say *Dana Mills*. There is no reason to make Dana Mills a name for anyone but someone who is long dead.

"Is it any wonder that my husband went back to those years of trauma and committed a crime motivated by it? I can only think that it was a horrific accident and I urge you to think the same. Today I grieve my son, and my husband both."

She pours wine with a heavy hand, into the glasses of journalists, Ben's whole staff, and half the lawmakers from around the state. PTSD specialists and grief counselors. She gives them a special look, an agonized one that nonetheless contains grit. No use looking entirely like a victim. It's a balance, her future.

She takes a slice of pâté delicately with the edge of her knife, lets it dissolve on her tongue. The cameras catch her, a tear in the corner of her eye, her dress for mourning. She'll run for office, eventually. She writes speeches in her head. Willa rises, her face in the expression that will telegraph compassion, grief, and strength in the newspapers.

"To us," Willa says softly. She doesn't say the silent part, but she thinks it. *To us, and people like us.*

"To us," echoes the table.

"Against the darkness," says Willa.

"Against the darkness," they reply.

"And to my brave son Dylan," she says. "Rest in peace."

She can hear them crying.

The train is ready to take Dylan into the city, and there's a band waiting to play the funeral march, and the cars are stocked with champagne, coffee, tea, and a funeral banquet, done delicately. There are donation cards in each seat where the tickets would normally be. Already checks are flying through the air and into the accounts. Already Willa is famous for her pain. Already the train is sold out for two months.

"You're brave to come tonight, and strong. You're all good people, doing hard jobs. Even in a time like this, perhaps especially in a time like this, beauty triumphs over horror."

The mothers sit down on either side of her and take her hands, and everyone bows their heads, and the train is there, perfect and shining and waiting for passengers. The singer begins to sing.

The first notes are enough to make Willa rise in her seat, but not fast enough to stop it. It's the song she heard years ago in her house, the song her son would not stop humming. It's the song that brought all this trouble into her life.

"*Listen*," sings the soprano, a trilling lullaby, a sweet and delicate soprano.

"*Down from the mountain*," she sings.

Down from the mountain and out of the dark.
Up from the ocean they march through the park.
They are coming, they are coming,
All the ghosts and all the men,
They are coming, they are coming,
When the moon comes up again.

Is Willa Woolf hallucinating now? Is she back in time, deep in her own memory of catastrophe? Is she clawing her way down the slope of a mountain, is she beside her husband, a monster?

Or is she a monster herself, flying out of her house and over the land?

Willa breathes in and out, listening to the song, and she feels a flutter in her heart, a rising that becomes a pounding. Nerves. Caffeine. Grief. Fear. Thole.

She opens her eyes and lifts her chin, almost imperceptibly, trying to look as though she is deep in prayer. She sees someone pass through the door of the station, and he is hulking, muscular, matted, and hairy.

He's something wild when nothing wild lives on this mountain. Everything's been exterminated. There are no bears, no wolves, no panthers. There are no predators left here. Willa's gotten rid of them.

But this song is a song of wolves, of lakes where sea monsters swim and ancient forests bloom.

"*Listen, in them sleep heroes*," the soprano sings.

Heroes in the mere
Heroes in the drear
Heroes who march down the hill to the hall.

Willa's husband takes a step into the station, and she's the only one who sees him. She looks into his eyes and knows that he knows everything she is, everything she's ever done, and that he has forgiven her sins and taken them for his own.

She is flooded with love for him, and even as she is, she knows that the sharpshooters must already be waiting, that bullets are whispering his name.

There is a sound from above, and the chandelier shudders, and the singer stops singing, and everyone but Willa looks up. Then everyone in the station is falling and shouting, screaming over one another, and guns are drawn and people duck, roll, and drop to the marble tiles.

Willa is the only still soldier in the center of the battle, and she looks calmly at what is coming into the station.

Look, she thinks, in some wonder, because what she is looking at is nothing terrifying. It's only a woman and her son. Willa looks into the eyes of her enemies for a moment, long enough to realize that she's alone, a frozen woman in the center of a battle film, the camera coming closer to her, her face too lit and her makeup too perfect. There's only one end to that kind of movie. She ducks her head and runs.

41

Now it begins. I'm already in the station when the funeral procession comes in. I'm in the ceiling looking down on them. Gren's beside me. We're the invaders instead of the invaded, for the first time.

I'm looking down at Ben Woolf's wife, a sliver of ice at the table, and she's the one who killed Dylan, and I'm the one who'll kill her. I've known her for years now, her yellow hair and painted face. The way she stood in the kitchen looking out at me. The way I stood on the mountain looking in at her.

I'm looking down at the coffin as they load it into the train, listening to an opera singer, singing something I don't know, and do know at once, something familiar. I can't listen to familiar. I'm here, in my own skull, paying attention to my own future, not my past. Gren is beside me, watching, his face wet.

Our plan is to wait. I've been teaching him, but there's only so much teaching to be done in five days. He can shoot, but he already could. He can use a knife, but he knew that too. Some part of me still thinks there's another option. The funeral will be over, and Gren will say goodbye. We don't have to die here.

Wait for the funeral to end. Wait for her to be alone. Wait for something to change, and then—

And then Ben Woolf walks into the station from outside, and

he's filthy and wounded, his face covered in cuts from when I found him in the tunnel.

I feel Gren move beside me, launching himself through the panel of the ceiling, and then he's down in the midst of the crowd, and running.

I tumble down into the table, among the chairs and banners, and throw myself at Woolf from behind, using my leverage to shove him down. He falls, crushing wineglasses and steak plates, smashing pitchers of water. He's fighting not me but my son, a boy screaming in a circle of anguish and fury. They're evenly matched. I shout directions at Gren, and Gren follows them.

His neck, his arm, his fist coming for your face, his chest, his size, punch, kick.

The crowd is panicking and people are stepping on one another and black balloons are everywhere and bags of black confetti. Tiny glittering trains shower from the sky.

I see Dylan's mother standing in the middle of the room, and she stares at me, and for a moment I think she's drawing a gun, but then she's running.

Gren is still so young, still so scared, but he's fighting for his life, and for someone else. There are police in this station, and I feel them aiming, but they can't shoot at us without shooting at him.

I scream my enemy's name. *"Woolf!"*

He looks up at me. His teeth are covered in blood. His chest is covered in blood. His neck is wounded. He has my son in his arms, clenched too tight, my son pressed against his bulk. Not a man, not grown. Did I give birth to him so that he could die in public, torn and shredded, innocent of anything but defending me, defending his friend?

No.

I throw myself at Woolf with all my strength, shoving him

out of the station, over the edge of the new tracks, and into the mere.

We drop down, through ice, seeking fire.

No kingdom will clasp Gren from below. There's no hole in the snow, no place in the sand where nothing becomes something.

It doesn't matter what form a child takes. He might be smoke and he might be a screaming monster flying across a mountaintop. He might be a boy with a tender heart picking up skeletons and trying to put them back together. He might be all that. You will know he's yours. He's nothing but your son, whatever he appears to anyone else.

I dive. I follow the man I see swimming before me, his hair bright in the dark. Into the fire, into the cave I can see with a vision that isn't mine. Who does it belong to? I don't know what I am. I'm Dana Mills, and I was a child and then I was a Marine. I was beheaded and I lived. I gave birth to a wonder of the world. Maybe every mother thinks those things. Wonders. Glories. Beloveds. I gave birth to a son.

Everything exists.

I have all of my memories in my mouth. I hold them in my teeth and I wait for Woolf to show himself. I'll drown, but I'll drown taking Ben Woolf down.

He's in front of me, and my son is in his arms.

We are in my territory.

I let all of my rage pour out of me. I let all the pain come through me, all the anger. I let all the blood of centuries of murders pour out of my hands, all the agony of childbirth and all the panic of waiting for someone to find us on that mountain, all the fury of keeping someone safe in the dark when you should be bringing him out into the sun and giving him all the things he deserves.

When my son should have had school and friends and diplomas and love, when my son should have driven a car and gone to college and been at the top of every class. When my son should have been able to fall in love. When my son should have grown old with his chosen one.

When my son should never have met this man.

We surface on the ledge, and Woolf has him, strangling him, and Gren is fighting, but he's losing. I'm on Woolf, battling him like I'd fight anyone on the other side, any enemy, but I'm gunless, swordless, all my weapons lost in the water. He's stronger than I am. More than that, he has my child by the throat, and fury isn't enough.

I watch myself, a woman projected on a shredded sheet, stretched between trees, trying to fight a man twice my size, even as he tries to murder my child. I watch it as a trailer for a film I won't see, fireworks falling overhead, missiles making their way across the sky, babies exploding like bombs, soldiers with their lips pursed to kiss, a river that's not a river, a bright star that isn't a star, a silver goblet from somewhere else, my hands cutting the cord that ties me to my child, and reaching out to Woolf, to knit him to me instead of to my son. I'm full of the history of my own heart, and the history of my family, and what does he have?

He should have nothing, but nothing is enough.

Gren, born here, from somewhere else. Gren, his eyes huge as he looks at me.

"Run!" he screams at me. "Mommy! Run!"

To hear that word is to know that your child knows he's not going to make it out.

I'm not strong enough. I'm not fast enough. I'm throwing myself into Woolf, but he's in a frenzy. He has a hunting knife in his hand and he yanks and screams as he drives it into Gren's throat, and—

My son—

I watch him die.

42

Now! something shouts inside Ben Woolf's skull. He's weighed down with decorations, old gold medals and imaginary purple hearts. His skin feels heavy too: tattoos of monsters and broken boys, flags of many countries, missiles and swords, the names of his gods and his animals.

He has something in his hand and he's leapt back into the lake.

He feels the breath he's held all these years begin to gasp out of his lungs, but he lived through all the things that have tried to kill him.

Good man, he thinks. This is his training. This is his history, protecting the innocent, saving the community. This is what he was meant to do, and who he has always meant to be. The man who saves civilization from horrors.

He surfaces from icy blue darkness full of drifting memories of people he killed, all of them swimming at him, their eyes open, their hands stretching to reach him.

There's a great deal of blood in the snow, enough to paint a masterpiece on a fresco, a brave resolution, a set of demons wandering hell.

He struggles out of the lake, sinking through snowdrifts, thinking about places he went once, the way he swam in a swimming pool tiled with gold tiles, pure gold, pried them up in a rage, and found out they were only ceramic. There are photos of a long-ago Ben Woolf, looking like a hero, swimming fast, diving deep. He posed for portraits, the president patting him on the shoulder, a somber smile, a handshake, and Ben Woolf alone carried the story of what he did in the war. And what did he do? What everyone does in war, for thousands of years. Kill the enemy and try to survive long enough to go home. There is no such thing as a war hero, he knows, and has known forever. There are heroes of daily life, and he is one of those. He has strong hands and a sharp knife. He is not a winner, but he has won. No one knows it yet. He has to show them.

Peace is written in blood, and has been and will be. Dana Mills knows it as well as Ben does. She served in a war and so did he. If someone wants to kill you, you kill them first. There must be walls to keep attackers out. Locks on the doors. Guns in the hands of the defenders. Society wants to collapse, and it is his task to keep it from crumbling. He was born this way, and there is a history of violence on Earth, more violence than calm, more blood than water.

Everything has changed in an instant, and he's too far gone to go back home.

His wife is standing at the edge of the lake. She's all in white. No, the snow around her is white. She's in red. No, she's in black. She's a crow.

"Willa?" he says.

"*What did you do?*" she screams.

He's followed the orders he's been following since the beginning of his career, the ones that've told him that all heroes lose things as they go. There is nothing simple in the end of a story. The battlefield is always piled with corpses in need of burial, and even the riches belonging to an enemy are not enough.

He has no army. He's alone with the rest of his life, and his wife looks at him in horror, and he knows he will never see his sons again, knows he will never sleep in his bed again. Somewhere, he hears women screaming his name.

Ben Woolf steps onto the train tracks and starts to climb the bridge, feeling his muscles move. All he's done is save everyone. No one is thankful. No one respects him. He has blood on his hands and it's still spilling out.

So it fucking goes.

43

Now Willa Woolf stands at the edge of the lake. The mere is greenish black, and the only things she can think of are shipwrecks, frost and chill, oil spills, dead dolphins and lost whales, all tangled together into this failure, this catastrophe, this swirling drain of all the water in the world.

Her mother isn't saving her. Her mother has fled with her friends, for safety. They're inside the train with Dylan's coffin. Willa watched them hide themselves there.

Let go, Willa thinks.

She feels the heart inside her, thumping. She sees a dripping woman coming out of the mere, and boarding the train at the back, walking onto it behind all the people who're inside it.

The woman is silent, but she turns her head and looks at Willa, and there's nothing about it that isn't familiar. Years of forgetting. Years of countertops and windows. Years of earthquakes and grief, babies born and now dead.

Willa yells and spins, back to where the police are. She points.

There she is, Dana Mills, there she is, the murderer, but they're not coming for Dana Mills.

Willa looks at the lake again, from which her husband is emerging, a form dripping with darkness, his hair tangled, his muscles too large, his hands too big, his face a strange mask of hunger and joy.

And now Ben is at the end of the rail bridge, holding a monster's head in his hand, his face blank and strange—

And the monster is not a monster—

Everything is a sea of shouting and barking, sirens and chirps, and the world is white, and Willa is in the middle of it, her arms around her chest. She holds herself.

The boy is just a boy—

"*What did you do?*" she screams.

Ben is there, and she is here, outside the station, surrounded by black balloons, emergency order, Herot Heritage, Dylan's face on them along with the train that was supposed to carry him to the city and bury him. All of this was supposed to be lovely. All of it was supposed to make hearts ache, not beat inside of Willa.

She thinks about *Winter's Tale*, trying to remember the plot. She was in that play once. A child named Mamillius is eaten by a bear. It seems like a joke, like a puppet interlude. The child exits the stage, the bear runs through a bit later, and later still you learn that the bear ate the boy, but you never see it happen. The boy is grieving his mother, who isn't really dead. She's hiding in a convent, accused by her husband of being unfaithful.

The bear was a shadow puppet piloted by two actors with sticks, paper, and a big piece of fake fur.

Wait. She's remembering it wrong. The bear doesn't eat the boy. The bear eats someone else entirely. The father recovers. The mother resurrects. There's a happy ending with a wedding and a veil, and the gods show up.

The son is dead, though, the little son, his little death, and for the entire play you think he'll return, but he never does.

Dana Mills is a woman in black, who should never have come back from any dead land, who deserves nothing.

Willa watches her, boarding the train, with longing, with

something she finally diagnoses as lust. It's none of her business, in the end, what Dana Mills is doing on that train full of the residents of Herot Hall. The mothers. The cowards. Abandoners. Kill them, then. Kill them all.

The last twenty years. This whole life. How can they leave Willa here? They should take her. She should die with her army if they're dying, if that woman is coming to put them out of their misery.

Willa is in misery. The dragon on her wrist is shining in the sun and it spins too quickly, through the hours, through the days, reddening into rust.

She turns her head slowly, and looks at all the people, the ones in the station, and the ones out here, the people running out of Herot Hall, and the people running up to see what there is to see. The police piling out of cars and sprinting out of the trees, her neighbors, the women of this mountain, the mothers on the train.

She can see them all through the windows, but they're distorted by the old glass. They're shifted, stretched, their faces mottled, their teeth longer than they should be, their manicured fingernails curving into—

Someone tells her she has the right to remain.

"Remain where?" she asks.

"Silent."

"Mother!" she cries, but no one answers. There's a camera, and Willa is immortalized, her eyes wide, with running mascara.

Inside her stomach she feels it still, beating, beating. It ticks like a bomb, her son's heart. She feels it now.

She remembers it all now, everything.

Willa looks down at her own hands and watches them change into something other than the hands she's used to seeing. Speckled and withered, the talons long and curved, pearlescent. She's not the only one. It's everyone, all the people of Herot Hall, the police and the babies, the men with their names all the same, the women with their perfect faces, all cracking and showing what's underneath, what's always been there, coarse fur and gaping maws, whipping tails, scales, claws and hunger, and teeth, and teeth, and teeth.

44

Now it ends. The currents of electricity, the calls of metal. This train will depart the station with all of us on it.

We are done with being mothers. He was our son, in law alone, and now he is our son-in-nothing, because we're finished with our daughter.

We have no children.

We run across the platform and onto our train, past the coffin, quickly, erasing with every footstep the nightmare that is already on the screens of everyone at the station. There is chaos, and there is a train, and there are doors that lock. Take shelter.

Here is your purse, and here is yours. Here is your coat. Here are your keys. Here is your phone. We have nothing to say at all. We are leaving the scene of a crime. There were shots fired. Some of us need our medication. Some of us are having palpitations.

Look at Ben Woolf. Look at the blood in his hair, the bones in his beard, the way his teeth are full of gristle, the way his whole face is red. Look at him, not at us.

What about the daughter? She's not our daughter. Never mind the years of cleaning up after her, fixing her life, mending her marriages, taking care of children she failed to raise.

So many years of marching. So many years of waking at

dawn to trumpets, cooking in the mess hall, mopping up the blood. We are entitled to exhaustion. We are entitled to this train we built with our own money, our bank accounts drained to buy crystal and chrome.

Are we ready? Ready? Yes, yes, we are on our way, yes, the stations of the cross. We pass a man crouched in the last car before the conductor's, who asks us if we saw her.

Which her?

We put our hands into our purses. Coins of many countries, credit cards, lipsticks, expensive watches, and ink pens. Our dead husbands' wedding rings. Tiny bottles containing both perfume and pepper spray. Phones full of bad news, videos about to be viewed a hundred thousand, a million times.

We drop everything. Look, it's your lucky day. Why don't you take our credit cards and sleep somewhere fancy?

We're past pills and cocaine. Now it's just Kleenexes, tissues wadded up.

This train is bound for glory. This train is bound away from Herot Hall. At least we'll ride it once. The conductor is already in place. We see the door shut behind whomever it is.

We're through the car with the coffin. We're clutching programs detailing our grandson's small life, and the history of this train, named, they claim, after him rather than after Tina Herot's dead husband.

Ben Woolf is being arrested, no doubt, and Willa is too, reported anonymously by one of us, and we have nothing to do with any of this.

We look at Diane, and nod.

We are dressed in black. We're heavy with ceremony. We seat ourselves in the dining car, along with the rest of the survivors of Herot Hall, and there is an unexpected whistle, and we begin to roll.

The train rumbles out of the station. Just as we leave the tunnel, some of us look across at the white, at the graffiti of blood, signatures on the snow. Others put on their sunglasses. This isn't over. There will be more to deal with, statements to make. In the city, they'll take the train aside and bring us all into the precinct, but for now, a last ride in luxury. It will be police escort, federal, and we will walk one by one into rooms, be questioned by men in suits. Bright lights and false-sounding condolences, and we will tell them we know nothing.

We'll say it like we're giving a press conference.

"I need to speak with my lawyer," we will say, in voices that offer no other option. We know our rights.

The train is moving at strangely high speed now, emerging from the darkness of the station and into the light. We blink at the vista, a view over the mountain and Herot Hall, a world beneath us, the lake frozen at the edges and steaming at the center.

We have a moment of uncertainty. Do we report the train's speed, or do we resign ourselves to it? Look at us, our eyes bright, our makeup perfect, our spines straight as dressmaker's pins. Look at how we sit, not screaming, as the train we're on begins to hiss and rock.

The train shudders silver, new paint flaking off names and dates and faces and places, dents from moments its metal has touched edges, windows cracking. We slide from seat to seat. We were the women at one side of the tracks, and now we speed headlong at the other.

And there he is. We see him now. We see what's happening.

On the bridge before us, Ben Woolf is standing, one hand in the hair of the child he's killed. He raises his gun and tries to shoot at the train.

Sometimes grace is speeding at the obstacle instead of avoiding it. We see our enemy on the tracks. We look into the conductor's car, and we see our other enemy, driving.

We surrender to the end.

Everyone sees this train, windows blazing, and its dining car full of passengers as it pushes its way toward Ben Woolf, standing, screaming, shooting at something larger and stronger than himself.

Everyone sees the train as it takes him from the tracks, as we derail, and fly out from the bridge and into the air, Ben Woolf pressed to the engine like he's marrying metal.

We watch him obliterated.

No one ever really knows who's holding them at night, that's one thing you learn when you're dead. We turn in our last moments and hold tight to one another, dropping through the mere.

The train maintains its trajectory, deeper, deeper down, and reclaims all of it, the graves of centuries, the blood that watered the land. Our husbands' secrets, and our own secrets. Our history and our regrets. We reach out, one by one, and take one another's hands, wedding rings pressing into wedding rings, fingernails stabbing like needles into wrists, as we sink into darkness.

We open our eyes and we let it all go.

45

Now we're all together, for the first time and the last. I'm driving the train, and Ben Woolf shoots at me, but he misses. He's scream- ing, but I can't hear him. He thinks he can take on a train, but he's a man. I drive it into his body, and like that, he's no longer anything to fear. His hands are open and his heart is revealed. The end of his story is simple.

We fly off the bridge, and into the mere. We fall away from the surface, and time is slower than it was. Time is listening to me.

Through the ice, I see Dylan's mother, her hands pressed flat against the frozen edge. She's kneeling, bloody, shouting, but I can't hear her.

We're going deeper, and as we go she's taken away, her wrists in silver bracelets, her head crowned with a hand, escorted into the rest of her life.

My son is with me, my son with his beloved, and everyone else, the bones and blood dispersed into this water, the history of my family, the sand and bullets, the old hotels, the train tracks, and the train. The mountain and the mere, the trees we touched, the rabbits we snared, the wolves we heard but never saw. The cats and the dogs bounding down the driveways, the children on the swings and the women on the bridge and the echo of the sirens, singing their way into notes for birds to mimic.

The mere is freezing over above us.

There's a silver goblet dropping through the water beside a silver train, both of them sinking slowly to the bottom. There are bodies, skin blue, clothing drifting. Champagne mixes with salt. Rain mixes with sea.

Am I dead myself? How long have I been here and gone at once? I feel something inside my heart, something that reminds me of someone I used to know, long ago, in a city no one remembers but me.

I feel old things running around this place, like we're in the center of the smoke of a burning book of wonders. As though all the pages have gotten stuck together and now it's a world of everything at once.

A pitcher of water in my hands. A stand of trees somewhere in the middle of a desert. A bed with white linen sheets. Above me the moon crescented, stars I don't know. Wine in a cup. Smooth wet sand around me, packed down, a cave, a tomb, a room. A rock rolling across the entrance. A stick made of old wood.

And here, a country of claws. A mob of monsters. Look at them as we fly, and look at us, all of us, the desperate, desiring humans of this place. No longer. The story is shifting. Things are changing.

All is well and will be well. I look down and see the candle lit in my chest, glowing, blazing.

And now: we are the wilderness, the hidden river, and the stone caves. We are the snakes and songbirds, the storm water, the brightness beneath the darkest pools. We are an old thing made of everything else, and we've been waiting here a long time. I'm part of the fossils and the tunnels, the swords buried in mud, and all of it sings to us, and all of it is us. We are the mere and the mountain. We are the dead and the bones they left behind. We are the birds and the rainfall, the storms and the stars, and all of us are named, and all of us are numbered.

Later, maybe, two thousand years after the end of this

century, the world will have parched and flooded, dried and become succulent again. There will have been deaths of continents, and new islands born where there were deserts. The world will be different from this one. Maybe all the cities will have crumbled away, and all the bridges fallen. Maybe there will still be a mountain here.

Someone will tunnel into the cave beneath it and find our grave goods: trucks made of plastic, a knife with a red case. A sword. Some guns.

The bones of two boys, their skeletons entwined, dressed in wedding attire.

In the pair's joined hands, the searchers will find a smooth stone and the tiny head of a plastic king.

✦

"Listen," someone said to me once. This was a long time ago, another life, the same woman, the beginning instead of this, which is not the end but something else. *Dana Mills. You're the one who gets away. You're the one who keeps living.*

"Listen, let me tell you a story."

"A story?" I said. I was on a bus going cross-country, and I was seventeen years old. I had all the time in the world.

"I was lost," said the old woman beside me. "I was lost and I didn't know how to get home. No one would take me in, and I didn't think I'd make it. Then I found something."

I turned my head, expecting a Bible. She handed me a rock instead. It was embossed with a fossil, a tiny sea monster the size of my thumb, a lizard face and swimming limbs. When I tilted it into the sun, it glowed, opalescent.

"You never know what will make everything change," she said. "They keep finding ancestors of humans in caves, and every time they do, it's a surprise! They keep finding miracles. This one is millions of years old, this miracle. Touch its spine and feel how it must've swum. It must have found its way through a sea that was here before anything else we see now. Maybe every monster is a miracle meant to change the world and maybe every monster is just an accident of biology."

I looked out the window. Corn and light. Me here, about to go running into it, alive.

"Somebody told me," my seatmate said. "Somebody told me that he didn't love me anymore, that he'd never take me back or let me come home, but there are billions of years out there, and who knows what's happened in them. If something's happened once, we could all find love again. If something's happened once, none of us are done for. None of us are the last of us. The story is all of the voices, not just the voice of the one who tells it at the end."

I was holding a rock with a tiny sea monster embedded in it, a child of some tremendous mother. How many millions of years had it traveled to come to me?

I was holding this rock when the old woman in the seat beside me fell asleep, and didn't wake up. I was holding it as I stood at the side of the highway, watching them drive her away to be buried. I'm the only one who knows her story.

When I was in labor with my son, I clenched the rock in my fist, feeling the bones.

When he was tiny, I told him its story, naming those bones, one by one.

When he was eight, I gave it to him as a brother, and joined its bones to ours, a single family, one line of miracles, one line of warriors, one line of swimmers through unknown waters.

"Listen," I told him. I whispered it into his ears. "In some places, no one's alone."

And they're all around me now, a market full of people, a city full of people, a world full of people, bright eyes, bright skin, bright voices—and nothing is what I thought it was.

I'm in a crowd, and hanging on to my hand is my son, tiny, learning to walk, learning to talk, learning to be alive.

I'm in a crowd and we are all walking together, my mother and my grandmother, my husband and my heart, my son and his beloved, my ghosts, the soldiers I fought beside, the people we killed, and the people who killed us. My saint with her breasts on fire, and my strangers with their hands out, telling me to listen.

The sun is setting, and the town is a skyline, black as the back of a whale coming up out of the ocean. My skin is cold, but the last rays heat me, making this soul into steam.

We walk past the fire and past the graves, under the stars, up the mountain, and up, and up.

ACKNOWLEDGMENTS

The original inspiration for *The Mere Wife* came during a 2006 residency at the MacDowell Colony, where I ran across a library copy of Richard Yates's *Revolutionary Road*. I typed the first few chapters of my own novel about monsters in suburbia eight years later, overnight on my sister Molly's couch in Paris, next to her newborn son Jasper, who was intermittently growling (it runs in the family). In 2015, I was a resident at Arte Studio Ginestrelle, on Mt. Subasio, Italy, where I wrote the rest of the first draft listening to the snuffling of wild boars and the howling of boar-hunting dogs. Thanks to Marina Merli, and residents Opal Palmer Adisa, Jude Harzer, Signe Lykke, Harriet Wheeler, Gosia Lipka, Aleksandra Syrenka, Nel ten Wolde, Susan Cornelis, Deb Berzsenyi, Nancy Ulliman, Reinot Quispel, and Neroni the cat. When I returned, my magnificent agent, Stephanie Cabot, took the newborn novel out on submission, and I owe thanks to her and the rest of my Gernert Company team, Ellen Goodson Coughtrey, Rebecca Gardner, Anna Worrall, and Will Roberts. I salute the generosity of Carole DeSanti and John Joseph Adams, both of whose thoughts on the first manuscript led to this version. At Farrar, Straus and Giroux and MCD, thanks to my editor, Sean McDonald, who acquired this wild beast and wolfherded it through several increasingly fangy versions, and to claw-tenders

Nora Barlow, Maya Binyam, and Daniel Vazquez. Also at FSG/ MCD, thanks to Katie Hurley, Jonathan Lippincott, Nina Frieman, Brian Gittis, Norma Barksdale, Debra Helfand, Naomi Huffman, Jeff Seroy, Alex Merto, and Keith Hayes, and to Miranda Meeks, who is responsible for the beautiful cover image. Thank you to the immensely skilled and ridiculously appropriately named Beowulf Sheehan (assisted by Sami Sneider) for the author portrait, and to the divine Mandy Bisesti and Greg Purnell for, respectively, warpaint and skull dragons. Thanks to Marika Webb-Pullman at Scribe, multiyear believer. Deep owing and love, as ever, to China Miéville, who read, annotated, and battled every bit of this book, ghosts to epigraphs. There are no margin dragons like his margin dragons. More love to Jamie Pietras, who fed my fires and feted me throughout the last year and a half of this project, all while listening to my revision roars, and to the rest of the large tribe who offered specifics during this dream: Chris Abani, Zay Amsbury, Nathan Austin, Jim Batt, Jess Benko, Kim Boekbinder, Brooke Bolander, Libba Bray, Myke Cole, Molly Crabapple, Kate Czajkowski, Junot Díaz, Matt Cheney, Chip Delany, Kira Brunner Don, Rebecca Donner, Kelley Eskridge, Patrick Farrell, Jeffrey Ford, Craig Franson, Larisa Fuchs, Neil Gaiman, Barry Goldblatt, Nicola Griffith, Adriane Headley, Mark Headley, Molly Headley, Dani Holtz, Kat Howard, Doug Kearney, Meghan Koch, Carmen Maria Machado, Kelly Link, Téa Obreht, Erin Orr, JoAnna Pollonais, Victor LaValle, Ben Loory, Sarah McCarry, Sofia Samatar, Joshua Schenkkan, Sarah Schenkkan, Elizabeth Senja Spackman, Jesse Sheidlower, Sxip Shirey. You're all listed in my book of wonders. Thank you, finally, to translators, to tales told, to scholars of crumbling manuscripts, to disputed definitions, to passionate readers. You bring me the brass balls and the talons to write my own versions.